wor

'*The Visitors* may be Mascull's first novel, but she writes with the fluency and dexterity of a born writer, deftly crafting an engrossing story that imbues her characters with tangible sensitivity, warmth and humanity.'
Sydney Morning Herald

'Haunting'
Irish Tatler

'Powerful'
No.1

'Beautifully crafted.'
TheBookBag.co.uk

'The writing is stunningly beautiful . . . immensely powerful and moving. Certainly my favourite book of the month.'
LoveReading.co.uk

'Very accomplished . . . The story is one of friendship, of love and loss, of adventure and at its heart a compelling and affecting ghost story . . .'
BookMunch.wordpress.com

'A won ... *tors*
is a bea ... our

About the author

Rebecca Mascull lives by the sea in the east of England with her partner Simon and their daughter Poppy. She has previously worked in education and has a Masters in Writing. *The Visitors* is her first novel.

REBECCA MASCULL

The Visitors

First published in Great Britain in 2014 by Hodder & Stoughton
An Hachette UK company

First published in paperback in 2014

1

A CIP catalogue record for this title is available
from the British Library

Paperback ISBN 978 1 444 76523 6
eBook ISBN 978 1 444 76522 9

Typeset in Plantin Light by Palimpsest Book Production Limited, Falkirk, Stirlingshire

Printed and bound by Clays Ltd, St Ives plc

Hodder & Stoughton policy is to use papers that are natural, renewable and recyclable products and made from wood grown in sustainable forests. The logging and manufacturing processes are expected to conform to the environmental regulations of the country of origin.

Hodder & Stoughton Ltd
338 Euston Road
London NW1 3BH

www.hodder.co.uk

To Simon, my rock
and Poppy, my pebble.

I

My name is Adeliza Golding. I am born breech and nearly kill Mother. I hear her muffled screams from within the dark warmth of her belly and kick my feet to rid her of me. I enter the world in a flood of fluid and blood, pulled by the hands of Doctor. When I cry out and open my eyes I see a grey blur. Within it crowds a host of faces; pale and curious, they whisper and nod. This is my first meeting with the Visitors.

Mother has suffered five who died inside her before me. I am the miracle who survived. But my eyes are wrong. I can see something placed before me, but little beyond that. I learn to listen and touch, so well that I can discern Father from Nanny from Doctor from Mother from Stranger by the click of the door and the pressure of heel on rug. The Visitors make no sound in movement, but I hear their voices. I am a good little talker, saying new words as a fish lays eggs.

When I am nearly two, the fever comes. A heat like boiling soup. My ears are inflamed and leak pus. Father's voice. Always Father, always close. Nanny's voice too, and Doctor's, all grow faint and I think they whisper to spare me discomfort. But, fade away they do, to nothingness and nowhere. And never return. My ears are spoiled. Even the Visitors hush and lose their voices, looking in on me from time to time, shaking their solemn heads in pity. I am in my darkling room for months. It is a year before I can walk again without an arm around me.

In the silence, my eyes strain beyond their limits of a foot or two, yet this too begins to fade from me. Feet become inches and inches dwindle to looming shapes in a wash of dim grey. Before long I have lost all useful sight. I turn my head to the windows during the day or to a lit taper in the evening, but that is all. Much later, I will learn the name of my new affliction: cataracts. Here I am, a girl born with little sight who loses her hearing from the scarlet fever, then cataracts ruin her eyes. By three I am totally deaf and blind. The words I had learned wither like muscles unused. I speak the same words over and over at first. 'Night,' I call out in confusion at the darkness. 'Night. Night.' But I speak less and less, till it is one or two words a day, no more. When the fever passes and I am recovering, Father carries me outside to feel the wind in my hair and the sun on my skin. He takes me to the hop gardens. I pat his face and find tears there. To distract me, he places my finger on a fragile new hop flower, plucks it from the bine and lets me roll it around in my hand and crush it. 'Hop,' I say. 'Hop.' It is the last time I say an intelligible word. Thereafter, I fall quiet. I am a blind deaf-mute.

Mother is taken queer. After all the babies and the blood and the tragedy of me she retires to a quarter-life behind closed curtains. I am permitted to visit once a day before lunch. I enter her bedroom with Nanny, who leads me to Mother's bed where I hold her moist, warm hand. I try to climb into bed with her at first, but I am always pulled away. I want to run my fingers up her arms, her neck, her thick long hair like mine, to caress her face and know her. But I am restrained. I forget what Mother looks like.

My fingers are my eyes. They search and find, they look and see. And I use my sense of smell and its sister sense, taste. I know things your eyes and ears cannot summon. Upon entering a room, it is obvious to me which sex spends most time there by their perfume or aftershave, soap or talcum powder. A man's bodily odours are rich and tangy, sliced with rank cigar breath if he is a smoker. I can always tell if it is that time of the month for a woman, if she has the curse, yeasty like drying hops. I can discern the age of the books on the shelves by the scent of leather, old and slack or new and taut. If there are flowers in the room, what kind, wild or tame, how fresh or how many days dying. I can smell the dust hidden in the curtains or a dead maybug on the windowsill. I know if the housemaid has skimped on cleaning, and I can even sniff out ampery crumpet crumbs under the sofa. Can your eyes tell you so much? After all, you are a mind connected by nerves to the orbs in the front of your head, and receive the invisible yarn of sound through holes at each side. You call this seeing, hearing. But it is only your brain that makes sense of it all. My stimuli enter through fewer portals yet my mind invents reality for me every second, as it does for you. And we both dream, do we not? When your eyes and ears are largely shut to the outside, we are on equal footing. And we dream of places we have never visited, sights and sounds we have never seen or heard, people we have never met. So we are not so very different, you and me.

Once able to walk unaided, I explore my house tirelessly. I know the shape, weight, density and warmth of every object, every piece of furniture, every texture of carpet, rug or curtain, every bump and line on wallpaper (the flocked design of the dining room is my favourite). I cavort from room to room and seize objects, sniff and handle them, dash them against the wall to see if they are brittle. I am acquainted, too, with the shape of the land in the garden, could build it up in clay from finger memory: the curve of the lawn to the west and the four undulations leading up to the orchards and the steep turn in the rutty path east to the hop gardens. I go down there and skip along the hop lanes, fluttering my fingertips across the sticky stalks or the new growth soft as eyelashes. But a worker will grab me, fearful of damage being done to the crop; then Nanny pulls me away, perhaps lets me play house in the hopper huts or climb the hobbly steps to the cooling loft in the oast house and lie down on my back on the slatted floor of the drying room. The other place I prize to go is the herb garden: delicious aromas of rosemary, borage, creeping thyme, lemon mint, hyssop, chives. I know each so personally by bouquet that Cook might send me to fetch particular ones for the kitchen, for I am the swiftest seeker. Or a maid bids me fetch lavender for the linen drawers. Or Nanny dispatches me to pick chamomile to make the tea that soothes my sorely eyes (they weep of themselves from time to time). I love to stand and jump my skippy rope at the four-went way of the triangular herb beds, the sweet and peppery fragrances mingling in the whim of breezes.

Further afield, I range around with Nanny, when she can keep up with me. But she is getting old and tired and at times, even as young as three or four, I settle her down beneath a tree and stroke her hand until I sense her rumbling snore. Then I throw off my boots and stockings, as I hate to imprison my feet. I feel with them almost as much as I do with my hands. I paddle in the beck and plash the bubbling water with my toes. I climb trees and search for nesties, swing from the branches and run pell-mell as fast as my feet can find the ground, prance through tall grass and clouds of dandelion seeds or pick up a stone and heave it into the air. At least once the missile falls down on my own head and wounds me. I have a natural fear of pain, but no love of caution. Besides, knocks and scratches are bright shards in a dull existence. I fall and bump and crash while Nanny dozes. She puts iodine on after and the sting makes me cry. I do not know how she explains my injuries, but Father keeps her on, so she must come up with some ruse.

I am no less reckless with people. I grab at a tweenie maid and she pushes me away so I fall against the coarse stone of the scullery wall and my ear bleeds. I poke my finger into the stream of blood and savour it. Father's hands wash it away. Those who love me are patient with me, but those who are paid to work in Father's house find me unsettling and do not want to be alone with me. I rock my body and sway my head from side to side. I press my fingers into my eyes to make stars. I bite at my clothes and flap my hands before my face to fan it. I bang my head on the bedpost (though when tranquil I like to fondle the runnels and knots of carven wood on my headboard, which tell a sylvan story of their own). I am an idiotic creature. Maids and cooks and gardeners come and go. Only Nanny stays, and Mother in her room. And Father. But there is his land, his precious crop, his staff, his work; he cannot be my prisoner.

I become such a trial to others that I am often seized

and frog-marched to my bedroom. I am a particular nuisance in the kitchen. I like the fire, always alight, which welcomes me but not the damp reek of wet woollen clothes hanging to dry before it. Once I grab at the pot used to scald the milk as I like to taste the skin on top, and burn my hand badly. I learn to spend every afternoon locked alone in my chamber with knitting or needlework to occupy me, while the household enjoys the freedom of my absence. I, too, enjoy the peace, brushing my hair a thousand times and braiding it into elaborate styles which later shake out crimped. Or sewing for hours in straight lines and curves and random shapes, using a variety of stitches, all of which I know by feel, from blanket to cross-stitch, zigzag to daisy. I might make clothes-peg dolls and dress them in rags, or knit woollen garments for my favourite cloth doll. She is as long as my forearm and stuffed plump with sawdust. She has buttons for eyes, and when I am older and understand my blindness I pull off her button eyes so we are blind together. She has no name, because I do not yet understand names. Nanny is not Nanny, simply the one always there, leading me and showing me, and sometimes using me roughly; Father is the mellow one with the bristly chin and kind arms, who embraces me too briefly then goes away for too long; Mother is the hand on the body that never stirs in the forbidden room. And I am the one with the hot cheeks and the tummy and thick long hair like Mother's down my back and the secret places and dozens of buttons on my underclothes and the starchy layers of dress and the stiff boots, dressed every morning by other hands, the one whose body I cannot escape from alone in my room so that it must be Me.

But I am not forlorn. You have forgotten the Visitors.

They are with me often. They come and go. I can sense them when my eyes are open. But the moment I drop my eyelids, their presence dissolves. I have no visual memories to understand the sight of them. But the Visitors are there. I cannot pet them as I do a person in the outer domain, but I am always aware of their company. With my family, I know their mood by touch, the tension in Father's brow or the impatience of Nanny's fingers. Yet I know if a Visitor feels melancholy, nervous, calm or cordial by an inner sense, a vibration that creeps into my brain as warmth or cold spreads through the skin; your body reacts without your control, but you feel it all the same. I cannot converse with the Visitors because I have no words. Yet I know they want to tell me things. They are waiting for me to act, to do something for them, though I have no idea what purpose this may be. They seem to reside in my mind and so my childish self believes they are actually living inside the bones of my head. In my isolated afternoons I hold my handiwork up to my forehead to please them; play with dolly and rub her against my hair so they can reach out as if to touch her. If I am mournful I close my eyes to make them go away. Sometimes a person needs to be wintry.

Some days I tire of my comfortable gaol. I kick the door and batter the walls and caterwaul. I get into rare trouble over that. Nanny might come; I know her entrance by her churlish manner of swinging open the door and its unique jar sends me dashing behind the ten-foot velvet curtains to escape a beating with her slipper. If Father comes he treats me tenderly and strokes my face. This is my favourite punishment. I love Father with a ferocious jealousy and fight against his efforts to escape me. Mother never comes.

As time goes on, I learn some basic manners and a sense

of politeness, but only in the way a chimpanzee can be taught to wield a fork, with no comprehension of why this is better than his fingers. I will wear the prickly starched lace collar without wriggling. I take my dose of castor oil weekly without protest and eat the fat on my meat. I love mealtimes and am fed well, preferring contrasts like cold meat and hot gravy or hot jammy pudding and cold custard. I learn to keep my elbows from the table and not to gulp down cocoa or grunt when devouring seedy cake. I am permitted to help in the kitchen, to stone cherries or top and tail gooseberries with Cook's tiny scissors. Nanny taps on my hand or my back to reprove me. If I am good, I am given locust beans whose odour is horrid but their flavour delectable. If I transgress out of reach, Nanny stamps on the floor. The jolt travels to my feet and makes me stop. When Father is out, Nanny hits and shakes me. Not hard. Enough to shock. Nanny is a proper martinet, but for my own good. I am a wild animal kept in a tame house.

My desires drive me: hunger and thirst, the need for comfort and closeness, a wish to move and explore, a spirit of enquiry into what I can feel and smell and taste, never quenched. I ask all the questions my mind can conceive without words, by grasping and probing and sniffing and tasting, by applying to my nose and tongue or thrusting at Nanny or Father, a need within my flexing fingers to have it explained, to understand. But I have no words to express it and no mechanism of mind to receive it. I understand routine, that the aroma of food from the kitchen means luncheon soon, or a flannel in my hand means bath time next. Eventually, I come upon a sign or two to assuage needs: tap my lips for hunger or stroke my eyes for fatigue. But these are not calculated, only the mimetic gestures that bring satisfaction, as a cat learns to wheedle its desires from humans.

I follow my senses because they are all I have. I have to fathom the world for myself. A normal child grows and learns by listening and watching, trying out tasks and asking questions through her eyes and her early sounds. They are not yet words, but their inflection imitates the adults around her and she is understood by those dearest. I have none of this. My mind fights to escape its confines, to race and leap, but the silence and the greyness smother it. My outlet is anger, clear, ice-blue rage. My throat brings forth great shouts of hatred and I am chastised for these sounds, any sounds, in fact. I quickly learn that the noises I make – which I know only as a throbbing in my throat, a tickling in my mouth – are abhorrent to others. By touching the lips and throats of those around me, I learn that people throw messages at each other I cannot catch. I clutch at Nanny's skirt or Father's sleeve as they pace with purpose around the house and garden. And I know very early, I do not recall exactly when or how, that I am singular. I do not think my animal mind perceives that I am blind and deaf. I know there is a land that surrounds me, but always lies just beyond my grasp. I feel its constant presence through everything everyone else can do and I cannot.

I find Father holding a book and when I try to take it, I tear the pages and he stops me. Later, I return and find him there, the book still stuck in his fist. Why does he clutch this lifeless object in his lap for such long periods? And Nanny, why does she stand before a frame on the wall and primp her hair? She wears strange appendages on her nose, circles of glass surrounded by wire. And the box – a sacred object I am only allowed to toy with under direct supervision from Father – the box containing a ridged disc. When the box is working, it pulses with life. I lay my palm against its side to detect the vibrations. But no one can explain these mysteries to me yet: books and mirrors, spectacles and gramophones. Or gas lamps, candles, clocks and paintings, the Christmas tree, the chessboard, the piano or Father's bugle, which hangs from a nail on the parlour wall. I only know that the others use them for some misty purpose of their own, from which I am eternally barred.

When the slow realisation settles that I am alone in my ways, I have no words to bemoan my fate. Only my fists, with which I can punch myself on the nose or pull out fat handfuls of my hair. Such self-violence produces the most spectacular results, chiefly the wonderful sensation of Father holding me down on the settee with his whole body and constraining me so tightly I can barely breathe. This makes me crow with delight. Yet afterwards, Father is always dreadfully puffed and puts a hand against his chest. Then I am sorry for my tricks. If Father is not at home, Nanny sometimes ties me to a chair. This is displeasing, but does not happen every day. Only when the madness grips me.

I know emotions as you do: boredom, disappointment, curiosity, pride. I know the house and garden where I reside. I know comfort and routine. But I do not know the meaning of home or family. My daily life is not thick with memories and understandings and connections as is yours, but rather it is thin and splintery, broken in places which let in the chaos of the unknown. I truly believe I do not know happiness. I cannot perceive of joy versus sadness, only the difference between loss and gain. I do not know myself or society or my place within it. I can enjoy or dislike a sensation, but not discern its relative importance;

say, between a sour apple or the death of a bird. What thoughts I have, if any, are unremembered. I have the tools of a mind, but not the method by which to use them.

A sad little shadow my soul casts. These are the years 1883 to 1889. This is the Time Before.

2

I am six years old. It is late summer and the perfume of plums and pears, apples and blackberries sweetens the air. I know that when the weather is hottest and the hops are ripe, many new people arrive on Father's land and stay for a while. The ground shakes with their carts and caravans and tramping feet. They bring an army of exotic fragrances: woodsmoke and baking potatoes, perspiration and latrines. And every morning, a remarkable thing happens. Father marches into my room carrying his bugle, opens the window that faces the hop gardens, lifts his instrument and blows a rhythm across the land. I am permitted to clutch his leg as he does this and I can perceive the toots of the bugle tum-ti-tum through his body and into mine. At this signal, the people beyond stir, their work and chatter soon drumming the earth. In my long afternoons, I sit at my window and sniff the air, aware of these hordes and aching to meet them. The oast house exudes heat which drifts to my window and makes my skin clammy. A dizzying wave of yeast-stink pervades the air for days. If Nanny comes, more rarely Father, I point outside towards our guests, eager to meet them. But the answer is always no, no. I am not allowed to mix with them. I can smell the parasite deterrents our farm-hands use to keep themselves free of the pests the strangers bring, the lice and the fleas and the bugs. But I do not know this fact as yet and I do not care. I only want to meet them. I point and point again. My arms are pulled back, down. My hand slapped. This makes my blood boil.

My tantrums grow worse. Now it is five or six outbursts a day. Afterwards I am exhausted and tearful, needful of arms around me. Yet the more I rage, the less I see Father. One September day I am tied to my chair all afternoon. The moment Nanny frees me, I escape and bound to my door. Careless Nanny has left it unlocked. I throw it open and hasten down the stairs. A maid's hands grasp at my blouse but I wrench away and crash into the umbrella stand, which spews its contents. I scramble across their spiky guts and reach the front door. Outside, I skip down one, two, three, four steps and on to the drive. I trip on a rock I have forgotten at the edge of a circular border and the gravel greets my face with a clawing scrape. Skin, blood and stone fuse. But I will not stop. I get up and run-stumble on eastwise down the twisty path. I follow my nose to the hum of strangers gathered along the hop lanes. My flailing arms meet with resistance as I pass, bodies to the left and right, solid, foreign. I reach the end of a row and stop, winded. Then I feel a hand touch mine. I pull away, ready to yell, but it is a new hand: cracked and cut, used to manual work, but slender, mobile and female. It touches my hand again. This time I do not recoil. It begins to move, making shapes. Two fingers lie flat on my palm, one touches the tip of my fourth, a hand grasps my outstretched fingers. And so they go on, these odd shapes. Now, a finger draws a line from the top of my thumb down its curve to the tip of my index finger, then touches the tip of this and then one finger flat in the palm, then three fingers side by side. I am utterly still.

The next hand is Father's, on my shoulder. I turn, use my free right hand to point at the shapes. But the hand withdraws. I cry out, stretch into space for that new hand. It comes again and I relax. I want that hand now. Father's nudge at my back, we walk slowly back to the house, the new hand still there, still making those shapes. We go to my bedroom and sit on my bed. I do not know where Father is, I do not care. I assess the hand, up the arm to the head. Thin arms. Hair tied back in a tight, neat bun. Curly, wild when free, I imagine. Warm skin, sharp cheekbones. Full mouth. The lips smile. A countenance so pleasant I kiss her cheek. A sharp whiff of hop, sweat and soap exudes from her skin.

The hand takes mine again. It makes more shapes, new ones, quicker and quicker. I love this hand now. I want it never to leave. Nanny taps firmly on my back and I turn in fury, want to grab her and snap her, toss her away. I want nothing but my lady, who now taps my face. I remember my grazed cheek. In my enchantment, I had forgotten the pain. I permit Nanny to cleanse my wound, but cling to my lady's hand. I want to explore her further so I let my hand roam, reaching down to her buttoned boots caked with mud, fingering her skirt of coarse cotton, covered with an apron stiff with grime, frayed and hole-ridden along its hem. I get up and retrieve my sewing basket. I will mend it for her and put everything in apple-pie order and she will love me. I feel someone leave the room but assume it is Father and do not care, as long as my lady is here.

When I return to the bed and sit, I know from its

flatness that I am alone. Now that I am calm they have taken my lady away. I go to the door and it is locked. I scream and beat the walls. My wrath is scorching. I have never felt such a longing and loss as I do for my lady, for that hand and its shapes. I will not eat, I will not drink, I will not succumb until I have that hand again. Time watches me, impassive. I sense the Visitors come. They are sad for me; I almost feel their touch like the faintest breath on my skin. They want to console me. But they cannot, they cannot do a thing for me, cannot act for me in my powerlessness. I despise them for being no help and no use. I close my eyes and shake my head to insensibility to rid it of their pointless pity. I fall on my empty bed, sobbing, gasping. In time, I wipe my face and take up my doll. I tidy her hair and straighten her clothes. I sit on the edge of the bed and cradle her in my lap. She sleeps.

Hours later, I have not moved. I do not understand patience, but I know that nothing will happen while I am screaming. So I sit still and wait. Then, a jolt as the door is unlocked and opened. I know two figures approach by the stirring of air and their tread. One is Father and the other follows: tiptoe-light, tentative. Father pats my tear-dried cheek. I grasp his hand, do not know the common way of begging, but do my best, a kind of drawing towards my heart, my head swaying, eyes tight shut. Please, please. Bring her back to me. And here it is, her hand again in mine. I straight away flatten my palm ready for the shapes. They begin again. If I fidget, they stop, so I remain static. Then an object appears in my hand. I know it well, it is a key. Daily, Father lets me unlock the tall clock in the hall and wind it up. She removes the key and makes three shapes: one finger hooked in the palm, a touch on my index fingertip, a pointed finger at the base of my thumb. Then the hand is gone. Back comes the key. The three shapes again. The key. The shapes. And so it goes on.

She stops. She wraps her fingers around mine. She takes my index finger and moulds it into a hook in her palm. Then she shapes my straight finger pointing at the tip of her index. Next I point at the base of her thumb. Now the key is back in my hand. Away again. I have to make the shapes myself. She helps me. I recall them exactly. The three shapes, then the key. The three shapes, always the same three shapes in the same order. She places my right hand over her own, so that I can discern the shapes it makes from her viewpoint. This helps me refine my style and I quickly become adept. I am good at this trick. It is new and it is fascinating. I like the complexity, the sense of purpose.

I remember Father and flail my hand out for him. He is there beside me. I take his hand, put in the key, remove it and make the three shapes. He grasps my hand and shakes it like a jolly gentleman. I do not think he appreciates how wonderful my new trick is, so I do it again and again. His hand is rigid with concentration. He stops me and throws his arms around me, lifts me and wheels me about the room. So I do it again and again, as it cheers him and makes him love me. He sits me down with her and this time my doll appears in my hands. I learn new shapes then hold my doll. There are four shapes this time and they are different from the others. Yet the last two are the same one repeated. I check this to make sure and yes, it is correct.

This day we pick up many objects around my room and make the shapes for each: bed, chair, brush, pin, shoe. Then parts of the body: ear, nose, mouth, eye, hair. As she demonstrates the new patterns, my face is screwed with anxiety to read it precisely and reproduce it correctly. I am delighted when I get it right. And I do get it right, repeatedly. I want to pick up more things and make more shapes, more and more. Everything. But she is selective, ignores some requests, proffers others. I learn at least twenty and make them over and over. Soon my fingers are fatigued. Not from motion, as my hands are habituated to doing fine work for hours on end. But my mind is tired. It is unaccustomed to such strenuous and peculiar activity. I want to lie down, but I do not wish her to leave me. I take her hands and pull her to the bed. I stroke my eyes to show I am sleepy. She makes new shapes for me, five this time, some I know already from other patterns. She strokes my eyes too then makes the five shapes. I draw her fingers to my breast. I am very frightened that she will go. But she does not. She is lying beside me and lets me squeeze her hands. Before my eyelids droop, the Visitors come and they are most excitable and congratulatory. I fall asleep with a merry heart. I dream of her. My dreams are a mixture of the real and the impossible, as are yours. I can run without impediment, I can leap and float, my feet above the ground. But I cannot miraculously see and hear in my dreams. Instead I feel through my body, my muscles' sense of space, my joys and terrors, as in my waking life. This dream is of my lady's hands, just her hands in mine. They move with mystery and offer a kind of hope I do not yet understand but I want it, how I want it so.

She never leaves me. She is there when I open my eyes in the morning and there until I close them at night. There is no extra bed in my room, so she must sleep elsewhere, but comes in before I wake to be with me and stays until I have fallen asleep. I have woken in the night to find her absent, and have shouted for her. Nanny comes and I shove her stupid old face away and yowl and reach for the other one, the lady with the hands. Nanny slaps me across the mouth but then Father's hands are on my hair. There is a commotion in the room. People are stamping and throwing themselves about. I reach out for Father. Instead she comes, the one I want. She helps me to lie down. She caresses my eyelids and helps me fall back to sleep. Nanny does not come again, not this night or ever. Nanny has gone.

At first I wake every night and cry out for my lady. I fear that she will tire of me and drive me from her presence. But she does not and soon I am comfortable with her leaving me when I am still awake. I know she is always there for me in the morning, so I do not fret. I am happy to sleep alone, knowing my days will be filled with her. I do not have to spend the afternoons locked in my room any more. I have her with me all day and we play and learn new shapes. She smells different now, of clean linen and Mother's soap.

I have never been so pleased with myself and my lot. It is the most exquisite treat to have a companion who stays with me always. I hug her and kiss her often, take down her hair and brush it, but I was right, it is wild. I find if I wet it first with water from the basin on the washstand it tames and lies flatter. I brush it damp like this and plait it or tie it in rags at night, so that there will be ringlets in the morning when she comes to wake me. Every day we play new games. I copy her when she shakes my hands or pats my fingers gently, we nod towards each other and at our closest I let her breath tickle my skin. We explore more rooms, more objects and more shapes. Two weeks pass and I learn dozens of new patterns. It is still novel to me and I enjoy it. But I have no clue as to its purpose. I make no connection in my mind between the shapes I am learning, the patterns they make and the objects she gives me. I can repeat them, but they mean nothing to me. I never make the shapes when the objects are not there, only when I hold them in my hand. I do not know that these patterns mean more than themselves. I am a mynah bird. Yet something grows in me, a kernel of thought, that there is intent behind this dumb show, that it is not a plaything like our other sports. It is important. But I cannot grasp why and my lady cannot convey it. Until she takes me to the hop garden.

I know from before that once the people leave Father's land, the bines go too. The plants do not return until the cold has come and gone and the warm days recur. My lady lets me grasp the bare poles. Most of the plants have been picked. But I find a single hop cone clinging to a forgotten spiny tendril straggling from a mound. I give her the flower as a present. She takes it, puts her right hand in my left and makes three shapes: her flat hand rests in my palm and brushes upwards across my fingers, she prods the tip of my fourth, pinches the end of my index finger. Then the hop flower is put in my hand. Again, the three shapes. Then the hop. Three shapes. The hop. Shapes, hop. Shapes, HOP. Shapes, H-O-P. I stop her hand. I stop dead still. I am thinking. I hold the hop flower, roll it around in my left hand, crush it. I reach for her hand. I make the three shapes, H-O-P. I give her the flower. H-O-P, again and again. The shapes are a word. The word is a sign. A sign that speaks. The flower I hold in my hand has a name and its name is H-O-P. I spell it.

'H-O-P.'

I drop to the ground, scrabble around for that hard, round thing I like to throw. I place it in my lady's hand, she gives me five shapes. S-T-O-N-E. Its name is stone. I spell it out.

'S-T-O-N-E.'

I laugh and jump and skip and grasp my lady's shoulders, which shake with laughter too. More, I want more. We tumble around the garden and we find G-R-A-S-S, a L-E-A-F and a T-R-E-E, even a N-E-S-T. I reach out and touch my lady's face. Tap my palm, rest my hand on her chest. What is my lady's word? What is she? She spells it for me. L-O-T-T-I-E. Lottie. I spell it back.

'Lottie,' I spell to her. 'Lottie.'

We are talking with our fingers.

But what is the word for Me? Does Me have a name? I pat my chest, I tap my hand. What is my name? Lottie takes my hand. One finger flat in the palm, a fingertip pointed at my middle finger, the side of the hand placed at an angle across the palm, a fingertip pointed at the thumb. L-I-Z-A.

'Liza,' says Lottie.

'Liza,' I say.

My name is Liza.

3

I learn hundreds of words. We go into every room and Lottie shows me the names for everything I can lay my hands on. I know the word for every object in my house now, from the simple 'copper' in the kitchen to the poetic 'marcella counterpane' in my bedroom. Nouns first, then verbs and adjectives. I can explain qualities: hot, cold; young, old. I can express opinions: like, dislike. I join words together and make pidgin sentences: Liza run. Liza drink milk. Liza love Lottie and Father. I lose all interest in those who cannot finger spell. Father learns it in a day, but he is not as quick as Lottie and me. I want to tell him things, but when he speaks back I have to wait a long time for his words and sometimes I push him away mid-sentence, bored. He evidently starts practising, for soon he is better and we talk every day. He takes me on walks and names flowers and herbs for me, gives me the terms for all the parts of the hop plant and the equipment in the oast house. He shows me precious objects in his study: a conch shell, a marble egg, a rose quartz crystal. I learn the names of all the soapstone chess pieces. He makes a special chessboard from wood, with raised rules between the squares, so that I can feel to move the King one space forward, the Bishop two spaces diagonally, the Knight up two and along one. He begins to teach me the game and shakes my hand heartily when I make a good move. I know he loved me in the Time Before, but I feel he loves me more now.

Next I learn about names. I discover that Father is Father and Mother is Mother. I know Cook is Cook but has another name, Martha. This is confusing so I call her Cook Martha. There is Maid Edith and Maid Florrie. And Maid Alice who is lady's maid to Mother. I still visit Mother every day and I am allowed to drip drops of lavender water on a handkerchief and mop her forehead. She lets me touch her hand and now I make shapes for her. She lets me do it into her outstretched palm, but never answers me.

Afterwards, I tell Lottie, 'Mother make no shapes.'

Lottie says, 'One day.'

I know I am Adeliza Golding, Father is Edwin Golding and Mother is Evangeline Golding. Lottie is Charlotte Crowe.

I ask, 'Why Lottie not Golding?'

She says, 'Different mother and father.'

'Where sleep?'

'Not this house.'

'What house?'

'By the sea.'

'What is sea?'

'Big water.'

'Like pond.'

'No. Very big. Salty.'

'Liza go now to sea and meet Lottie mother and father.'

'One day,' says Lottie.

Soon I stop calling myself Liza and understand the word 'me'. Later, I think that my two years of hearing before the fever helped to store in my mind a plethora of ideas derived from my ears which must have been locked in some piece of dusty furniture at the back of my head. Lottie has the key. She not only teaches me names for objects or feelings or ideas, but she does something else: she talks with me all the time. She sits or walks with me and finger spells long sentences into my hand. Many of the words I do not know, but others I do, and I can work out some from their context. She treats me like a hearing child, one who cannot yet understand all the vocabulary the adults use, but who learns through listening and repeating and constant exposure to language. She does not engage in baby talk. For the first time in my life, I have found a person who does not treat me like an infant, an object of pity, or an animal. She treats me like a person.

I become very clever at the finger spelling. I want to do it all day, all night too. Any time I am alone, if Lottie must be absent for a moment, I speak to myself through finger signing into my own left hand. Lottie and I do not hold our palms flat any more to converse. When we talk, I hold my hand before me, curved downwards as if holding an invisible plum, while Lottie makes the signs rapidly within the curve of my hand. I do the same. My right hand is so pliable now and the left stiff to compare, as it never speaks. Our minds and our hands think in words, not separate letters. When you listen to a person speak, you do not notice every letter, nor do you read each letter separately when you look upon writing. Our conversations are the same. Our fingers move so fast in forming our words, I challenge anyone to follow the quicksilver speed of our conversations.

I ask Lottie, 'Why do you know finger spelling? Why only you?'

'A man taught me a long time ago.'

'Why?'

'I had a sister once. She was like you. She could not see or hear.'

'Did you talk with her?'

'Yes. The man who taught me was a vicar, a man of the Church. He had travelled far and wide and knew many things. He had been across the sea to a big school once and learned the finger spelling. When he knew we had a baby sister who was blind and deaf, he came and taught us how to finger spell.'

'He taught you and your mother and father?'

'Yes, and my brother. We taught her and she learned quickly, like you. We all had such happy times together. She was a lovely girl.'

'Where is she now? Can I meet her?'

'No, Liza. I am afraid she died.'

'How did she die?'

'She had a dreadful fever when she was about your age.'

'A fever like mine, the one that hurt my ears when I was a baby?'

'Yes, but it was too strong for her and it killed her.'

'What was her name?'

'Constance.'

'Constance Crowe.'

'Yes.'

'You loved her very much.'

'Yes, I did.'

'I am sorry.'

'Thank you, Liza.'

I kiss Lottie's hand. A Visitor says, *Why are you sad, Adeliza?*

* * *

The Visitors speak with me now. It began the same day I spelled 'hop'. The moment my mind opened to language, they came streaming in, desperate to communicate with me. As with Lottie's long speeches, I did not understand them at first, yet learned to converse with them gradually, as I learned to finger spell with Lottie and Father. Yet they do not make the shapes in my hand, as they do not share the same territory as my family and the servants. But I can hear them inside my head. I know that you too can hear words in your head, yet they make no sound. Somehow, your thoughts create the voice in your mind, with no sound waves to make it real. But hear it you do. It is the same for me and the Visitors. They are equivalent to my thoughts. Yet I know they are not mine. They are other, but choose to stay with me and now speak with me, only when my eyes are open. Some have names. Others have forgotten them. They do not speak to each other. They do not seem to know each other exists or anyone beyond my head either. But they talk to me and tell me things. Sometimes, I need to organise them, say, *Hush! Wait your turn.* Otherwise, if there is more than one, they all talk over each other and the cacophony in my head drives me mad.

At night, when Lottie has retired to bed exhausted from my constant need for her, I stay awake listening to the Visitors. I talk to them in my mind. These are strange conversations with the Visitors, not like with Lottie or Father. They are quite rude. They do not really listen to me, only waiting for me to finish a sentence so that they can say what they want. And what they want most of all is to talk about themselves. Or rather, one thing over and over. They do not discuss, only harp on this one thing. It is different for each. It may be a boat trip or a dog they once had, a fall from a tree or a scratch from a rose thorn. This one thing they are obsessed with, and they speak of it again and again. I try to ask them about other matters, who they are and what they are, where they come from and why they are here, but they do not seem to understand such metaphysical enquiry and instead tell me again about their obsession. It is as if they are stuck in a groove and cannot escape this one event. One is charming, telling me of a day spent building a dry-stone wall with his son. But another is angry, twisting his rage into knots while damning another man for spooking his horse, causing him to fall and crack his head. I ask this one to calm down and mostly he does. I do not like him. They were easier to live with before I learned language, before they could talk.

I decide to tell Lottie about them. I know them and I am accustomed to them, but I fear she will find them strange. She has never mentioned them to me and neither has Father. I worry that they do not visit Father and Lottie, as they do me. And that is when I name them, the Visitors. I explain them to Lottie. At first she does not pass comment. I ask her if she hears the Visitors in her mind.

She says, 'No. Those are my thoughts. You can call them Visitors if you like.'

'No,' I say. 'The Visitors are different. They were with me before you, before I learned words.'

'They were your thoughts then too. You always had a mind. But no language. Now they talk with you because you know words.'

I shake my head. I am sure she is wrong, but I fear she thinks I am touched, a little crazed due to my years of isolation. And I do not want there to be the least shadow between myself and Lottie. I ask her often, 'Are you very fond of me?' and she always answers, yes. I do not want her to think of me strangerly. So I stop talking about the Visitors. All I know is that I am different from Lottie, from Father, from everyone. Not just with my ruined ears and eyes, but in another way I cannot explain. I live in another country. With language, I bring dispatches from the abyss. I cannot say I am happy there. It has been my prison. But at least it is familiar. The area beyond my fingertips is bigger than me. It is marvellous yet frightening. I wonder if I will ever feel at home in that other world, your world.

But then Lottie begins to teach me more than language. I learn the laws of nature by exploring the gardens, picking flowers and berries, peeling bark or digging for worms, making a rain-catcher and bringing snowballs inside to feel them melt in my warm hands. I understand that animals cannot talk with their fingers. I am hugely disappointed in this and think they must be very feeble-minded. I learn biology by finding a dead bird and lifting its wings to understand flight. Physics by climbing trees and dropping apples. Geography through placing a stick in the beck so that I can feel the flowing of water and understand currents. I know that the water on Father's land runs into a river downstream which feeds into the great wide sea where the Crowe family live. Beyond there are other lands where many live and others have travelled. Our planet is made of land and sea, mountains and valleys, stretching forth from my little life across the globe and back in time for millennia and forward beyond my short span for ever. I cannot encompass how large the earth is.

One day Lottie takes my hand and leads me to Father's study. He has bought me something new. She lets me find it. It is half as tall as me, twice as fat. Round, curved, I am feeling over it, down it and below it. Upon its surface, peaks and troughs, rough terrain and smooth sea. I have guessed. It is the earth. It is a globe. We talk about countries, about our little England and the provinces beyond it, all encompassed in a sphere. She is astounded at how quickly my fingers move across it and how my mind knows it so completely so soon. By touch, I have a special knowledge of it which perhaps a sighted child would not gain from a flat map. In a morning I learn the continents and the oceans and some of the countries. Europe gives me trouble, so many little nations on one slab of land.

'Do they not argue in Europe,' I ask Lottie, 'living so stuffily?'

I like mountains, as they ridge pleasantly beneath my fingernails. The first I learn are the Alps. They do not feel so very far away from England. I ask Lottie if we can visit the Alps tomorrow. She explains the globe is a scale replica, that I have to multiply the distances I feel by hundreds and thousands of times. That the miles from here to Australia are almost beyond imagining. My mind aches at this. But one day, I will be able to comprehend it. For now, the globe gives me a shape for our existence.

But what is beyond the globe? The sky. And beyond that? The stars. And beyond them?

Lottie says, 'Your father wants to talk with you about that.'

'Why not you?'

'Your father does not want me to discuss such matters with you.'

'About the sky?'

'No, about God.'

'What is God?'

'Ask your father.'

So I ask him, 'What is God?'

Father tells me God created the world and the universe and everything in it. He is all-powerful and all-knowing. God wants me to be a good girl, kind to others and always mind my parents and my teacher. God knows when I have been bad. He sees me always and knows my every thought.

'Does he live in my house?'

'No, our Lord resides in heaven.'

'Is it by the sea?'

'No, it is above the earth, way up above the sky itself.'

'When you look up, can you see heaven with your eyes, Father?'

'No. It is not in our sphere.'

'How can God see me then?'

'He has the all-seeing eye.'

'How can he hear my thoughts?'

'He can do anything He pleases. He can enter your mind and eavesdrop on you.'

'Like the Visitors?'

'Who?'

I stop there. I am not ready to tell Father about the Visitors. I do not want him to think I am a lunatic.

Now I know about the world and about God, and I can speak about them. I believe I know everything, that my education is complete. What else is there to learn?

4

Lottie brings me something new. Slips of paper with bumps on them. She lets me feel the bumps; they are made of lines and curves, like the carvings on my headboard. She puts a pot of glue beside me. She gives me a cup. She helps me to paste the paper to the cup. Then she spells C-U-P in my hand and directs me to feel the bumps on the paper. Now my mind is at work, it does not take me long to realise that the bumps are letters. Put them together and you can make words. Not in the hand, but on paper, where you can pass the paper to someone else and they can hear it by touching, even take away the paper to somewhere else and give it to another person, who can hear the word too, without even being in the room with you. I understand it is a kind of portable finger spelling. Lottie explains further that others can recognise these letter shapes with their eyes, while I use touch. Later I know this to be called reading and writing.

We paste many labels on to objects and I start to learn the sequences of shapes, relating them to my finger alphabet. Pointing to the tip of my thumb corresponds to the shape A on the paper, and so on. Then I am given the separate letters of the alphabet on paper and I organise them myself into words, arranging them side by side to spell cup, key, apple. I put the words together to make sentences: water in cup, apple on table, key in door. I use the letters to make more words, the ones that are not objects you can hold or actions you can show, the useful words that hold language together: the, is, as, it, her and all the rest. I make long sentences. Lottie and Father read them and pat me on my head to show their approval.

One morning I ask Lottie, 'Is it only you and Father who can read?'

'No. Many people can read.'

'Can Mother read?'

'Yes.'

I get straight to work. I arrange my letters with great care. They stretch across the table in the dining room, which has become our schoolroom. Lottie wants to help, but I tell her not to look. It is private.

'Will Mother come down here?' I ask Lottie.

'I don't think so.'

So she helps me paste it on a sheet of paper. We collect a selection of spare letters and put them in an envelope. We have to wait until lunchtime to see Mother. I go in and take her hand as always. I give her the paper and the envelope. I wait while she reads. It says: 'Mother. Please talk to me. I love you.'

I wait. At first, there is no movement. I wonder if she is sleeping. Then I feel the bed shaking. I reach out and find her hand is wet. She raises mine to her cheeks and there are tears flowing down her face on to my hand. She takes my face in her hands and holds it there. She is looking at me. I smile and nod my head, to show her all is well. She takes me in her arms and holds me so tightly. I am nearly eight years old and it is my first hug with Mother. I cry also and we hold each other for a long time. When we have recovered ourselves, she takes the envelope and places letters on the bed. It is soft and bumpy, not ideal for messages, but I take each letter and feel it, reading slowly. She has written one word only: 'Sorry.'

The next day I am allowed to see Mother for longer. We bring the envelope and a tea tray on her lap on which to place them. I begin. It is a question I have wanted to ask for a long time.

'Do you love me?'

'Yes.'

'Why not finger spell?'

'Ill.'

'Where are you ill?'

'Body. Mind.'

'When will you be well?'

'Better today.'

'Why?'

'You.'

Our first conversation. It is laborious, finding the correct paper letters, placing them on the tray only to find they slip and slide; and for speed's sake we are forced to form simplistic sentences which frustrate my meaning. After, I tell Lottie that the paper letters are driving me to distraction. They are flimsy and crumpled, getting greasy and dog-eared from constant use. She tells me a printer in Maidstone made them, an expert in embossed paper. But Father is working on something much better. I must be patient. Soon, it comes. Father has constructed metal types for the alphabet and a wooden board with holes, where the alphabet blocks are slotted and can be removed to rearrange and spell out words. I am delighted and spend hours a day making sentences. I have to be dragged away for exercise and other lessons.

Lottie brings me books. I open one and find the pages are full of raised letters. I can read whole sentences without having to make them myself. I remember in the Time Before trying to destroy Father's books through ignorance and want. Now I can go away from Father and Lottie and sit on my bed; I have my own books, books I can read alone, without any help from another, without any explanation or filter from those who love me. I read of the alphabet, numbers and animals, picnics, jungles and the stars. I demand more and am given fairy tales, intrepid adventures, caves full of treasure, a child's Bible. I dote on my books and hug them to me in bed, discarding dolls for a time. They are my new friends. I want more, yet I am told there are few books in raised letters and by now I have most of those from the catalogue. Yet still I yearn for more. Then I learn a new way of reading, no raised letters, instead bumps in patterns that stand for letters. Lottie and I learn the bumps and I spend hours applying them to new books Father has found for me. The patterns have a special name: Braille. Lottie explains that the blind use Braille to read quickly, that it was important for me to know the alphabet first, for I will use it in another way one day. Yet Braille will help my reading take off and there are far more books published in this way. Once learned, it is much swifter than reading the embossed alphabet and soon I am flying through longer and longer books.

One day Father brings me a special gift, a particular book he likes. I sit and begin the first sentence: *Marley was dead: to begin with.* I read *A Christmas Carol* by Mr Charles Dickens. I never knew there were voices like this. I never imagined life jostling with other minds and bodies, all going their own ways in their own lives with their own stories to enact till their own deaths take them and they are remembered in the minds of others always and for ever. The act of feeling the bumps on paper transports me from my confinement in a way not even a conversation can. Only now do I understand why Father sits so long with a book in his hand. He is a time-traveller. And now, so am I. There is one curious thing: as I read, I am not disturbed once by the Visitors. It is as if there is no room in my mind for them, as it is filled with the book. It is a relief. I love my Visitors and talk with them often. But their absence is a release. I read my book in a day.

I have many questions about the book. I ask Father first: 'Are ghosts real?'

'No, I believe not.'

'But Mr Dickens writes of them.'

'It is a story and one can write whatever one pleases in a story.'

'Is this not a lie?'

'Stories are not lies. They imagine a thing to be true, to entertain us.'

'Can Mr Dickens see me?'

'Of course not!'

'But he talks to me as I read his book and I think he knows me. He can see me when I do wrong.'

'No, Adeliza. That is God.'

I am not satisfied. I ask Lottie: 'There are ghosts in this book. Father says they are not real.'

'Some people believe they are.'

'Do you?'

'I do not know for sure. Perhaps.'

'Did God make ghosts?'

'I do not think so.'

'But God made everything.'

'Some people think that.'

'And you?'

'Your Father would not want me to talk to you about this.'

'Father is not here.'

But Lottie will not explain further and I cannot persuade her. She says instead she has a present for me. I hold it and know it. It is a pen. The sighted use it for writing, as I use my metal type. Not for me. But she shows me how to hold it and places a piece of paper beneath my pen and tells me to make my mark. I scratch a wild stroke then touch it. I can feel the wet ink, quickly drying on my skin and the paper. Now I understand why I needed to know the letters of the alphabet, for now I will form them with my own hand.

'But I cannot read it.'

'No, but others can. And you will be able to write to them. Write letters and put them in the post. And your letters will be taken in coaches to other people who can read them hundreds of miles away. And they will read what you have written.'

'But I do not know anyone who lives far away, except your family. And they do not know me.'

'Learn to write then and you can write them a letter, introducing yourself.'

'I cannot write to old people. I am shy of them.'

'Write to my brother Caleb, then. He would like that.'

In winter, the smell of burning hop bines drifts through the air to my table as I labour over my writing. In the New Year I forgo my annual activity of helping make the first hole for the hop poles so that I can practise my letters. It takes months to write each letter of the alphabet distinctly and to separate words from each other. By March, the stilt walkers are stringing up the new coir twine to the overhead wires for the hop bines to grow up, and I am learning punctuation. In May, the farmhands thread the bines around the strings, training them to grow clockwise. They pinch out the pipey bines that promise long stems but no fruit. I can now write legibly enough for others to decipher. It is hard and long and daily work, doubly difficult as I cannot check my own writing and see my errors. But I persevere. I think about my finger spelling, my first language. Though we think of it as talking, I realise that I have been writing all this time, that my flat hand is the paper and my finger is the pen. Using ink is merely the next step, to make it conveyable. The growing season is well under way, my father's workers busy protecting our cherished harvest. They place ladybirds on the leaves to eat the flies and stop the hop-blight. Later they trundle the crop washer down the alleys, spraying soft soap to kill pests. Meanwhile, I complete my first unaided letter, which reads thus:

> *Dear Caleb Crowe Liza writes letter to you Liza will come to sea and bring doll Liza will talk with Caleb Liza will give love to Caleb Liza will come home*

It may not seem much, but it is a great leap for a ten-year-old deaf-blind girl whose first six years were lived in the land of the dead. My wooden board with the metal type becomes only a toy for filling a spare moment, gathers dust, then is put away. Mother has learned to finger spell. She comes downstairs and even takes short walks with me, my arm linked with hers, my hand stroking the material of her leg-of-mutton sleeves. As we walk, I say to her with my other hand, 'What do you see?' and she describes things to me. She has a particular way of speaking, a turn of phrase I like, a way of stating the heart of things. She still sleeps every afternoon. I am told she will always be weak. But I have my mother now. And Father and Lottie. I have my hands to talk, my books to read and my pen to write my thoughts. Now I am a person.

A few weeks pass and Lottie brings me something wonderful. It is a letter from Caleb. She reads it to me:

Dear Miss Golding,

I was pleased to receive your letter. I think it would be a fine thing for you to visit us in Whitstable. Bring your doll and I will take you both out to sea. I will show you our oyster beds. You can feel an oyster in your hands and I will crack its shell open for you. Then you can eat it. Have you ever tasted an oyster? There is nothing better.

Yours sincerely,
Caleb Crowe

It is finer even than Mr Dickens. But I am worried about the oyster.

I ask Lottie, 'Is it not very cruel to crack the oyster's shell? Does it cry out?' She assures me it does not and that they are indeed delicious to eat.

From that moment on, I beg and beg Father to let me go to Whitstable.

He says, 'You are not ready to go into the world yet.'

'Why not?'

'There are still some things for you to learn. About the way you are with people.'

'What things?'

'The noises you make.'

'But I have voice. Why cannot I use it?'

'You know the hearing people find it disagreeable.'

'But I want to practise so that I can speak with my mouth.'

'We do not think you will ever speak with your mouth, Adeliza.'

I consider this. 'Is this true? Does Lottie say it is true?'

'Charlotte and I agree. You will never speak with your mouth.'

'When I go to God in heaven, I will see and hear, you told me. So I will speak with my mouth in heaven.'

'But not on this earth, Liza. So it is best that you keep yourself quiet.'

'I will try to be silent, Father.'

'And another thing. There are times when your face is . . . a little odd.'

'Am I ugly?'

'Not at all. You are a beautiful girl. But perhaps others would find strange the way you make faces sometimes. And the way you sniff at objects and even at people.'

'You mean the world is not ready to see me.'

'You know I love you more than anyone else. But other people are not used to your ways, as we are at home.'

'I will work hard on my vices, Father.'

I am true to my word. I always do Father's bidding, of course. But my most powerful incentive is this: every time I grimace or shout, I think of meeting Caleb Crowe. I think of his aversion when he sees the peculiar deaf-blind girl. From then on, I am composed and serene, neither a murmur from my throat or a flinch of my face. I know I must be a curious creature to behold. Not the wild animal of my early childhood, yet I am prone to great excitements. Now I strive to be an angel child. I ask Lottie to hit me every time I make a horrible noise or repulsive grimace, but she says she will never do that. She will tap my back when I do wrong and pat my head when I succeed. Lottie and I make a secret bargain, that I repress my urges all morning, but in the afternoons when Father is out, I can go to my room and do as much yelling and crying as my heart desires. At times I hark back to my old barbarous self, going on capers in my room, slamming doors to feel the quaking thud and jumping on the bed till the springs wince.

Before I get a chance to travel to Whitstable, or anywhere else for that matter, it is the hop-picking season once more and the rest of the Crowe family come for their annual visit. Lottie disappears for a whole day. I do not begrudge her time with her family. But I miss her dreadfully. Mother takes a short walk with me in the morning and I mope around the house all afternoon, reading my books and knitting and pacing in and out of the scullery, waiting for the door to open through which my Lottie comes and goes from the house. But she does not return and I go to my room that night and it is Father who helps me to bed and to say my prayers and my only prayer is that Lottie should tire of her family soon and come back to me. The next morning she wakes me up and I throw my arms around her and weep. I want to tie her hands so she cannot leave me.

'Do not go away again,' I say.

'I have to sometimes, my pet. You are my special one

but I have others who love me too and who I love very much.'

'I know. I am sorry. I am selfish.'

'Come and meet them.'

I dress with care. I insist I do my own hair but ensure it is carefully checked by Lottie. We walk down to the hop garden and find the Crowe family around their hop bin. They cannot stop to chat too long, as they only earn by the weight of flowers they pick. I know that Lottie sends money home to her mother from the wage she receives from Father. But they need more, I am told, and the hop picking helps a lot. It buys them winter clothes at least. Mr Crowe does not come to the hops; he stays by the sea to manage the oyster beds.

There is Mrs Crowe here and three boys younger than Lottie. Their names are Clarence and Claude, twins aged five, and Christopher aged three. And there is Caleb. He and his mother can still finger spell, though they are rusty due to a long time since use. The children do not talk with their fingers at all, as they never had a need.

Mrs Crowe says, 'Pretty girl.'

I say, 'Thank you.'

'Very grown up.'

'I am already eleven years old.'

Mrs Crowe touches my cheek and her hands are rugged as bark. But kind. We pause and I think she has nothing more to say to me at present. I reach out and Lottie knows who I want to meet next.

Caleb says, 'Hello.'

I say to Caleb, 'Thank you for your letter.'

'Welcome.'

'Lottie says you are twins. Were you in your mother's tummy together?'

'Yes.'

'Lottie is twenty-two years old. Are you the same age as Lottie?'

'Yes. Same birthday.'

'Do you look the same?'

He takes my hand and places it on his cheek. The edge of my hand brushes his tickly moustache. I feel his features with trembling fingers. He has the same sharp cheekbones as his sister, the same long nose, the full mouth. The hair is less wild, wavy and thick, long at the back and swept away from the front. I touch his eyelids, his eyes large like Lottie's. I think of my eyes. Father says the cataracts are cloudy and look spectral. I hope they are not unsightly. I close them as I feel Caleb's face. I do not want him to be scared of my eyes.

They have to work on, so Lottie leads me away. I want to see them every day but Father says no. I believe Lottie spends the evenings with her family when I sleep. She is weary the next day, every day of the hop-picking season. Her fingers move slower than usual. I am allowed to meet her family once more. It is the last night before they leave for home and there is a hoppers' party. Father says I can go for one hour, but must come home forthwith for bedtime. The ground shakes with dancing feet and thumping rhythm. I try to dance with Lottie, but tread on her toes so much I am embarrassed and stay by the side, feeling the swoop of dancing couples as they whirl by. I tap my feet and clap my hands to the pounding beat of the music. Lottie takes me to meet the musicians. There is a woman playing a hollow drum stretched with smooth skin, striking a double-ended beater on it. She lets me hold it while she beats a pattern and the rhythm resonates along my arms. They say she is from Ireland. I know from my globe it is reached by boat across the western sea.

There is a violin and I touch the hand that holds it. Is is Caleb, I know instantly. He stands behind me and lets me hold the instrument in my left hand, my fingers wrapped around the fingerboard while he supports the scroll. The violin sits under my chin and I grip down with my jaw. In my right hand, he places the bow, curves my hand into the correct shape for gripping. We place the bow on the string and he pushes my hand upwards and gently pulls it back, the string vibrating and sending rays of delight through my body as the sound waves travel through the violin's wooden frame into my own. I can feel the music come alive as we play the long note again and again, push up, pull down. He takes the violin and kneels beside me, lets me place my hand on it and plays me a tune, a jig or a reel or some such dance and I can feel the thrust of the bow and the jagged short strokes it makes to speak the tune. And the rhythm tap-taps through my hand and into my bones and I tap the tune all evening before bedtime and tap it again on my headboard that night. And I never forget it.

I understand I have passed a kind of test. Now the hop pickers have met me, Father agrees I am fit to be seen. New friends come to the house. People have heard of the little deaf-blind girl who can talk with her fingers. I undergo the touch of dozens of new hands – friends of Father's, local dignitaries, scholars and professors of the blind and deaf, the curious and the nosey, the sentimental and the avaricious – all come to see Adeliza Golding. Some come more than once and I know them in a trice by their handshake. You may glimpse a person once and not see them for a month or more. If you see them again, will you recognise them? I do, but by contact. A person's handshake is unique, a slight pressure of the index finger in this one, a perpetual dampness with that one. My new acquaintances are amazed that I know them by a touch of their hand. I call them acquaintances as they are not friends, not true friends. They come for many reasons, mostly of their own – to study, to sate curiosity, to gawp, to feel pious or grateful for their own lot – but not to be my friend. I admit them as it seems to please Father. He can be proud of me now. For these visits, he wears his cutaway morning coat, high stiff collar and ascot tie. I am dressed smartly too. Apparently, since I have controlled my 'blindisms' I am quite a pretty girl. He shows me off and it makes me proud too, with my heavy hair and tricky fingers. But I must wear a ribbon across my eyes, so they do not distress the ladies. I hate the ribbon, but I do it for Father. My doll has a ribbon across her eyes too.

We meet the people and feel their copperplate calling cards, each one unique. I smile for them, talk through Lottie of the things I can do with my hands. I would like to tell them about the Visitors, but know I cannot. I ask them many questions about themselves, to learn of life beyond my house and land. But they do not wish to talk much of their lives, as they live them and therefore find them dull. They only want to talk about me. They have some curious ideas about the deaf-blind girl, that I can see colours with my fingers or that I can read their thoughts and divine their futures. I am jaded and ask for rest. One silly woman says how clever I am and compares me to a parrot. When Lottie has spelled this into my hand – for she does not believe in shielding me from what people say – I stand up, raise myself on my toes, and with an expression of sheer disgust on my face I thrust my arm out towards Lottie and I spell: F-O-O-L. No, they are not my friends.

They are a means to an end. Once I can prove that I am fit to be seen and heard, I am allowed to leave my home at last. I want to go straight to the sea. But Father says no. Instead, I am to travel on the train to London with him. Lottie is coming too. Father tells me I am famous. They write about me in the newspapers. An important person has read of me in *The Times* of London. He is a doctor. He has written to Father about me, asking many questions. He wants to meet me. He knows more than any man in England about one special subject.

Eyes.

5

The year is 1895. I am eleven years old. I have never left my father's land. This morning, Mother brings me new travelling clothes: woollen jacket and skirt, embroidered blouse with a lace trim, shirt collar and a ruffle jabot. My hair I wear down topped by a neat boater. I cannot abide the large hats favoured by Mother, as they make me topple. I want to impress the doctor but I must be comfortable for I am to walk and travel by train today. I have been worrying about my eyes.

I ask Father, 'Please can I leave the ribbon at home? I am sure the people who see me will not be afraid of my eyes. I think they will stare more if I wear the ribbon.'

Father agrees and I kiss and hug him with gratitude.

After breakfast, Lottie, Father and I begin our walk down the gravel driveway to the lane that leads to Edenbridge and the railway station. We have no need of the carriage as it is a short walk and a pleasant March day. There is the scent of early blackthorn blossom as we reach the bottom of our driveway, the furthest I have ever been from home. The moment we cross the road and find the path to the village, I have a sense that someone new has arrived. But not outside. As we walk, I find a new Visitor, a very old man who tells me he cannot find his wife anywhere. He is most anxious and questioning. I tell him I cannot help him. Another Visitor comes, a girl who complains she is wet through and cold. They talk over each other and make my head ache. *Go now*, I scold them. *I am busy.* And they do go, they always do when I tell them. Then I stumble.

Father takes my hand and says, 'Shall we go back? We can take the carriage.'

'No,' I say. 'I am fine. Please let us walk. I am very happy.'

Lottie finger spells for me as we walk, telling me of the travellers she sees on the roads, their horses and wagons, their clothes and hats, those who wave and those who stare. I can feel the deep rumble of cartwheels on the road as they pass, tramping footsteps on the path, the tendrils of scents they leave behind, pipe smoke or coal dust. They know I am blind, perhaps not deaf. I hope they stare a little as Father has told me I look pretty today. If I close my eyes, the Visitors do not come. I know there is a crowd of new ones waiting, but my eyes remain shut and this keeps them away.

We reach the railway station and wait in a line to buy our tickets. Father hands me the money and allows me to pay the man in the ticket office. He shakes my hand with civility. He smells of boiled eggs and something else, something smoky and bitter. As we walk out on to the platform that same odour is overpowering. I feel a tremendous thundering in the ground and Lottie tells me the train is pulling into the station. The air is moist with steam and its acrid flavour piques my nose. We climb the steps into the carriage and Father leads us to our seats. There are Visitors on the train too, I can feel them waiting, watching. There are two other people in our carriage and I am introduced. A lady with leather gloves who is a teacher and a gentleman with hair on the back of his hands who is going to see his grandson in London. They ask me questions about myself through Lottie. I am accustomed to these interrogations from Father's associates. But I feel these are more amiable, a chance encounter on a train with a deaf-blind girl brings a kind of casual curiosity absent from the analytical meetings at home.

I am most looking forward to our railway picnic devised by Cook to be eaten on the train. Almost as soon as we are seated, I ask Lottie if we can eat. We have potted cheese, pickled gherkins, cress sandwiches and cold tongue, with ginger beer to swill it all down. I imagine our other passengers must be very envious, so I ask Lottie to offer them some, but she says they decline. I cannot think why. Perhaps they have their own hamper.

One of them opens the window and I beg Father to be allowed to put my head out. He agrees, but says I must not lean out too far, just as far as my rosy cheeks. He holds firmly on to my waist. I cannot think the door will fly open but he is being very careful. It is my first time away from home, after all. I can feel that the window slides down and I want it open further as I can only just reach my nose above it. Father shows me the leather strap to slide it down and now I can tilt forward. The wind rushes against my face and makes my eyes water. I shut them tight. When I open them again there are three new Visitors all talking at once. One says he works on the railways but cannot find his train. I perceive a colossal blast from the front of the train and the camber of the track changes, the rushing wind is gone and I feel crowded. A Visitor calls to me, says, *Watch out, miss!* I pull back in and Father tells me the train has entered a tunnel. As we rush out of the other end, I put my head out again. The train describes a sharp inward bend in the line and the steam buffets me as it is blown towards us from the engine. Tiny bits of stuff are flung into my eyes. I jam my fists in to rub them. Father pulls me inside and tells me my face is a mess of soot. I did not know steam was so dirty. Lottie is dispatched for water and a cloth to clean me up. I must look my best for the doctor.

I sit and commune with the train's tempo. I speed across the land. I am a traveller. I feel a new Visitor, who says he has been standing on the bridge all day, watching the trains come and go.

I ask him, *What do you see from the bridge?*

All the trains. Golly, they're fast. The fastest thing on land.

Another comes. The railwayman. He was in the tunnel, now he is riding the train with me.

Why were you in the tunnel?

I'm the signalman, miss. A sheep strayed from the field beyond and I came down to shoo it off. We don't want blood on the tracks, do we?

Where is the sheep?

Gone, miss. Gone.

Lottie touches my hand. 'Not long now. The conductor is here. He says we shall arrive in London soon.'

I shake hands with the conductor. He has a hole punch for tickets and lets me play with it. He gives me a bit of paper and I make long lines of holes which veer into circles and diamonds. I give it to him as a present. Lottie says he is grinning from ear to ear. I have made many friends on this journey. The train begins to waver and rattle from the driver applying the brakes. We are approaching the station. There is movement up and down the walkway; I can feel people's feet stumbling along with the train's halting pulse. As we pull into the station, Father takes my arm and helps me to find the door to the platform. My first train journey is over and I have loved it.

As we descend on to the platform at Victoria station, the stench of too close humanity engulfs me. I have never conceived such a potent concoction of people, bustling and bumping and sharing the same close air and space. As we begin to walk, I know once more that there are dozens of new Visitors waiting to speak with me, but I shut my eyes to dismiss them. It is curious this, that new Visitors come when I travel. I cannot explain it. Something tells me that when I board the train again later to return home, I will leave these behind. I do not understand why, it is just something I know.

I feel the ground shake when a rocketing eruption comes from the train as it lets off steam. Those with ears must suffer. Lottie tells me a porter is asking Father to carry our luggage, but we only have the picnic box and Father shakes his head, saying to Lottie that he will not be forking out money to someone to carry a basket when he can quite easily do it himself. Lottie tells me there is a Nestlé's chocolate machine but we would need a penny from Father. I know she is shy of asking him, so I stop and take his hand.

'Can we have some chocolate from the machine?'

'How did you know about that?' asks Father.

'I could smell it.' It is a white lie. Lottie and I devour the chocolate as we walk along, though Father declines.

I grab his hand. 'Have some, Father, please!' But he will not. Something in the quick movements of his wrist tells me that he is anxious. And I remember why we are here in London, not to have picnics or eat chocolate and other adventures. It is to see the eye doctor. I work the melting mass around my teeth as I think about what this doctor wants and why Father is nervous.

Outside Victoria station the air broadens and the rumbling chaos of my first city street assaults my senses. Father is looking for transport to the doctor's office. I am overwhelmed by the reverberations from the pressing of huge wheels into the road, the clip-clop of a thousand horses' hooves, the throb of machines all around, the thrum of numberless feet pounding the pavements. You may believe a deaf-blind person is immune to the teeming roar of a city street, but you would be wrong. Our sense of physical awareness is attacked in precisely the same cacophonous way. It is exhilarating and terrifying, exhausting and vital. I feel the dust and grit speckle my skin and inhale smoke and dirt and horse manure and produce of every kind.

'Tell me everything,' I press Lottie.

She says the wide road is packed three deep each way with carts, coaches, trams and trolley buses of every description, all drawn by horses clattering by each other with hundreds of near-misses every second. Trams and omnibuses are stuffed with passengers, the upper deck reached by a half-spiral staircase with a rail, topped by mottled crews of men in bowler hats and cloth caps, handlebar moustaches and side whiskers, women with their hair pinned up and wide-brimmed hats furnished with cloth flowers, artificial fruit and masses of feathers. Carts are driven by men and boys with dusty coats and mucky boots, some with blankets across their knees, their goods secured with tarpaulin and rope. A coach and pair of the well-to-do is directed by a coachman and groom riding on the box with a top hat and plume on the side, while cabs have men in bowler hats with a whip. There are two men pushing a board on wheels advertising tea along the edge of the road. The lanes clog at turnings, where two-wheeled hansom cabs and four-wheeled growlers queue quite patiently. Nearby is a stoppage where a horse has slipped on the cobbles and men are placing sacks all around so the horse can regain its footing. Pedestrians negotiate the roads at their peril, old gentlemen with canes and top hats, little messenger boys with cropped trousers and working women with tight-waisted coats dodge in and out of the bustling traffic. But there is a kind of method to it, Lottie says, as everyone seems to know what they are about. And where on earth are they all going? All these individual lives acting out their progress simultaneously in the tumult of the city street, just like Dickens. I dare not open my eyes as I know there are hundreds of Visitors clamouring through this tempest to speak with me and I cannot bear the din.

Father finds a cab and helps me up the one step into the sprung seat inside. I sit between Lottie and Father and we are off, moving into the stream of traffic and bouncing with the trit-trot of our driver's horse. The rattle of the clanking wheels jostles my bones and jogs me against my companions.

Father finds my hand and asks, 'What do you think of London?'

'Noisy!' I joke.

We dismount in a quieter street, the stiller air punctuated by a coach or cart here and there, but much more subdued and welcome. Lottie tells me it is called Wigmore Place. I did not know streets had names. She says it is a very smart street and there is even a motor car parked at the far end, the first she has ever seen.

'There must be someone ill nearby,' Lottie tells me, 'as the road has been covered with straw to spare their ears.'

We wait to cross the road. Lottie describes an old man with a long beard who is called the crossing-sweeper. She says all along the kerbs are horses and carriages top-to-toe and our man must find a place for us to squeeze through on to the pavement. Lottie says two little boys further up are crawling under a horse's belly to get across.

We mount five steps and I feel Father rat-a-tat-tat on the door knocker. The door scrapes open and we tread on dense carpet. As we progress down the hall, I flutter my fingers along the wall. Thick wallpaper and heavy curtains absorb the vibrations from outside. We are in a haven of peace from the stormy seas of London.

We enter a room that smells of Brasso and a hand finds me. It is a man's hand: warm, chubby and good-natured fingers grip my own in a confident handshake and I am at ease. Lottie tells me this is Dr Knapp. He smells of medicines, a minty flavour lingering about him, but its sharp clean lines are comforting. He lets me feel his face, which is fat and jowly with a soft beard and kindly smile. I am led to a chair that has a reclined back and Lottie says I should sit and get comfy. She tells me the doctor wishes to examine my eyes, so I must sit very still and keep them open. I like the brush of his fingertips on my eyebrows and do not mind his attentions. Lottie says he is holding up a succession of instruments to look carefully into each eye. At periods, she asks me to look up, left, right, down and straight ahead. Then a change comes.

'I can see that,' I tell Lottie.

He has shone a light into my eyes. I perceive it, as I do the bright sunshine when it shines directly on to my face at noon.

Lottie says, 'That is good news.'

The examination continues for some time, then Lottie tells me the doctor has thanked me for my patience.

I go to sit down in a chair like those in our dining room at home, flanked by Lottie and Father. The doctor sits opposite me and takes my hand. In it, he places a curious object. I feel it all over. It is a sphere, like the globe, but bumpy and lumpy, and it comes apart into pieces. Lottie feeds me information through my left hand, as my right hand explores the curious thing in my lap. The doctor has given me a model of an eye. Liza tells me the names and they are beautiful: iris, cornea, lens, retina. Then I am asked to leave the room, so that Father and the doctor can talk. But I will not. I want to know everything. I reach for Father's hand.

'I want the doctor to explain it to me. Please. I want to understand.'

Father agrees.

Through Lottie, Dr Knapp tells me about my eyes: 'Your eye lets in light. It travels through the lens. This helps to focus the light on the back of your eye and lets you see clearly. When you were born, you were very short-sighted. We call it high myopia. Your eyeballs were too long. When the light came in, it couldn't reach the back of the eyes. Your vision developed well as most of a baby's preserve is seen closely, such as your mother's face. But your myopia grew worse as you grew older. Then you developed cataracts in both eyes. These make your lenses cloud over. And you lost your vision completely. Both of your problems lie in your lenses, which help you to focus. I can give you an operation that will take the problem away. I can remove your lenses. This will remove the cataracts and change the way light reaches the back of your eye. Other parts of your eye will still be able to focus light for you. If the operation is a success, you will be able to see. You will be able to look at distances quite well. You will need spectacles for reading and close work. But you will be able to see for the first time. You should also understand that there are risks with any operation. You could have an infection afterwards, which could harm or even destroy your eyes. Or make you very ill. In the worst cases, infections can be fatal. But we will do everything we can to stop that from happening. You do not have to have this operation, Adeliza. But it is your best chance to see.'

I cannot believe what I have just heard. I had no idea this was why we had come. I thought we were meeting another associate, another nosy parker to poke and prod and study for their own ends.

I reach for Father's hand. 'Why did nobody tell me that the doctor could make me see?'

'We did not know for sure. The doctor had to examine you first. We did not want to raise your hopes to have them dashed.'

'Is it really true? Can he make me see?'

'There are risks. And I am worried about those. You might lose your eyes or become very ill. You might even die. And I cannot bear the thought of it.'

'I do not want to die.'

'I know. And I would never put you in harm's way. But I believe you are old enough now to understand the risks of this. And I believe you have the right to decide your future. If you accept the dangers, and choose to have this operation, I will espouse that decision. Mother feels the same way. And I believe that God wants you to see the wonder of His creation and He will protect you.'

'Ask the doctor what happens in the operation.'

Lottie narrates: 'He says you will have special medicine to make your eyes numb, then he will use a very sharp knife to make a small cut in each eye and remove your lenses. Afterwards, you will be bandaged for many days and stay in bed in a dark room. The eyes should heal on their own. When the bandages are removed, we will know if the operation has worked.'

I ask Lottie, 'What should I do?'

'It is your decision.'

'But what would you do?'

'It is not important what I think.'

'It is, it is!'

'What do *you* think, Liza?'

A Visitor says, *Where is the nurse? She said she would bring remedy and it hurts, it hurts.*

A creeping fear takes hold of me. I twist my fingers. I do not know what to do. I have never felt the need of counsel more. I think and think. Of the operation, the medicine, the knife. Of the time after in the dark room, of infection and destruction, of the boiling fever when I was two and how I suffered. To go through all that and to make it worse, perhaps become so ill, maybe to die, to die, to die. But to see, to see, to see . . .

I say, 'Do it now.'

6

I have to wait for the operation. Dr Knapp is very busy and treats many people. The waiting is agony. I feel sad in my eyes all days. A legion of hopes and fears punish me.

I try to imagine what it will be like to see. I turn my face to the light and sense its benevolent warmth and try to stretch my memory back and back to the time before the Time Before, when I was a happy child without cataracts. Yes, my eyesight was bad then, as the doctor called it, high myopia. But I could see things close by, my parents' faces, the breast, my hands and toes, the blanket, the bottle, the spoon, the dummy, nappy and pin, the hundred little things of a baby's days and nights. These sights were stored in my infant brain somewhere, but are atrophied through neglect. I cannot apprehend how they looked, what looking was like, how seeing will be. I have talked with Lottie many times about colour and still do not understand it. She helps me by linking colours to other things I know, thus white is clean and black is dirty. But I have great difficulty accepting that a white shirt can become grubby when rubbed in mud, or that a blackbird's wings can be smooth and speck-free. I feel an object and hold it up to my eyes, try to see myself seeing it, but I cannot imagine comprehending an object through anything but the feel of it, the shape, the weight, the texture and the space it inhabits.

Does all this also come through sight, or is it something so different it cannot be conceptualised, as different from touch as smell is? Another country, another language, another arena of sensation? I ache for it. I open my eyes wide and strain to see, to make it happen myself. And all the while, this corkscrew dread, that it will never happen, that the hope will fizzle like spit on a hand iron.

One day, Father brings me a letter from the doctor. He reads it to me: 'Adeliza Golding is requested to attend at the London offices of Dr Lucius Knapp for an operation of cataract removal, the sixteenth day of October, 1895.'

'I will be twelve years old by then.'

'Old enough,' says Father.

Mother packs a bag for me. She puts in all my nightdresses, as I am to stay in the doctor's house for the first two to three weeks, or until I am able to travel. Then I will be brought home all the way in a coach and recuperate in my own bed.

'The doctor must ask us for a fee. And the coach will be very expensive,' I say to Mother. 'Where will we find the money to pay?'

I know we are quite well-to-do. I know we are richer by far than Lottie's family, that we have a large house, fine belongings and land. But we are not aristocrats. And Father always says hop farming is where fortunes are made and lost.

'Do not worry,' says Mother. 'It is all in hand.'

But Mother knows nothing of such things.

I ask Father, 'Where is the money for the doctor and the coach? Do we sell enough hops for these? Will we go hungry?'

'We do very well. These past few years we have had high

yields and neither the mould nor the flea, and prices are good nowadays. We can pay for the coach. But, very kindly, Dr Knapp has offered to do your operation for free.'

'Why would he do that?'

'Because he knows you need it and he is a good man. Some people would call him a philanthropist, which is a person who acts kindly towards others for no reward.'

'Are there such people in the world?'

'Yes, and Dr Knapp is one of them. Also he is very interested in your eyes and your being deaf. He wants to study you. So he is getting something out of it too, to satisfy his scientific interest.'

'I am a very interesting person,' I say. And in this way, we resolve it.

We take the train, as before. A dizzying collection of Visitors calls to me from the streets of London: here a lost boy crying, a young woman with a baby who will not feed, an elderly lady who cannot find her hat with the little birds on it, a man who says the omnibus company must pay, must pay, it is not safe. I realise that after the operation, my eyes will be covered for weeks, and I will not be able to sense the Visitors. I wonder if I will miss them.

When I arrive, I am settled in a bedroom upstairs at Dr Knapp's house and Lottie helps me change into a night-dress. A nurse comes to show us to the operating room. We meet Father in the hallway.

'My brave girl,' he says. I reach to touch his face but he stops me. I insist and feel his wet cheeks.

'I will be well,' I say.

He tells me he has to wait outside, as they cannot have too many people in the room. But they have said Lottie can be there to hold my hand and tell me what is happening. I say goodbye to Father and go into the theatre. It smells of disinfectant and metal. I am asked to lie on a hard bed. They place a folded cloth over my mouth and chin, and another across my forehead. My nose is left exposed for easy breathing and, of course, my eyes.

A Visitor is here, another and another. They are all afraid.

They said it would be over now. Why am I still here?

Where is the nurse?

My wound, how it throbs.

Now I am very frightened. I want to say no, I have changed my mind. But I do not want to let everyone down. I think how much easier the lives of everyone I love will be if I could see. I think perhaps they will love me more if I am not blind. And I know I must do this, for everyone. Lottie takes my hand and holds it tight. She asks if I want to know what the doctor is doing.

'Yes, I want to know everything.'

She signs into my right hand, then leaves it free for me to ask her questions. The doctor talks to her and she tells me what he says.

'He is going to put some drops in your eyes. The liquid is a mixture of water and something called cocaine. It will make your eye numb. It is called an anaesthetic. When the doctor touches your eye with the knife, you will not be able to feel any pain.'

'How will he know? Before he touches my eye with the knife, how will he know if the drops have worked?'

Lottie asks the doctor. He pats me gently on my arm.

'He says he will test it first with something soft. Do not worry. Nothing will hurt.'

We wait while the doctor readies himself and his tools.

'He is going to give you the drops now.'

I feel the liquid meet one eye, then the other. I blink several times and it runs down one cheek, swiftly swabbed by someone. It is cooling to the eye. It does not sting or smart. I wait.

'Now, Liza. This is very important. You must not move at all during the operation. You must keep as still as a rock. If you move your head, the doctor could cut in the wrong place or damage your eyes.'

There is a pressure in my right eye, but the medicine has done its job. I cannot feel anything against the eyeball itself.

'Is he touching my eye now?'

'Yes.'

'With what?'

'Do not worry. It is going well.'

'Tell me!'

'Do not agitate yourself, Liza. It may make you restless.'

'Tell me then.'

'He is putting a tiny stitch into your eyelid to hold it open . . . Now he is using a very fine knife to make a cut in your eye . . . He applies a sharp hook . . . He takes a tool called forceps in one hand and applies a little spoon with the other . . . The lens is out! He has taken the lens out of your eye and placed it in a dish. He says this part of the operation is complete. Well done, Liza! Keep still.'

'Do you feel sick?' I ask Lottie. She must be able to see the knife cutting into my eye. I wonder if this is gruesome.

'No, it is very interesting.'

Next comes the same procedure in my left eye. Another

success. Lottie says each eye has taken only fifteen minutes to complete. But to me it feels like hours. The moment Lottie tells me it is over, I faint.

I wake in bed. My eyes are bandaged. They are sore. As I cannot open them, there are no Visitors.

Lottie is there. She takes my hand to ask, 'How do you feel?'

'It hurts.'

'Wait here.'

I grab her hand tight. She uncurls my fingers and signs, 'I need to tell the doctor you are awake. It is not far. Half a minute.'

My eyeballs pulsate.

The doctor comes and feels my forehead. He says to try to sleep. He says I need lots of rest. So that I will heal, I must stay in bed for up to three weeks.

I drift in and out of sleep for the first few days, and suffer baffling dreams which are heavy and stifling. I wake only to drink a little warm milk. Soon I feel brighter. I eat eggs and toast. Some stewed apples, very sugary. After sixteen days, I sit up in bed and I am bored. Now they know it is time for me to go home. Lottie helps me dress. Father comes and I can tell he wants to embrace me heartily but he is careful with me as if I were thin china. I am taken to the door. Here I ask for Dr Knapp and he is there. He shakes my hand.

I instruct Lottie: 'Please tell him thank you very much for me.'

'He says you are very welcome.'

'Say well done for being so careful with the knife.'

Lottie puts her hand on its side in my palm and wobbles it. This is our sign for laughter. I think I amused the doctor.

Father escorts me to the coach. It is much more comfortable than the London cabs; it has softer seats and is less bouncy. A thick blanket is placed around my legs and we begin our long journey home. The coach sways on southwards from the capital through Surrey and into Kent. I have slept most of the way and am grumpy on waking. I burrow my head into Father's sleeve.

I feel Mother's hand. She has come to welcome me.

'You should be in bed,' I say, as the late sun is cooling.

'Not me, you. Come and rest,' replies Mother.

I do not need help to walk but there are many hands around me. I am cared for. I am led to my bedroom where, exhausted by the journey, I sleep deeply. I must remain in my darkened room for another week, black blinds and heavy curtains at the windows. I cannot sense anything behind these bandages. I used to be able at least to perceive sunlight, and I miss its warmth. I am more in the dark than ever.

I recover well. Everyone is thrilled that I have not developed an infection, that the pain in my eyes has receded after only a day or two. I am healthy and happy. Soon, I am bored in my room, bored of sewing and knitting. I ask for lessons again with Lottie. We are learning arithmetic using a special metal frame made for the blind. It helps me count and add numbers. We read the book called *Mental Arithmetic* and a problem may say, 'If a boy buys five apples and has six friends . . .' and so on. And I say to Lottie, 'But why does the boy buy the apples? Why does he not go scrumping with his friends? And why does he not buy enough apples? Is he not a bad boy to forget one friend so?' Lottie laughs at my questions, but I become vexed. I am wearisome when learning arithmetic. I am forgetful and my thoughts waste. I frown so much my head aches. I say to Lottie, 'Are you not very tired of living? Does your heart not tire of beating? Does your head not tire of thinking?'

Lottie says, 'Let's end our lessons for today. You can stop thinking now.'

'How can I stop? Can I close my think as you close your eyes?'

'Let me explain,' says Lottie.

I say, 'No more today. My think is tired.'

When Lottie is not here, I wish to talk with the Visitors. But I cannot, as my eyes cannot open. I am very curious about them now that I know there are others. I want to ask them: *Why do you stay here? Why did you not come with me to London? I met other Visitors on my journey. Do you know them? Are you sure you do not know your name? Why do you not visit Lottie or Father? What do you want with me?*

I predict they will never answer my questions, only prattle on about their obsession. I understand them a little more these days. I have an obsession of my own now: my eyes. Every day I use my number frame to count down the days remaining until the bandages are removed. Dr Knapp is coming all the way from London to be there. If I had my choice, I would go to a quiet corner of the garden all on my own and take them off. I do not want an audience. If I have failed I want to find out alone, and will hate the pity of others. But Father will not allow it. It has to be executed with care and the doctor must do tests.

The day is here. Father, Mother and Dr Knapp assemble in my bedroom. The air is stuffy with their breath and expectations. The black blinds have been removed and the curtains are opened. I sit on my hard-backed chair, where Nanny used to tie me. Now I wait upon it for the most important moment in my life. Lottie kneels beside me, holding my hand. I feel the doctor untie the binding at the back of my head. I am relieved to feel the pressure lessen, and want to shake my flattened hair free. But then I am gripped by an almighty terror. I squeeze Lottie's hand so hard she squirms, then quickly sign into her palm: 'No. Tell him to stop.'

'Why?'

'I am afraid.'

I have lived with my blindness all my life. Only weeks ago, I was given hope that I might see. Now the moment comes I cannot face it. The disappointment would break my heart.

'Be brave,' says Lottie. 'We are all here with you.'

I can feel tears well up behind the bandages. As they loosen, the tears escape. Lottie rubs my hand in comfort, Father and Mother touch my arm. The bandages are off, only two pads remain. Dr Knapp removes one, then the other. I keep my eyes fast shut. I see nothing. I will not open them.

'It is time,' says Lottie.

I flutter my eyelids, awash with tears. My hand grips Lottie's so tightly. I open my eyes.

There is a flickering blur of haze. And I want to cry out, it is a failure, my eyes are still damaged. But I realise immediately that it was my tears, as I open my eyes wide and blink them away. I am hit by light. The most dazzling, incandescent explosion of light assaults me and makes me recoil. I cover my eyes but hate the darkness it brings. I uncover them again, and the colours hit me. I do not know their names yet, but they are irresistible, these shapes; these white ovals with tinted halos that approach me. And I remember these are faces, as the shape of eyes, nose, mouth and hair imposes itself upon my new vision and speaks its name – face. I am surrounded by faces all laughing and weeping, and I lift my hands up and can see my fingers reaching. I touch Father's cheek and his salt and pepper hair, and next to him Mother's is faded gold. And the big round face must be Dr Knapp, with a shock of white hair and a beard. And I turn to find my Lottie and her face is the most beautiful of all, with glorious blue eyes so wide and round. And red, red hair, which curls in waves around her pink smiling face, and her eyes shining with tears – how they shine – and I throw my arms around her and I cry and I cry with joy.

I stand and stumble to the window. I am surrounded by green, greens everywhere. Later I know these for grass and bushes. It is November so the leaves are lost from many trees, and there are stark black lines of bare tree limbs against the white sky and the monochrome contrasts are so shocking that I almost turn from them, but I do not, I stare on fascinated at this cracked puzzle of sky and branches. Then I turn. I reach forward for Lottie's hand. My, how her hair blazes. Father and Mother are holding on to my shoulders and the doctor is nodding. And Lottie holds her own hand up to me. But there are others behind her. Other faces. At first I think they are the servants, come to share our joy. But these faces are different. They are smiling and friendly like my family, yet they are not the same; they seem lit from within, a bluish-white glow as if a lamp shone from their eyes, their cheeks, their hair. And

I realise all at once, they are not my family and they are not the servants. They are the Visitors. And they are real. I can see them.

One stands close behind Lottie – a woman with black hair and black eyes. Her skin glows violet-white, and she is in perfect focus, as if she were made from different stuff than the others. I realise from the way people are talking and looking at me and moving around that no one can see the Visitors but me.

Are you real? I ask the dark woman. I think it, inside my head, as always. And she can hear me. When she answers, though she moves her mouth, I can still discern her words inside my mind.

I only came selling lavender. Now I cannot find my way home.

Her dark eyes are like holes in her head. I move towards her, and Lottie thinks I am coming to her and steps forward. But I stretch to touch the Visitor and my hand reaches her face. There is almost nothing there, but there is something: a wisp of matter, the caress of a cloud. The woman takes a step and the mist of her is cold on my hand. I withdraw it, chilled. Foreboding comes upon me, a ghastly idea of who the Visitors are and why they are here.

Go away, I say.

And she does. She turns and the blue-white glow flares briefly, then she fades and is gone. I shudder, as if ice water has trickled down my neck.

Lottie takes my hand and finger spells to me. I realise for the first time that she looks at my hand as she spells, she does it by sight. I always thought she did it with eyes closed, to be like me.

'Are you well?' she asks.

'Never better,' I say and we smile and smile. How white are teeth!

'What can you see?' says Lottie.

I look up at her face. It is so beautiful, I cannot get enough of it. I drink it in.

'Everything!' I say. I see her turn her head towards Father, Mother and Dr Knapp and watch her lips move. So that is speaking. She is telling them what I said.

I turn to Father and touch his face again. His dear old face. It is wet with tears. I look at Mother too. Her eyes are dark brown and sad. Father's are light green and sparkly. I sign into his palm, 'Bring me a mirror.'

There is none in my room, as it has never been required in here. Lottie goes out and returns, a small round object held aloft. I reach to take it and miss completely. My hand grasps air. I have yet to connect seeing with movement. I almost want to close my eyes to reach for it, as this seems easier, but I do not. I never want to close my eyes again. Lottie places the mirror in my hand and I hold it up to my face. But the image is blurred close to, so I move the mirror to arm's length until it comes right.

There I am. My hair is yellow, so yellow that I think it must be hot like fire. And my eyes are dark like Mother's. I have her eyes precisely. They are the same. I never knew I was so like Mother. I touch my hair and toy with it, as I know ladies do in mirrors. I reveal an ear. It is ridiculous! Such a huge, flapping thing curled round in horrid knots and channels, extended for yards beyond my head, and I check to see if the other is so hideous and it is exactly the same. I look up horrified, that I am so ugly, but I see that everyone has these appendages thrusting out from the sides of their heads, and the men having short hair and the ladies wearing theirs up, I can see their ears, and they seem preposterously big to me. And the nose jutting out, a mountain splitting the face, and eyes, wide, impudent saucers, and the mouth a great maw opening and closing with speech. The proportions I knew with my fingers appear all wrong with my eyes. It will take some getting used to. Yet, despite its peculiarities, it is all more ravishing than anything I could have surmised. I conclude what poorly instruments my fingers were, when all along this actuality existed and I had no sense of it. I grieve for the blind. It seems a crime to me now that anyone cannot see this glorious world. I want Dr Knapp to cure them all.

He wants me to sit down now so that he can examine me. He holds up some curious objects and looks into my eyes. The shock of their closeness is strange and I quail, afraid he is going to poke me in the eye. But I realise that I am still a novice at judging distances, and trust him to examine me. He looks carefully in both eyes and Lottie says he is very pleased. They have healed perfectly and my vision is good, though I will need to come to London again to have spectacles made for close work. I wiggle the fingers of my other hand close to my eyes. There is a blur, like the moment I first opened them and was blinded by tears; I look up, terrified my eyes are failing me already, but soon realise that it is indeed in proximity that my eyes do not work so well. They are good at middle distance and best far away, beyond the room and the undulating treetops to the stately rain-clouds. The closer something is, the less clearly I can see it. Except the Visitors. They are in perfect focus, wherever they stand in the room. I do not know what to do about them, so I tell them to leave. One by one, they fade and depart. I will deal with them tomorrow. For now, I have a world to know. I have opened my eyes and created light and colour. I have invented the world anew. I can see.

7

On this, my first day of sight, I begin by exploring the house. I am allowed to leave my parents and the doctor behind and walk across the hall and down the stairs. Lottie is with me all the time, to stop me tripping, to explain this and that. One of the strangest things is trying to reconcile my brand-new visual images with the knowledge I gained previously from touch or description. Some objects I know presently and others I cannot make sense of at all until I touch them. I see a painting on the landing of something green and frilly, with layers of shapes and a long thin line at its centre. I stare at it and cannot decipher what it might be. Is it something you wear?

I ask Lottie, 'What is it?'

'Hops. A painting of hop flowers, the leaves, the stalk.'

I am dismayed. I know this object intimately by touch but its visual image means nothing to me. The next painting I know immediately. I have never visited this place, yet I know that this grey mass bordered by a flat expanse of yellow under a louring sky is the sea. Somehow the linguistic description I had read so often in books or discussed with Lottie had painted an image in my mind more powerful than that of Father's beloved hops, which I have handled countless times.

I go on through the house, astounded at how much there

is to see. The wallpaper and painted walls are all different colours, and the upholstery is patterned with leaves and flowers and birds in every shade imaginable. Clothes, too, are covered with checks and dots and swirls and lines, on Mother and Lottie, and even Father's waistcoats and his shiny shoes and buttons. I am bewitched by the myriad tints of colour within one object, such as Lottie's eyes: the pupil is black, the aura deep blue while the iris is light fringed with green. It is how I picture the Mediterranean. Even my own eyes – not as bewitching as Lottie's – have two tones, dark brown at the centre with a paler edge.

We move from room to room, our speed as always hampered by clutter. But once outside, my first instinct is to run, and I launch myself from the bottom step and hurtle across the gravel driveway to the grass. I stop short, panting, and move forward again, the vertical trees and the horizontal ground hurling themselves at me at a terrifying rate and bewildering my eyes. Lottie catches up with me and I drop to the grass. I look at her face and see her eyebrows lowered, her eyes intense, her mouth slightly pursed. I know these shapes with my fingers. Her expression is concern for me, she is worried. I will have to learn a whole new language of reading other people's faces and bodies, applying my knowledge of touch and vibration to what I see and correlating the two.

'Go slowly,' she advises.

I have crossed the threshold to a new country, the land of the sighted, and it has its own laws of which I am ignorant. I stand again and move forward, with care this time. My surroundings move quite quickly, but I am becoming accustomed to it. It may be better to walk with my eyes closed, but I cannot bear to. I look to the sky and the clouds race across it. I see them reveal the sun, and stare into this white heat. I gasp and cover my eyes. It hurts to look straight at the sun – is this just me or everyone? Lottie tells me it is a flaming ball of fire, of course it will hurt to look at it, everyone is the same in this.

I see my first animals, little birds flitting from tree to tree or flapping across the white of the sky. The way birds move brings me to tears. I have felt a bird's feather many times, found them in the grass or stuck to a twig. I have held a bird's body and drawn out its miraculous wing and named the different types of feather along it. There are stuffed birds in glass cases in the parlour, and Lottie would take one out for me and let me touch it. I had a caged bird for a time. I would open the miniature door and put my hand in the cage, feel around for the vibrant fluttering and hold its little engine of a body, feel its heart beat furiously in its tiny chest. One day I found it inert, lying on its back at the gritty bottom of its cage. I cried for it then. But to see birds now, as they flutter from branch to branch and hop, hop, hop along the paving slabs and peck, peck, peck, almost too quick for the eye to comprehend; and then the miracle, as they lift up and fly, small black shapes against the brightness scoring the sky with their wings, the absolute liberty of it. I never knew what happy creatures birds are. I assume they are happy, though I cannot see them smile. To think, I once allowed that sovereign creature to be locked in a cage in my house. My defence is that I did not know, I could not know the joy of emancipation myself. We envy the birds theirs and lock them up. I wish to open every cage and free them, as I have been freed.

The elegance of water. Lottie takes me to the beck and I watch the water shimmer and slide over pebbles, sparkle and glint, endlessly mobile. It feels delightful, water, as it slips through your fingers and surrounds your skin and cools your throat. But who could know how purely it declares its life as it moves endlessly downstream? I realise that when I was blind and moved my hand through water, I had thought I cut it as a knife slices butter. I am amazed that it runs on, through and over my fingers. As I am splashed by the skittish brook, I think of raindrops and look up, willing those rainclouds yonder edged in thunder to loose their load and show me rain. And I want the sky to bring forth snow, hail, fog, lightning – and oh, a rainbow! – so that I can see all weather all at once.

Where is the wind? Can we not see it? I am astonished to discover that the wind is invisible. It was never, in all our lessons, something we had got round to discussing. The wind moves the trees and plays a thousand dances along every bend of leaf and lift of branch and blade of grass, and plays havoc with my hair and blows it playfully into my new eyes – but it is all invisible. One can see its effects, but not itself. What is wind made of? Air. What is air made of? Lottie tells me about microscopes and says Father must get me one. A telescope too. Then I will understand about the universe beyond our eyes, the realms of the very small and of the very large and far away, that even our wondrous eyes are limited. But our marvellous brains have invented tools for us to overcome our limitations. The utter complexity of the world. Only now, as my eyes drink in the intricacy of it, do I think of God. Is even His mind big enough to encompass this endless variety? I conclude this is impossible, that these limitless features could not have been contrived by one mind, that it is all too much.

We come back into the house through the scullery. Our

cook and three maids are there to meet me. They are all smiling, and though they are servants and I am the young lady of the house, I do not care at this moment and I hug them.

I say to Lottie, 'Please tell Martha, Edith, Florrie and Alice I want to know them, if they do not mind and would like it.'

'You do not need to say this,' spells Lottie, frowning.

'I know I do not need to, but I wish to. I wish to know everyone alive, and I want to start here, with these kind ladies.'

I watch Lottie say my words. Edith speaks to Lottie, who tells me: 'Edith says from this day on we are all friends.'

Edith holds her hand out to me and we shake on it. They all laugh and some speak words and there is more smiling. I comprehend how much I have missed, the constant flutter of communication that speech and sight afford, the asides and glances, a flick of the hand or a cocked head or the twitch of a nose, the raising of one eyebrow and the palm covering the mouth. All this has been occurring while I have been laboriously finger spelling my way through the last few years, thinking myself so grand in my intercourse with others and placing myself at the firm centre of the universe. How much else was going on around me of which I had no clue, and what an almighty fool I feel.

As they chatter, I watch their mouths and a new envy grips me.

'Lottie, I know I cannot speak, that with no hearing and no memory of sound this would be very difficult. But can I learn to read what people say? Can I learn the movements people make with their mouths and perhaps see a word or two there?'

'Yes, you can,' says Lottie. 'It is called lip-reading. You will learn this, starting tomorrow. I have been reading about it. And I have another surprise for you. While you were recovering, I spent my evenings learning about another kind of language for you, which will give you more freedom to speak and a greater range. It is a language of signs you make with both hands in the air in front of your body. They call it sign language and I will begin teaching you this afternoon.'

'Why did you learn it while I was recovering? You did not know I would be able to see. It might have been a complete waste of your time.'

'I just knew you would.'

'Did you pray for it?'

'No.'

'Why not?'

'I have not prayed since Constance died.'

And for the first time with my new eyes, I see real sadness in a person's face. And as it is Lottie's sadness it near cracks my heart in two.

'Oh, Lottie. God was cruel to take her from you. How did you bear it?'

Lottie pulls her hand from mine and makes a few curious shapes in the air between us.

I take her hand back. 'What is that?' I say.

'They are signs. I spoke to you with them.'

'What did you say?'

'I said, "I found you."'

Cook Martha beckons us to the table. While we have been talking, she has laid out my luncheon. I sit at the broad oak table with its knots and cracks and grain and I touch its surface and see with my fingers and my eyes how ornate is even this most prosaic of objects, a kitchen table.

'Are all tables like this?' I ask. 'Beautiful, like this, with the shapes and shades of colour?'

Lottie relays my question and Cook laughs and shakes her head. People's faces are so odd when they laugh, teeth are so broad and fill up their mouths which seem too small to house them all.

My lunch is a thick juicy slice of pink ham fringed with a golden honey glaze, a hunk of pure white bread with a brown crust warm from the range, apple slices of pale yellow flesh and bright red skin and vibrant orange carrots cut into sticks. I cannot believe how radiant are ordinary foodstuffs! The maids watch me smiling and Lottie sits beside me, but where is their lunch?

'We will eat later,' Lottie tells me.

'Are you not hungry?' I say.

They exchange glances and again I see a milieu of which I have had not a moment of experience, of shared meanings and secrets conveyed through the eyes only.

'Please eat with me, everyone,' I ask Lottie to tell them. Cook Martha nods and places five more plates on the lovely old table, and we all eat together. It is the best meal of my whole life.

I look around the room as I eat. The tiles on the wall are blue and white check and around the range a mixture of earthy reds and browns. I love the kitchen and all its bits and bobs, its pots and pans and paraphernalia. It is as rich in treasure as Aladdin's cave. On the shelves there are dozens of packets of food and other goods, I know not what, with pictures of people and objects on them and writing in different colours. People store these items in cupboards and throw away the packets after they have finished the contents. They do not see the beauty in them as I do with my new eyes. I ask Lottie to pass me some and examine a box of Reckitt's Bag Blue, patterned in red, blue and white – so bright and cheerful. And Nixey's Black Lead, which they tell me is for cleaning the Kitchener and yet the picture on the front is so eerie, it gives me a chill; there is a woman in her kitchen and a figure reaching to her, giving her the Nixey's Black Lead. The figure is wearing a black hat and has a glow all around her.

I ask Lottie, 'Is that a Visitor?'

'None of that nonsense,' she says and takes my cleared plate away.

I must talk with her later about this. I have something to tell her.

We spend the afternoon learning new signs. It is beguiling, this visual language. It allows me to express myself in space; there is a relationship between yourself, your hands, your face and the movement between your hands and your body. My favourite so far is this: you pinch your fingers together and place them against the side of your head, move them away and catch something. This is 'remember'. If you fail to catch it, open your hand and let it escape, this is the sign for 'forget'. There is a playful quality in sign language absent from the mechanics of finger spelling; it sometimes uses ideas and gestures to approximate life in a way pure letters do not. I love it more heartily even than my beloved manual alphabet which set me free from the Time Before. I feel a quickening in my understanding of the world, as Lottie and I labour together all afternoon to learn the rudiments of the new language from a lovely book she has, each page filled with line drawings of the hands making signs for vocabulary. But as the doctor said, I will need spectacles for close work like this, and so at the moment it is rather blurred and irritates me. Once I have my eyeglasses, I will be able to buy my own books and look at the pictures and read the words. I know I have another huge mountain to climb.

'Will I learn to read words?'

'Of course,' says Lottie. 'I will teach you.'

'When? Now?'

'Give me a moment! We will begin everything tomorrow. But now, you must dress for dinner.'

I am very excited about my first formal dinner with Father and Mother. I am permitted to sit at the grand dining table with them as a special treat. Father says grace. I never knew one has to close one's eyes for prayer. Only once this prayer has finished and we have thought about it are we allowed to eat. But eating is not easy for the newly sighted, trying to negotiate knife and fork with food and mouth. As with walking it might be easier to close my eyes, but I am determined not to and will not accept any help. The worst is the tomato soup which causes gory havoc down my napkinned front. My dinner is quite cold by the time I finish it. But it is nice to sit with my parents and share their delight as I stare around the gorgeous dining room, seeing at last my favourite flock wallpaper which always felt so luxurious. Now I realise it is scarlet on a pearly background, I delight in it all the more. I like to watch my parents eat, pronging a fork so delicately into a potato glistening with gravy and slicing it dextrously, placing the piece so accurately in the mouth and chewing. This eating business is serious here in the dining room.

Now I understand why Cook Martha gave me finger foods for lunch, which I jammed in quite easily, and I love her for that.

I use a specially shaped knife for the fish, which is engraved with a picture of two salmon leaping from a river. Our dessert forks are wrought with flowers and leaves spiralling the handle. How can such exquisite things be used only to stuff food into mouths? Even the crumb scoop used by Maid Florrie has an ivory handle decorated with heliotrope birds. After dessert we have three different types of cheese: Cheddar, Stilton and something French. I like the French best and Father disapproves. He takes a knife from his pocket and begins to cut shapes in a lump of Cheddar. When he is done, he passes it to me. He has carved an animal, I believe. Tall ears, big feet, whiskers. I reach across and finger spell for him: 'Rabbit!' He nods and smiles at me, then bids me eat it, but I cannot. I want to keep it. I place it on my plate and stare at it.

At bath time, I see my own naked body for the first time. I look down at my skin and chest and between my legs, perturbed by the absurd shapes. My body seems all out of proportion, arms too short, legs too thick. I ask Lottie for a full-length mirror, but she tells me this is rude and I should never gaze at myself naked. I know of course that nakedness is forbidden in polite society and only savages go around with their bits and pieces out. And I have to admit that clothes look so gratifying, that it is vastly preferable on the eye to see them. But skin is striking too, the shadows in the curves and the subtle flesh tones so pleasing to the eye, just as skin is pleasurable to the touch. As I sit in the bath and watch the play of water against my skin, I want to touch my body, but I know Lottie will say

I must not, as ever. I think, now that I can see, I will not need Lottie at bath time any more. And I realise that sight brings freedom and my heart swells with the possibilities.

At bedtime, Mother kisses my cheeks and my eyelids.

'Today was the first day of your new life,' she says.

When Father comes he brings with him a curious object. There is a curved piece of leather to place over your eyes and extending from it a frame holding two pictures that look exactly alike. Father tells me it is called a stereoscope and bids me look through the eyepiece. I expect to see the two pictures but instead see only one, a mass of white and grey without form, yet strangely deep, leaning out towards me as if I could reach out my fingertips and touch it.

'What is it?' I ask with my free hand in his.

'It is a famous waterfall called Niagara Falls. The two photographs are taken a short distance apart, the left one showing what the left eye would see and the same for the right. It makes the one image seem real. Does it look real to you?'

I stare and stare at the blurred image before me, but can make nothing of it. I do not wish to disappoint him, but it seems a poor trick.

I lower the stereoscope and spell out, 'I do not know what a waterfall looks like, Father, so I do not know if it looks real.'

'Of course not,' replies Father, a short line creasing his forehead. 'You have much to learn. But what a joy it will be for you to see God's creation in all its wonders. In the beginning, He gave you Charlotte to bring you the word. Then Dr Knapp was His vessel to bring you light. Let us pray.'

He kneels down beside me and closes his eyes. I watch

his lips move and try to catch a word. I interrupt him by unclasping his hand and asking, 'What are you praying for, Father?'

'I am thanking the Lord for the miracle of your sight. Are you not doing the same?'

'Yes, Father.' But I lie. I was doing nothing of the sort. I think of what Lottie said earlier and I want to ask Father why God gave me sight yet took Constance away. But he might be angry, so I close my eyes and put my hands together and instead I thank Dr Knapp for my miracle, my parents for their kindness, Cook Martha and the maids for sharing luncheon, and Lottie for being Lottie and being everything to me. But I do not wish to thank God, as I cannot see His part in all this. Besides, the Visitors never talk of God or heaven. The Bible is a pleasant story, but I cannot think that it is real. Father tucks me in and I believe I can read two things in his face: happiness and exhaustion. His eyes sparkle, yet the wrinkles around them make him seem ancient. As he bends down to kiss me goodnight, he puts his hand to his chest and grimaces. Perhaps today has been a trial for him.

'Sleep well,' I say.

'I will, for the first night in ten years.'

I snuggle down in bed and wait for Lottie. I relive my first day in my mind, now filled with new, visual memories. I am fascinated by eyes. It seems a very intimate thing to stare at someone's eyes, perhaps more rude than undressing. I have decided I do not like pink. It is insipid when light and garish when dark. It is a shame as one of my favourite blouses, I discover, is pink. I ask Mother how she could ever have let me wear such a ridiculous garment and fling it across the room. But I do not mind pink flowers so much, as they are natural and cannot help themselves. I pity them, for not being sunshine yellow or blood red, but instead this pointless half-colour. I adore clothes. When blind I preferred the nap of particular fabrics and had my favourites based on texture – velvet, voile, satin. Now I am in love with patterns, ideally those that are not too busy as these seem to aggravate my eyes. Rather, I am partial to representation of nature: flowers and leaves, animals and clouds, rainbows and waterfalls. I see these shapes in certain curves and swirls of decoration. I see faces in patterns on the bathroom tiles, the knots in tree trunks, my bedroom curtains. I see faces everywhere. It is as if they have been waiting all my life for me to see them, these hidden faces that only show themselves to those who are really looking, those who are as obsessed with what they see as I am. I point them out to Lottie, just to make sure I am not 'seeing things', as they say. But she can find them too, and delights in sharing them with me. I feel her load is also lifted by my operation. She was indeed devoted to me, the deaf-blind girl, as she was to Constance. Now we can simply have more fun together.

I survey my room and realise there is not one picture on my wall. I never needed them, I suppose, and I resolve that tomorrow I will ask Father if I can buy some. Then I think with a shock that I could learn to draw and paint now, and make my own pictures. And my mind gladdens at all the marvellous things I have waiting for me tomorrow and the next day and the next and for the rest of my sighted life, this new life, this new adventure. And I put my hands behind my head and lean back against the headboard, elated.

At the foot of my bed, a blue-white phosphorescence

glows into being and there stands the Visitor woman with the black eyes, watching me, unsmiling. Beside her is a child with a crimson sash around her waist, cuddling a doll and kissing its button nose.

Is this your daughter? I ask the woman.

But Lottie comes in and sits beside me, takes my hand.

'What a day!' Lottie says.

'I can see the Visitors,' I tell her.

Her face changes. Her eyebrows lower. Yes, this is a frown. She disapproves.

I go on, 'They have a strange light about them. And they are in perfect focus, never blurred.'

I have been glancing from Lottie to them as I explain this. Lottie cannot help herself, she turns and looks at the bottom of the bed. I find it difficult to read her expression, but from the way her hand lies in mine, I sense she is annoyed.

'I know you cannot see them. No one can but me. What are they, Lottie?'

Lottie takes my hand firmly. I glance back to the Visitors. They are waiting for me to finish. They want to talk to me.

'Look at me,' says Lottie emphatically.

Leave us, I tell them. They fade and go. I still find this shuddery.

'Liza, now you are more normal, you need to banish your blindisms. The Visitors is one of these and it is time to dismiss them.'

'But they are real.'

'No, they are not. I think you are not yet used to your new eyes. Everything is odd to you and you are mistaken.'

'I know what a person looks like. And these are people, as real as you or me. You do not believe me?'

'I cannot believe in something I cannot see with my own eyes.'

'Once I was blind and could not see the world. But I believed in it.'

'That is not the same. You could touch it. You had the physical proof. Can you touch the Visitors?'

'Not really. But I can see them and hear them in my mind.'

'Eyes can deceive you, the mind can play tricks. You would need to bring me greater proof.'

I think, I will. Someday I will prove it to Lottie. I am determined.

'Until then, you had better keep quiet about the Visitors, or others will think it is a kind of madness and lock you up.'

'Father would never do that to me.'

'I do not know. But I fear it.'

I hug Lottie and tell her not to worry. I know that I cannot speak of this to her again, or to anyone. I will work it out for myself. Lottie retires and shuts my door. I find myself in the dark, a new dark, the dark of the seeing. It is not frightening, as I have read some children are afraid of the dark. I find it comforting. I stare into it, fascinated. I perceive that it changes the more you look at it. Outlines emerge, things take shape and the dark recedes. Colour is absent, night is achromatic. I do not know if this is normal, or just me, or some magic the Visitors are working. I go to my bookshelf. I find by touch my old copy of *A Christmas Carol*. Now I can see, the raised type seems ridiculous, but until I learn my letters by sight, I still read like a blind person. And I can read these books in the dark and do not need a candle.

I find the part where the spirit of Christmas Past appears. I read: *from the crown of its head there sprang a bright clear jet of light.* It does not quite tally, but I think Mr Dickens is hazarding a good guess and he has never seen a spirit. Perhaps it is because he had not had his lenses removed, that within the space left by the emptiness in my eyes is a realm where violet light exists, and this is where the Visitors live. And that is why I can see them, the Visitors.

Ghosts.

I cannot sleep so I go to my window, part the curtains and look outside. The gardens gleam with an ashen lustre. I know the source of light must be the moon and I look up, desperate to see it. And there it is, bright white and spectacular; I like it better than the sun, as it does not hurt to look at it. A drift of steel-grey cloud floats across it and I think perhaps this silvery vision is the most beautiful thing I have seen yet. Then I see the other lights in the sky, white dots, here, there. The more I look, the more I find. So that is a star. And I think, Why are they so tiny and the moon so large? And I recall something Lottie explained earlier, that objects far away look smaller and those closer look bigger. The stars must be a hundred miles away, maybe more. I should make a wish; after all, it is the first star I see tonight, or any night. But I have nothing left to wish for, have I?

8

It is a blustery April afternoon and all the ladies, young and old, fight to keep our hair presentable and hats in place. My first railway journey with my new eyes is to Whitstable, to visit the Crowe family. The excitement of my first train ride to London is multiplied a thousand-fold by the delightful sensations of seeing the painted and polished engine puff into Edenbridge station. We board the train and find our carriage, which Lottie and I have to ourselves to begin with, reclining on the clean, soft cushions. I see the guard with his flag and whistle on the platform and he winks at me. I blush and turn to Lottie. Her face is serene. For her, this is going home.

On the way, Lottie and I eat cold slabs of pudding-pie and play the trade game, a new pastime Lottie has taught me to improve my observation skills.

She asks me, 'Please, I've come to learn the trade.'

'What trade? Set to work and do it.'

She mimes a trade and I have to guess it. Then it is my turn. I beat her on apothecary and she wins with pantry boy and funeral mute. We make up stories about the people we see at every stop. We talk now in visual signs. It is quicker and more expressive than finger spelling. I still use the latter sometimes, as I miss it. I mostly dream now through my eyes, but sometimes I dream in darkness through my fingers. It was my mother tongue and I cannot abandon it. Lottie tells me that her mother, father and brother still remember the finger spelling, but have never had cause to learn visual signs, so I will speak to them in the old way and I can lip-read their words.

I am rather good at reading lips nowadays. I have worked hard over winter. I now have my spectacles and can read words well, write tolerably neatly. As I could already write letters, reading was not an undiscovered land to me. I just had to impose upon my visual sense of letters the shapes that I had made with my hand and a pen for all this time. So I soon learned to read by sight and the world opened up to me again, for now I had access to all of Father's library and could order books from catalogues and read whatever I pleased, without being restricted to the paltry editions available in Braille. The first book I ordered was one about ghosts. But it had no pictures and I think that the writer does not know how the Visitors appear. I love to look at pictures in books, try hard to reconcile this flat thing of two dimensions with the actuality it portrays, and marvel at the trick of the eye that makes it look real.

So, along with reading and writing, I can lip-read and speak with hand signs. I use a mixture of these to communicate with people. It is, of course, easier for me to receive than give when it comes to words. Most people do not know the signs, so I need my Lottie to translate my signs into speech for them. It frustrates me that the world does not know my language or take the time to learn it. I am a disgruntled Englishman marooned in a Far Eastern port, where no one knows or cares about the British Empire and its tongue. He must get by with gestures and befriend a local if he requires more complex transactions. But bluster and complain as he might, he will never persuade his fellows to learn his language universally.

What perturbs me most is that it will be virtually impossible for me ever to assimilate completely. There are some deaf people who lost their hearing later in life, and learned to speak before their tragedy. They are able to express themselves through speech and lip-read the words of others. How I envy them. When hearing was lost at an early age, like mine, or perhaps never existed, as for those born deaf, it is extremely difficult to learn to speak adequately. I have been told that some congenitally deaf people *have* learned, but I understand it is a difficult and time-consuming process, taking hours of daily practice for years on end. And quite frankly, I do not want to spend my youth in a schoolroom with a mirror and a speech teacher toiling away at this far-flung dream. There would be precious little time for other lessons. What must be sacrificed at the devouring altar of speech? They say too that the results are often quite bizarre, with only close companions able to understand the learned sounds. So what is the point?

Lottie takes a nap as we travel. From the window I watch the grassy banks and neat fences whizz past, as we snake our way to the coast past fields of sheep or cattle, orchards, hop grounds. A winding river flows slowly by, banked by tall grasses waving at me in the invisible wind, birds flitting from tree to river bank, butterflies – how I adore butterflies. I found a dead one once before I could see, touched its paper wings. But a dead creature is nothing when you can see the life in something. They say you kill a butterfly by touching its wings, and that seems to me an evil thing to do. Flying things should be free; you can touch them with your eyes. It is enough, more than enough.

As Lottie dozes, I talk with the Visitors on the train. There are two in our compartment. One sits opposite me and the other stands by the door. As ever, neither knows the other is there and at times they talk over one another. The seated lady is most interested in rifling through her handbag.

I know I had it in here somewhere.

What did you have?

My medicine. I take it to get rid of that blasted pain in my arm. It grates on me so. Sometimes I take too much and I get a little woozy. And then I am a fright! Tripping up and walking into things! One of these days I'll come to a bad end, if I'm not careful.

I want to tell her, *You did come to a bad end. You are dead, I'm afraid.* But I have tried this, first with the dark-eyed gypsy ghost in my room. She had frightened me, and I thought, if I tell her she is dead, perhaps she will pass away and leave me alone.

I said to her, *I am very sorry to tell you that you have died. You are a ghost.*

Take care who you curse, my dear. I can curse with the best of them.

Her eyes, like black pits in her head.

I am not cursing you, I assure you. But I have to tell you that you are dead. Please believe me.

She stepped threateningly towards me. But I stood my ground. I am quite sure that the Visitors are too airy to hurt me.

You a witch, eh? I'll string you up!

Go away for ever! And never come back.

And do you know, it worked? I have not seen the gypsy ghost since. I did it with the angry one, who I think now must have fallen off his horse and died that way. I did not like his wrathful face, his accusing comments. I was too scared to tell him he was dead. I asked him to go away for ever instead and never return. I have not seen him either. I do not know if these commands are permanent, but I do have a degree of control over the situation.

The Visitors are not to be reasoned with. It is as if they suffer from their own form of deafness and blindness, from the truth. I wanted to tell every Visitor I saw what was truly happening to them. A child I told cried and cried, a sweet-tempered man became angry for the first time and shouted at me. Or they simply talk over me. I have given up trying to persuade them. It does not end well. I think of them now as idiots, who need to be humoured. If I am bored, they entertain me, I like to hear their stories. But sometimes I look at them and only feel sad. It is that way with family members. I have met Father's relations many times. Before I could see, I knew of them, but did not know they were my family. Once I saw their likeness to Father, and to me, I guessed them for ancestors. I believe I have met the Visitors of his own parents, and their parents, and some cousins and siblings too. They dawdle about the house and grounds. The man who built the stone wall is one – he might be Father's uncle. But I cannot ask Father to confirm, as I have still not told him about the Visitors. I want to talk to them about their lives, about Father when he was a little boy, but they have only their fixations and cannot be drawn to discuss anything much further. They welcome my company as I am their only friend. They ask me questions at times, engage in some conversation, yet mostly return to their obsession. I know now what it is: the day of their death. The Visitors never recall the moment of death itself, only the minutiae of the hours leading up to it, the little details of their lives that seem so important to them, a look in their eyes saying that there is something crucial they have forgotten, or more aptly, they have forgotten that they have forgotten it. It haunts them, a lost thought just out of earshot, in the corner of their eyes. They are distracted and troubled, then sunshine passes over their faces – the light of recollection – as they relate another incident from their lives.

The man by the door looks like a navvy. His clothes are those of the working man and his face is smeared black with mud and dirt. He smokes a long-stemmed pipe and does not speak. I smile at him and nod, to let him know everything is all right. Sometimes they get agitated and you have to calm them a little.

Then he speaks up: *Excuse me, miss. I don't have any flimsies left. Could you lend me a penny to get something to eat? I've been working so hard and I'm very hungry, miss.*

Very polite he is. I tell him I cannot help him. The truth is, I could not put a penny in his vaporous hand if I tried.

He says, *I was put away for begging once. I know it's wrong. But it's for food, see? Not for booze. Just so I can get my soup.*

I wonder how he died. He does not bother me. Often they drift off in their own thoughts and forget I am there. Why I can see them and hear them, when no one else can, I do not know. Why they come to me, when I seem unable to help them, I do not know. Perhaps one day my purpose will be revealed to me. For now, I accept them as something one has always known; like hunger when hungry, thirst when thirsty, they are a fact of my life.

I survey the curves of countryside for my first glimpse of the sea. I have seen it in pictures, but cannot imagine the real sea, the size of it, the weight of it and its movement in time and space. The smell of it. Will it have a scent? Everything does. The guard walks past and people start busying themselves up and down the train. It must be soon. Then, there it is. Across the broad way to the sky, a triangle of grey appears at the horizon, flat, unmoving. I know no fields of grey. The sun catches a sparkle in it and it gleams blue, traversed by shifting lines of spray. I nudge Lottie and she looks startled, then sees her native landscape and grins. We gather our bags and fix our hats and feel the train gradually pull and pull in, reluctant to slow its cheerful progress through the land, but obliged to, as beyond Whitstable station would be only water all the way to France. It is the end of the line.

My first impression of Whitstable is one of industry. The railway station is dirty and smelly, yet thriving and full of endeavour. It is beside the dock, and the air is filled with coal-dust. They build boats nearby and the yard stinks of pitch, paint and tar. Nonetheless the bustle of the place, with its horses and goods lifted from ground to wagon by a hand-worked crane, or hoisted on the backs of burly, greasy men, is full of fascinating detail to me. My upbringing has been more than usually sheltered due to my condition as well as my sex, and I have not travelled much. To see these lives played out before me in all their grimy detail is a privilege. If I did not want to hurry so to see the Crowes, I would happily explore the docks all day and insist on conversations with the men, to know what they are doing, where their goods are going, how they feel about their lives. I want to speak to everyone in the world, regardless of age, sex, class or nation, and if I had Mr Wells's time machine, I would want to speak with everyone who had ever lived. How else am I to know the world?

This part of the seafront is not a glamorous place, as one might expect from a seaside town, but it is somehow picturesque in its very ordinariness, with a jagged collection of squat, pitch-black weather-boarded cottages that face the sea, resolved to stay put whatever the elements hurl at them. They border the bright-pebbled beach, the throngs of polished stones glimmering white, caramel and grey under the cornflower sky and tumbling down to the hungry sea. Oh, the sea. It is restless and mighty, silver-metal here and green-blue-black there, facing the clouds with belligerent agitation. The ships in the port slice the sky with their huge criss-cross masts, peppered with men engaged in maintenance, packing, unpacking, cleaning, heaving and working their backs off. Further along, the bay is filled with a cluster of boats, many of which have the same graceful curve to the sides and tall stretch of sail. Their masts reach high into the salty air, fencing with the invisible breeze. Lottie tells me these boats are the 'oyster yawls', used by her family to sail out to the oyster beds to tend the crop and fetch it in.

Even on this squally April day, there are brave souls on the beach: family clusters, girls in cotton dresses and canvas shoes, hair tied back in white frilled bonnets against the breeze, zephyrs ballooning their aprons; young women in confidante pairs sit awkwardly on the lumpy stones, legs crossed beneath their ankle-length skirts, grasping a shawl with one hand, boater with the other; groups of larking boys playing cricket or chucking stones. To grow up by the sea, to have the luxury of ignoring it only to find it there whenever you wish, waiting and wild, at the end of every street. How I envy them.

I become aware of others who walk the beach, the Visitors. They are harder to discern on a bright day like this. Somehow their white-blue light obscures them and makes their glassy outline melt into the blue sky and white light from the sun. But they are there: a few women and children, but most are men, fishermen dressed for the sea and wandering alongside it, staring out. One stops, scans the sky then turns to me, says, *They must get their hauls aboard before it blows.* Others look round at me, seem as if they want to talk, but my mind is closed to them and they know it. I have gained more control over them recently; by force of will I can repel them with a look. I do not want their chill today. They are drawn back constantly to the water, gazing beyond it, beyond everything to a realm only they can see. I turn from them and we walk away, Lottie and me.

The streets that lead from the station towards the Crowe home are narrow and muddy. Around a corner, we come across two boys dressed in green woolly jumpers, short trousers, long socks and cloth caps. Small, aged faces. They stand beside a neatly stacked pile of shells and when they catch sight of us, they reach out their hands, palms aloft, and the older boy speaks. I can read his first couple of words: 'Remember the . . .' but the third is a mystery and I turn to Lottie. She dismisses them with a gesture and walks on, calling out, 'Come back in the summertime!' The younger boy kicks the dirt and thrusts his hands away in his pockets. The other boy has forgotten us already, calling to two other arrivals as they walk up the alley.

'Remember the what?' I ask Lottie.

'"Remember the Grotter". It's an old Whitstable custom. A tale that a knight was saved from the sea covered with clinging oysters. The children make an oyster shell grotto on St James's festival, end of July. They light them up at night with a candle and get a penny for the best ones. Those cheeky rascals are trying their luck with the tourists in April! I know their mother, she won't be pleased.'

We exit the maze of lanes on to a broad street of clean pavements and larger houses. I see two little girls collect horse manure from the roadside in a dustpan and run off with it. For their garden, I presume. Lottie stops before one of the neat, white houses. Each has a gate, a small flowerbed before the front window and a boot scraper beside the door, which Lottie uses and I do too. The tiny front garden is immaculately kept, with a ring of daffodils and crocuses surrounding a holly bush with leaves so shiny they seem hand-polished. Lottie opens the front door and marches straight into the house. We stand in an alcove filled with coats on hooks and a boot rack behind the door. I see our box standing at the end of the hallway, sent before us two days ago filled with clothes for our stay and presents for the Crowes. We take off our boots and stack them with the others, a heap of footwear from Daddy Bear to Baby Bear size. Each heel is clogged with a mixture of mud and shingle. My pristine boots look ridiculously out of place. I am suddenly aware of my piled-up hair and hair pins and silly ruffled shirt and I feel my cheeks flush.

I tap Lottie's arm. 'Do I look silly?'

She signs back, 'You are amongst friends here.'

We take four steps and reach the end of the short hallway, white walls brightening the narrow way. On one side, I glimpse the parlour, crocheted antimacassars on the two armchairs I can spy. Ahead is an open door, from which moist air issues into the hallway.

'Monday is washday,' says Lottie and steps inside.

The air is thick with steam. There is Mrs Crowe, arms elbow-deep in a large bucket on the kitchen table, grinding a garment against a washboard up and down, up and down. Behind her I can see through the opening into the scullery, where a boy who must be one of the twins, Clarence or Claude, holds a washing dolly and bashes it into a tub on the floor. The other twin and Christopher are playing at knights, wooden spoons for swords, the copper lid for a shield, their faces screwed in competition. The twin is winning, as he has a few years on his opponent and a more brutal demeanour.

I have met them all before, but by touch, never by sight. Mrs Crowe's hair is sable, greying at the parting and above her ears, with small eyes, dark and piercing, red cheeks from her exertions and a small, pretty mouth. Clarence and Claude are identical twins – astonishing to look upon in their absolute likeness. They are sparky boys, with twinkling eyes and active hands, hair and faces like their mother. Christopher is pale-faced and angelic, a shy little one, only as tall as his mother's hip, with Lottie's red curls and blue eyes. Perhaps their father is the red, white and blue one. They must get it from somewhere.

They all look up at the same moment and see Lottie. Mrs Crowe throws up her hands in delight and warm sudsy drops spatter my cheeks. Lottie is assaulted by arms flung around her, the children getting there first. Her mother wipes her hands on her apron first, then she too reaches her and they all hug together. I watch them, hot in my ridiculous layers of underwear. It is the little ones who peel away first, so curious about this frilly visitor to their home. Mrs Crowe steps back and sees me, reaches out her hand and takes both of mine. Her hands are deeply wrinkled and damp, scarlet and furrowed with cracks that when dry will be sore. She draws me close and squeezes my hands, looking with great interest into my eyes. And I realise it is the first time she has seen my eyes without my affliction.

'Her eyes are lovely.' She speaks to Lottie. 'Why, she's a young woman already. A beauty!'

'She's only thirteen, Ma.'

'She looks a lot older,' says Mrs Crowe. 'Better watch out for hungry men round here!' And I realise she has no idea that I can understand a word she says. She takes my hand and finger spells creakily into my palm: 'Happy to have you.'

I spell back, 'You can speak to me. I can read lips now.'

Mrs Crowe's mouth drops open and looks to Lottie. 'Is this true?' I see her say.

Lottie says, 'You can talk to her, Ma. She will finger spell to you, but you can talk back.'

The boys are watching all this, their hands folded across their fronts.

'Well, I never,' Mrs Crowe says. 'That is a relief! My finger talk days are long gone and I've forgotten that much. But the little ones have something for you, my dear.'

She motions to them and they all lift their arms deliberately; their hands held up, palms inward, they bring their hands in short repeated movements towards their chest, as if they are saying, Come, come closer. It is the visual sign for: 'Welcome.'

I lean down and kiss each one on his cheek, followed by blushes and giggles all round. Their hair stinks and I wrinkle my nose. Mrs Crowe says, 'It's Rankin's ointment, my dear. For nits. Good time to do it, when they're not going out. They're having a holiday from school this week, so that's why they're here, helping me with the washing. We're very clean in this house, aren't we, boys? Am I talking too much for her, Charlotte, too fast?'

Lottie and I both shake our heads.

One twin covers his mouth and whispers something to the other.

'It's rude to whisper, Claude,' says Lottie.

His hand drops. 'But she can't hear me!' he says.

'Miss Golding can see what you say,' Mrs Crowe scolds him, 'so don't cover your mouth. It's ignorant.'

I take Mrs Crowe's hand and spell out, 'Please, call me Liza.'

The organised chaos of washday continues. It does not stop for me and I would not wish it to. Lottie takes off her coat and hangs it on a hook, as do I, and we begin to roll up our sleeves. But Mrs Crowe grasps at Lottie's arms and rolls her sleeves down.

'None of that nonsense. You two are visitors here. Now push off out. Go and meet the men from the boat.'

'Let's all go!' pipes up Clarence. 'Come on, Ma. Come and have a bit of a skip with us.'

But Mrs Crowe stands firm, puts her hands on her hips

and glares pointedly above the fireplace. We all turn our heads and see hanging there a cat-o'-nine-tails. The boys' faces sink and they are given soap and a bowl of socks and sent to the backyard to get scrubbing.

'Don't think I'd ever use it!' says Mrs Crowe, and I can tell from her mouth that she is whispering. 'But they don't know that, eh! Off you go.'

We go back into the hall to fetch our boots, but as we step on to the tiles, I see another child has joined us in the parlour doorway, a little girl. She has a cloud of red curled hair, just like Christopher's – in fact, she so resembles Christopher that at first I think it is him, playing mischief by sporting a dress. But she is radiant. She is a Visitor. She has nothing to say to me, just stands there, smiling, in her hand a rag doll which has lost its frock and much of its woollen hair. Lottie moves past without an inkling and pulls on her boots, the little girl only inches away from her, her head down, looking at the floor. I see that she has her eyes closed, no, not closed, but shrivelled, her eyelids rest against no eyes. She has lost them. She raises her head and reaches out her hand to me. I feel a faint tickle, like a downy feather resting in the palm. She is finger spelling for me. I have to watch it, as there is not sensation enough to read it by feel. I catch only the end of what she says: . . . *and I was so hot, so very hot. Can I have my cup?*

Lottie turns to me, passes my boots and gestures for me to get on with it. I look at the Visitor and my eyes prick with tears. I know who she is. I want to tell Lottie that her sister Constance stands behind her and she is thirsty. But I cannot. Lottie has made it clear she does not accept the Visitors, that she thinks they are a sign of madness.

Rest now, I tell Constance. *I will speak with you later.* Her mouth twitches into a faint smile, she fades and leaves us. Sometime during my stay here with the Crowes, Lottie must hear some home truths, whether she likes it or not.

9

We explore Whitstable. Its coal-dusted alleys are soon replaced by the delights of a flourishing seaside town, packed with shops and places of refreshment, holiday-makers and locals, enveloped in the tangy scents of seafood and salt, fresh air and wet shell. We wander down the High Street, festive flags strung across the street above. The road is full of bicycles, wagons and donkey carts, while a couple push their great black perambulator at the side of the road as it is too wide for the pavement. We pass a shrimp stall reeking of the sea, a man in a fez selling the creatures in pints and halves. I watch the O-shaped mouths of street sellers shouting their wares, two men in long black coats with salt blocks on a cart, another man with a broad-brimmed hat and fly-catching strips hanging from it, stuck with the poor dead creatures. I read his lips as he walks sedately past: 'Flies, flies, catch 'em alive!' We peer in shop windows at fancy goods. I see an advertisement for sand shoes and bathing drawers and stop Lottie to see.

'I have no bathing things. Father would not let me pack them.'

'Why not?'

'He does not approve of bathing. He says paddling is mischievous, as it makes your feet cold and sends all your blood to your head. And I'd need ginger wine if my lips turn blue or cornflower petals soaked in brandy on my eyelids if they should become inflamed.'

Lottie laughs, her head full back. Men glance at her as they pass by on the pavement. Her red hair and blue eyes are so very striking. And she has an ease about her, as if to say, I do not care tuppence what you think of me.

'What nonsense!' she signs. 'Your father fusses too much. He is always imagining illnesses, in himself too. He's as healthy as an ox and so are you. How do you think we managed, growing up by the sea, if paddling was so evil? When we were children, we'd light a fire on the beach and undress before it, then run down to the sea in our underthings or the little ones naked. All the mothers had no bathing costumes, they'd go in their nightdresses which would float around them like giant mushrooms.'

I look at the mannequins in their bathing costumes.

'Perhaps Father would think it is unladylike to wear these.'

'We won't need those. It's April and far too chilly for bathing. But if you want to pop into a hut and take your stockings off on the beach for a paddle, I won't tell your father, will you?'

We are conspirators.

I am giddy with the freedom of my first sojourn in the world. I think, I am a visitor here in Whitstable. And as the saying goes, When in Rome . . . We walk on and pass a tavern called the Two Brewers. I notice the sign, because from one side you see the backs of the eponymous gentlemen drinking and as you pass, you look up to see their faces. A beer wagon has stopped outside and barrels are being offloaded. A couple emerge, clearly the worse for drink, as they reek of it and cannot stand up properly. They fall out of the doorway and bump headlong into the delivery man, who pushes them aside with his great forearms thick as a hunk of ham. They rise and mouth angrily at him; a bullish confrontation develops. Lottie hurries me on. I glance back and see the sign waving above their arguing heads in the breeze, and I see the name of the brewer is written across the top: Shepherd Neame. It is one of Father's customers. I think of Father and the hops. It is the first time I have ever considered the ends of my father's living. He is a good man, the best. But the products of his business can bring shame to those who use them. He even supplies a barrel of beer to the Head Drier in the oast house and all his men. It seems to me that to bring forth food from the sea, as the Crowes do, is a more noble enterprise than growing hops to make beer which ends with this intoxication. Perhaps Father does not know everything about morals and goodness after all.

As we reach the seafront, we mingle with the thronging promenaders, an ocean of parasols and hats bobbing like sea spray, the white puffs of pipe and cigar smoke punctuating the air above them. A well-dressed woman carries a lapdog resting on her fur muff. We pass a puppet show taking place on a wooden stage. Lottie translates the puppets' speeches for me, but I ask her to stop. I am too old for such childish things these days. We turn to an ice-cream stall and I buy us each a penny lick. I have never tasted ice cream so good, rum and raisin with nuggets of ice in it. I work my tongue into every crevice of the little glass cup, handing it back with a broad grin to the Italian ice-cream man who has glinting dark eyes and makes me blush. He smiles with yellow teeth and gives the cup a quick wipe out with his apron, before replacing it on the counter.

'The boys would love this,' I say to Lottie.

The ice-cream man watches us sign, interested.

'They were born here, remember,' says Lottie. 'It's all new to you. Old news to them.'

I glance at my Italian, but he has new customers now, pretty young women. I have ceased to exist.

I ask Lottie, 'How old are the boys?'

'The twins are seven and Christopher is five.'

'There must have been a big gap, before Clarence and Claude came.'

'Yes. I was seven when Constance was born, thirteen when she died. Your age now. Then Ma went deep into mourning. She wore black clothes for three years straight. Slowly, she started to come out of it. Then she fell with the boys and they were born, five years on. They have given her much joy. And Christopher, who looks so like Constance, it is remarkable.'

'I know,' I say. 'Very like her.'

Lottie frowns at me. 'How do you know?'

'What?'

'How do you know Christopher looks like Constance?'

'I meant, he looks like you.'

'You signed *her*. *Like her*. Not me. And you've never seen a photograph of her.'

She is suspicious. Almost angry. Yet there is a kind of hope in her eyes. Is now the time to tell her? I am too afraid. I cannot. I look away, a coward, pretending to find great interest in the view.

'Come on,' she says when I look back at her, as I must.

Her hands sign grumpily, her eyes elsewhere. 'No time for paddling now. The men will be here soon.'

We walk down the beach to the place where we must wait and squeeze on to wooden benches beside others who watch the sea and chat merrily. I want to tell her about Constance, I do. But it is too black an idea for this blue day at the beach. I must wait for the right moment. I will know it when it comes.

We are never awkward with each other for long. We cannot bear it. Lottie breaks our miserable spell by pointing to a patch of sea beyond the beach where the men will come in. She says they will be in the oyster yawls, from which they will disembark to the smaller boats to come into shore. We stare out at the restless sea for a while, comfortably wordless. I think of Charlotte Crowe sitting beside me, that this is her home, the province of her childhood and family. She gave it up to live with me. I want to ask her something, but I am loath to interrupt this peaceful seascape gazing. The trouble with visual sign language is that one cannot stare at the view and keep talking. I feel for her hand and finger spell in our old way, so we can converse and still keep watch for the Crowe men.

'You must miss your family terribly, living with me,' I say.

'I love my life,' she says.

'I never really asked you. How you came to live with us. What happened?'

Lottie lets go of my hand, turns to me and begins to sign. She has a story to tell.

'I was hopping with my family, as we did every summer. The oyster season goes to sleep in late spring, early summer. The oysters just need cleaning regularly and moving from one bed to another. It is a good time to earn money elsewhere. Our family has been hopping on Golding's farm for three generations. We had heard of the deaf-blind girl up at the big house. We talked about Constance and it made us sad. It was not long since she died. We never guessed that the daughter of such a rich family would not have been educated. But I suppose the finger spelling was quite a new thing in those days. We were very lucky that our local vicar was an educated man, a well-travelled man who had worked in schools overseas and studied at a college they have in America called Perkins. It's where they teach the finger spelling and he taught it to us, as you know.

'When I saw you running through the hop garden, I took your hand because everyone was shouting and coming at you. I thought they would corner you and give you a dreadful fright. You were like a wild animal trapped and I feared you would hurt yourself. I took your hand and I said, "Hush now. Calm down." Those four words, over and over. And I knew that you had never been taught. Your father came. We all had a lot of respect for him. He had always treated us hoppers fairly and paid well. The huts were clean and he did his best to provide facilities. I was glad to help. When we left you in your room and you went crazy, I wanted to go back in. But he would not let me. He thought you would hurt me. But I knew you wouldn't. I told him that you would change when you got words, that it was frustration making you angry. I told him our story, of Constance and the vicar. He listened with great interest but would not allow me back in to see you. He really was worried you would lash out. He sent me back to the hops. I think too he was a bit uncertain about having a girl like me around you. No, no. It's not what you think. He's no snob, not really. Just aware of his own station in life and what's right for his only daughter. The big house would never usually mix with the likes of us. But come back he did, a couple of hours later, to find me. And I'd already discussed it with Ma and she said I should offer to teach you daily for as long as we were hopping. Then your father might be able to secure a proper governess for you, who could be taught the finger spelling and bring you on.

'But your father had done his own thinking and came back with a wage, room and board. He liked me, he said, and believed I was the only one that you would trust. I told him I'd had a pretty decent education from the vicar, better than a lot of the other Whitstable children from the local school. But I could be no governess to a girl from a big house. And he just smiled kindly and said we should wait and see. So I talked with Ma and she said it was a great step up for me and I should do it. Only that month we had been talking about me going into service, as there was never enough money at home, and the thought of being a housemaid filled me with dread. This was a much better position. I knew I would miss my family – the boys were only tiny then and I loved to see them grow. But this was something I would never have thought could happen to a girl like me and I was thrilled to do it. To leave my life planned out for the rest of my days, and move to the big house, with all its possibilities.

'I was happy to come. And when I met you properly, and spent my days with you, I had not been so happy since the times I had spent with our darling Constance. I loved you soon and suddenly and I have never lost that love. It has grown over time so that you are family to me, Liza. I have watched you grow from that wild girl into a person, a beautiful young lady who found her eyes and now has the world spread out before her and can do anything she desires. I think of the time not so many years from now when you will find a man who deserves you and who will love you and be beside you, your equal and helpmeet as he should be. Then you won't need me any more, which is as it should be. But it will break my heart to leave you.'

To think, all these years, apprehension has grown in me of Lottie being the one who would tire of me and find a man, move away and leave me bereft. To discover she has the same fear is so aching to me in my heart, my blood runs quick and I quiver with the life of it. And we hug and hug, and cry like fools and laugh too at our foolishness.

'But I will never leave you,' I say. 'I love you much more than anyone else in the earth. What man would have me anyway?'

'Are you mad? Have you any idea how lovely you are?'

'But would it not be very inconvenient for him to sign to me?'

'He can learn.'

'But it will be years before I am old enough. You. You are the one who will go first. Have you never had a beau, Lottie? You are the beautiful one.'

Lottie dries her eyes and composes herself.

'There was a man once, when I was much younger. He was a fisherman, a good man. His name was Tom Winstanley.'

'Did you love him?'

'I liked him. Very much. I was interested in him. He was

a thinker. He used to write long poems about the sea. I liked that.'

'What happened?'

'Oh, I don't know. There was something about him. Something sad. He'd come from the workhouse, and he used to steal books to teach himself to read. He apprenticed as a fisherboy. He went to live in a fisherboys' home, with rougher boys. It was a hard upbringing for a soft bookish boy like him. And he never got over it. He made me sad. I didn't want my life to be like that, trying to take his sadness away. Something told me it would never end, as deep as the deep sea. I would be doomed to sink with him. I ended it.'

'Did he repine for you?'

'I believe so. He used to come around and ask me to change my mind. He wrote to me when I first came to live with you, long letters full of hope and coaxing. But I never changed my mind.'

'Does he still live here?'

'Round about. He fishes for plaice and brill at Ramsgate. He lives up there. Done very well, owns his own boat now. I've seen him around Whitstable sometimes. He always looks away. He never married.'

'Has there been no one else for you?'

'Not yet.'

'There will be, Lottie. I just know it. There will be a kind and good man out there for you some day,' and I gesture beyond us, as if we might see him coming towards us beyond the shore.

She shakes her head, then looks up abruptly. A sound has come from the sea. Here come the yawls, four of them fairly whizzing in with the brisk April breeze filling their sails, each towing a rowing boat behind it. We can see them drop anchor a way out. Three men climb down from each yawl into their rowing boat, pulling into shore, the man at the back pulling at two oars, the front two with one oar each. From this distance, they are so alike in dress as to be almost indistinguishable: chunky Guernsey sweaters up top, thigh-high leather boots below, drooping moustaches like Father's on every top lip and a cheesecutter cap on some heads, on others oilskin sou'westers.

Lottie on tiptoe waves her arm to and fro. In one boat, two of the men wave back. As they approach, their broad oar-pulls briskly bringing them home to the stony beach, I can see that, beneath their caps, these two men have terracotta hair, lustrous in the setting sun, large eyes turned towards us I know already are blue. The older man leaps out first, in a hurry to see his only daughter. He casts down his oar and rushes up the beach, his stride long and loping, grinning from ear to ear. The son, slower, more deliberate, smiling to himself, tidies the oars into the rowing boat and heaves a sack over his shoulder, resting on his back. He saunters up behind, in no particular hurry, not surly or rude, but a man unto himself. Caleb.

Mr Crowe greets Lottie in just the way her mother did. He lifts her off the floor and whirls her round. A tall man, he does it easily. Lottie is laughing and smoothing her hair. Caleb comes after and puts down his sack. There is an odd moment when Lottie and Caleb regard each other, a sizing up, that they are who they were, that all is well. A swift kiss on the cheek from Lottie and Caleb squeezes her arm, holding on while their foreheads briefly touch and Lottie steps back. Nothing is said. I think of how they dwelt in the womb curled into each other, companions betimes.

Mr Crowe greets me most generously, shaking my hand and trying to say 'Hello' in finger spelling. Lottie instructs them both on my new skills, heads nod and we are easy together. Caleb picks up his sack and we all move off towards home, Caleb and Lottie behind, murmuring of I know not what. Mr Crowe tells me things slowly with clear lip movements, a little laboured, but I appreciate his efforts. His protraction does not affect the amount he says, he is very loquacious.

'Do you like our yawls? Pretty boats, eh? And they can put up with some weather, they can. You know, it's a good job you've come in April. Only eat oysters in a month with an "r" in its name, you know that? 'Cause in May and June and July and August, they are not fit to eat. They're spatting soon, you see, and the sea'll be filled with spawn, just like confetti it is.'

I turn to Lottie. 'Spatting?' I spell out to her.

'Producing young,' she signs back.

Mr Crowe watches us. He adds, 'They're making their babies, if you know what I mean. Not like we do, as they have both parts and do it themselves.' He glances at Lottie. 'I'm not being impolite, am I? It's only oysters we're speaking of, eh?' And his face creases up in mirth and we are all laughing; even Caleb smiles and looks down, shaking his head. I do like Mr Crowe.

When we reach home, we are greeted by the aroma of baked bread. Three large loaves rest on the kitchen table, beside a pat of golden butter. Plates jostle with tea-cakes, scones and a huge fruit tart. There is no sign of Constance, as yet. We find Mrs Crowe in the yard, emerging from the ash closet. Piles of washing have been through the mangle and are now pegged, heavy and clingy, on the line stretched across the yard, propped up by a sawn-off branch for the line to reach the glancing wind. One last item is being squeezed out of the mangle by Clarence, a beige shirt with linen buttons which will not get broken by the crushing cylinders, while Claude holds it straight as he can as it comes through. Christopher is assisting by patting rhythms on the turning wheels, almost getting his delicate fingers trapped and crushed by the contraption, which makes me gasp. Claude swills out a wooden tub of grey water over the fence into the alleyway, wiping his brow with the back of his hand and yawning.

Mrs Crowe calls to Claude, 'Hurry up! Don't you have any gumption?'

'All right, all right,' he says, nettled. 'I'm doing it directly, Ma. Don't keep all on at me.'

I cannot imagine speaking to Mother or Father in this manner. Mrs Crowe raises her eyebrows at a neighbour, who passes her a cup of steaming tea, engaged in her own washday in her own backyard beyond the low wall, on which hang two tin baths beside the meat safe.

There are smiles all round as the Crowe men are welcomed and Caleb hands the sack to the lady of the house.

She says, 'Normal we'd have cold meat and bubble and squeak on washday, or whatever's left from Sunday. But we have our special guest, so we are having an oyster feast tonight, Miss Liza.'

Once we are seated at the kitchen table, oysters are passed around several to a plate, the adults grabbing a shucking knife and opening up the stubborn beasts. Mine are done for me by Lottie and put on my plate. I am shown how to loosen them and pop them in my mouth.

Mr Crowe taps my arm and says, 'Some say swallow it whole and others say savour it and chew. It's up to you.'

The Crowes all swallow whole, so I try to knock it back like medicine and end up with it caught at the top of my throat and nearly gag. I cough and all eyes are on me. Lottie whacks my back and my first oyster lands on my plate. Everyone laughs, and though I am not wholly mortified I do feel embarrassed before Caleb and take a quick glance at him, to secure my shame. He is watching me.

'Chew it,' he says.

I try and find it much more accommodating. The texture is disagreeable, the flavour indifferent, but the experience is not altogether unpleasant, something of the wildness of the sea and the wash of saltwater and the embrace of the tides swilling in my mouth. I take a hunk of bread roughly sawn by Mrs Crowe and spread a large swathe of home-made butter across it. The bread is still slightly warm and the butter melts in my mouth and fills me with warmth and comfort. With that in my belly, I try another oyster and the new taste grows on me. I try another, and another.

Mr Crowe says, 'Nothing better than an oyster, eh? They call it a kiss from the sea.'

I steal another glance at Caleb. He is dipping his bread in the juices on his plate and taking great bites. He picks up a shell and tips his head back, the grey cargo slipping into his mouth. I watch his Adam's apple rise and fall as he swallows it down.

After dinner, we sit by the Crowe fire and Caleb plays his fiddle. Perhaps afraid that I would feel affronted at so aural an activity, he asks if I would like to place my hand on the body of the violin and feel its vibrations. I stand beside him and he shows me a place I can hold it, as I had done in times past when blind. Now I close my eyes again, to feel the rhythm of his playing travel up my arm and down into sinew and bone. He plays songs with curious titles that summon up stories of wayfarers' lives, such as 'Captain Ward', 'The Bold Fisherman' and 'Banish Misfortune'. The table and chairs are pushed back and I take to dancing with the others on the tiles before the fire and feel the stamp of their feet and glimpse the clap-clap-clap of Mrs Crowe's hands to guide me. When I tire of dancing, I sit for a time by the fire and watch the Crowes.

Constance appears beside me. The Crowes dance and Caleb fiddles and they do not know their sister is here. I see her hand reach for mine. I spread out my palm along my thigh as if it aches and I uncurl it. I feel her tenuous fingers like a glimpse and watch her spelling.

When Charlotte comes, I like her best. She braids my hair and never pulls it. Ma is rough and pulls my hair, but she is always sorry after.

I look up and smile at the entertainment, so no Crowes suspect me.

I say, *What is your favourite thing to eat?*

Satin pralines. You can suck and suck and then your teeth crash through and it is soft and sugary and like heaven inside.

Lottie is watching me, one of her frowns. I smile and nod my head to the pounding feet. She looks away. I have one more question for Constance.

Did you have a secret with Charlotte? Something only you and she knew?

Constance smiles and nods her head. *She had a secret name for me. She would spell it in my hand at bedtime, over and over. It was my lullaby.*

What was your secret name?

That is my secret with Charlotte. No one else knows of it.

You can tell me.

I do not think so.

I am your friend. I am Charlotte's friend. You can tell me.

It was Tanty. She used to spell it in my hand. I love Tanty, Tanty is my love.

Thank you, I say. *Time to go now.*

Constance turns and wanes.

I come back to Caleb and he nods to me, assenting to my holding the edge of the fiddle again and feeling its spell. Between tunes, he asks me, 'What do you think of music?'

I motion for his hand and he places his palm out, lets me spell into it.

'I love music.'

'How do you love it?'

'I feel the beat as I do my pulse. And the notes have different vibrations. I feel them all.'

'Do you know a sad song from happy?'

'Yes, by its rhythm, by the look on your face.'

'What do you wish me to play?'

'Your favourite.'

He closes his eyes a moment then sets to, my hand receiving it. It is slow, so slow, with graceful bows and shudders as if the bow itself is weeping. Oh, for sure, it is a sad, sad song. His chosen one, his favourite. He closes his eyes and raises his eyebrows, his chest fills as he breathes in the beautiful music. He has a sculpted face, calm eyes. All stop in the room and listen, their eyes mournful, their bodies sunken. It is the saddest song I ever heard.

When he is done, I tap his arm: 'What was its name?'

He spells it out for me: 'Twa Corbies.'

'What is that?'

'They are Scottish words. It means two crows. They watch a dead knight in a ditch, a soldier. No one knows he lies there. They will take his blue eyes for dinner and pluck his golden hair to warm their nest. And over his bare white bones, the wind shall blow for ever more.'

One of the boys pipes up something and I see Mr Crowe say, 'Oh yes, Caleb, tell us one of your ghost stories. He is marvellous good at it, Miss Liza. You must sit here by me, where you can see him. He'll give you shivers up and down your back, you mark me!'

We seat ourselves by the fire. Caleb has put his violin on the sideboard and takes his place leaning on the mantelpiece. The three boys sit at Caleb's feet, eager faces upturned.

'There was once a beautiful young lady with long golden hair and large brown eyes, name of Nell. She worked for a canon at the Cathedral of Canterbury back in fat old Henry VIII's time. She loved the canon and was an excellent cook. One day another young woman came from the shires to live with the holy man, who said she was his niece. But Nell discovered the lady never slept in her own bed. She beleft they were lovers and fell with a fearful jealousy. Now there was no bounds to her. She spied on the couple every moment she could, listening to their laughter and torturing her soul with their twinkling eyes. She could bear it no longer and took a great crock from the shelf and in it baked the most sumptuous pie of her career. When the canon and the lady had eaten of the pie, they grasped at their stomachs, they tore at their insides, they bled from their noses and ears and eyes and all their other holes . . .'

At this, the three little brothers squirmed on the floor in gleeful horror.

'They clutched each other one last time in agony, and fell . . . down . . . dead. The monks from the priory came the next morning to find the two stone dead on the floor, a look of hideous agony writ large across their tortured faces, the poisoned pie half eaten on the table and crumbs of it smeared around their blue lips. All called for Nell the cook, but she had run away, never to be seen alive again. They buried the canon and his lady in a secret ceremony, to avoid a sure scandal. Years later, three stonemasons were called to repair a loose flagstone in the Dark Entry, a spooky walkway of the cathedral. When they lifted the stone, what did they find? A skeleton huddled in the corner of a secret crypt, its flesh worn away by time and nibbled by worms and cheesy-bugs and all manner of creeping things. Beside the bones lay a rock-hard crust of . . . what else, but the poisoned pie. Was it Nelly's bones they found? Within a year, all three unfortunate masons were dead. They say two murdered the other one, though nobody knows what drove them to such a grisly deed. The murdering masons were hanged, strung up by coarse rope, their necks broken, their feet kicking their poor lives away. And now whoever dares to walk the Dark Entry late on any night, if he sees the ghost of poor Nell a-wandering there, he will be cursed and not live a year! Would you dare? Would you, eh?'

Caleb points at the three rapt boys who jump up and vie to be the bravest before their big brother, 'Oh, I will!' says one, then another. 'I would do it! I'm not afraid of ghosts!'

Mrs Crowe gestures to me. 'What about you, Miss Liza? Do you have any ghost stories to tell us?'

And I want to tell them about the gypsy lady with the black eyes, the signalman who cannot find the lost sheep on the line, the navvy begging for soup. But I feel a heat from Lottie's glare and know I cannot.

'Oh, no. Not me,' I sign and make my meaning clear with a shake of the head and shy eyes.

Caleb moves from the fire and wraps his violin and bow in a cloth. He walks to the kitchen door and lifts an arm.

'Night all,' he calls, eyes down, fiddle under one arm.

All raise a hand and Mrs Crowe embraces him before he goes. He has his own room, the eldest son's privilege.

I am thinking of his eyes. They do not seem to me the eyes of a happy man.

'Is Caleb content?' I ask Lottie.

'Tired, I think is all.'

'Not only now. I mean, is he happy in his life?'

'What a question! Mind your business!'

'But is he?'

Lottie studies me a moment. 'You are getting too good at observing. You see much, don't you?'

I nod. She glances around, then realises of course that we can speak of whatever we wish, as no one here can read our signs.

'He yearns for things beyond this life, this house. I know not what. He has had lady friends, but none is good enough. He is a fine oyster farmer and a quick hopper, but he takes little pleasure in either. I believe if he could, he would escape it all as an animal flees a trap. No, he is not happy.'

Mrs Crowe moves our feet to store toys beneath the couch. The Crowes have been tidying around us and we have forgotten ourselves. We rise to help and are shooed away as ever, Lottie and I treated as ladies here. When all is done, the boys are put in one large bed together and Lottie and I are given mugs of cocoa. We share a single bed in Lottie's old bedroom, spread with a handsome quilt of Noah's ark, faded and care-worn, clearly handmade a generation ago and used to warm many Crowe children's beds through the years. We rest our heads on hop pillows mixed with lavender, the scent transporting me back home to late summer days sitting by my open window. We curl together in the darkness and finger spell memories of our day. We hug and kiss cheeks. Now is the time.

'I saw Constance today.'

Lottie is still.

'She stood in your hallway. Her eyes were shrunken.'

Lottie pushes my hand away and sits up. Through the thin curtains the eerie green flicker of the street gaslight seeps to illuminate her curled hair wild about her head. She reaches again for me and spells, 'You are wicked,' into my palm.

'She looks just like Christopher, the same blue eyes and red hair.'

'A wicked child, to make up cruel stories.'

'Her favourite sweets were satin pralines. She liked it when you braided her hair, how you never pulled it but your mother did.'

'Ma told you that, she must have done.'

'You had a secret name for her. You'd spell it in her hand at night, before she slept. It was Tanty. "I love Tanty, Tanty is my love."'

Now the tears roll down Lottie's cheeks and she buries her head in my lap. I smooth her hair as she weeps. She looks up, looks past me, about the room.

'Is she here now?'

She believes me.

10

Tuesday is ironing day. We have been slugabeds and wake late. When we come into the kitchen in dressing gowns and slippers, rubbing the sleep and dried tears from our eyes, the room is filled with steam and heat like a Turkish bath, deliciously cut through with the draught from the open scullery door. The table is spread with a folded blanket topped with a grey sheet, and Mrs Crowe is sprinkling water on a shirt to get the creases out. She ploughs through the stiff cotton with one flat iron, a cloth round its hot handle, while the other iron heats by the range fire. She holds the iron close to her cheek, shakes her head, dissatisfied, and swaps it for the other. After every few swishes of the new iron, she places it on a hunk of Sunlight soap to make it glide better. Outside hang the clothes already ironed since dawn that morning, the scent of clean cotton wafting in on the air.

Breakfast is porridge, keeping warm in a pot on the range. The younger boys have had theirs and are in the street playing. Mr Crowe has been out on the boat for hours. He will be home for his breakfast soon, kippers for the working man. Lottie tells me Caleb is still resting. He will work the yawl later. She serves our porridge, which we eat on our laps by the range, feet on the rag rug, the oilcloth beneath worn and cracked. We sprinkle brown sugar on top and pour on cold milk, creating a moat around the lovely gelatinous heap of coarse oats. I watch Lottie line up the husks around the rim of her bowl and do the same. Our oats at home are more refined. But I like these better. They have more gumption. I watch Mrs Crowe place the kippers straight on to the hot coals and the salty smell of hot fish fills the room. I think of our engraved fish knives at home and consider what is necessary in life.

When we have eaten, I lay down my spoon and ask, 'What are we doing today?'

'A boat trip.'

'How exciting! Where are we going?'

'Just you, Liza. I never get time to spend alone with Ma and Pa, so we are going for a walk together this morning. Caleb has offered to take you on a boat trip out to the oyster beds, so you can see how they grow. You don't mind, do you?'

Then her head cocks and she signals that Mr Crowe is coming through the front door. I tumble back into her room so he does not see me in my bed things. As I dress, I think of it and grin: a boat trip with Caleb.

We leave the house, dodging the Crowe boys as they play rounders in the street, one bashing the ball with his hand before hurtling past us, then yowling as he gets thumped in the back with the ball. Caleb says, 'Don't forget I got you that golf caddying today. Make sure you give your thruppence to Ma and don't lose it on the walk back.'

The boys throw their heads back in protest, then forget it as easily as the breeze blows clouds and beat on with their game, dodging in and out of neighbours' front gardens. Caleb shakes his head at them and smiles. We walk down to the beach together without conversing. I am worried about my clothes. I am not accustomed to dressing for boat trips and I only brought three outfits for our three-day stay. I have plumped for the outfit I packed for inclement weather, my tailored tweed jacket and matching skirt. They are warm and thick. I have plaited my hair and tied it up so that it does not blow about in a troublesome way and chosen my smallest hat, a little boater, which I have secured with extra pins so it is not stolen by sea winds. Caleb does not make comment on me, so I am hoping he approves. Most of all, I do not want to be an embarrassment to him, trip over any ropes or fall overboard and require rescuing. At this moment, I would like to be a burly man in leather boots and woolly jumper. But I am a slip of a girl in tweed and must make do as I am.

We cross the stones to the rowing boats and Caleb takes my hand, helping me into the boat where I sit on a wooden ledge facing the sea. He pushes the boat into the shallows, climbs in and takes up the oars, rowing us out with a languid ease towards the waiting yawl. Two men are already aboard, smoking and laughing, watching our approach with surreptitious comments that I cannot read beneath their heavy moustaches. I worry I am a ridiculous burden to them and there are a hundred other things they would rather do than take this silly girl on a tourist trip. As we pull alongside the bobbing yawl, Caleb stands and takes my hand again. One of the men on the boat touches his cap and nods at me, holds out his hand and helps me climb aboard. I am very glad my skirt is wide enough and I do not trip like a fool. I smile at the men and nod back, my version of thanks. I can see from their downturned eyes and half-hidden smiles that they are a little timid with me. Caleb is aboard and ties up the rowing boat to the stern.

The others set to pulling at a rope to raise the main sail, which billows with the wind, and soon we are off.

The yawl is beautiful. It has three sails, three triangles of descending size down to a long beam that juts out in front of the boat, pointing its way through the water. We weave along merrily with the April winds and I grab on tight to the edge as the boat tips this way and that. Caleb has seated me at the prow of the boat beside the smallest sail, while the men work at the back. We reach a forest of poles proud of the water. The yawl is manoeuvred to the proper place.

Caleb comes over to me and says, 'These are our oyster beds.'

I look at the sea and the clutch of posts, all the same to me. I reach up and spell into his hand, 'How do you know which is yours?'

He smiles. 'Oh, we know.'

The men watch our talking hands with shy, shifting eyes. They turn, take up large nets topped with wooden handles like a carpet bag, and throw them overboard, each linked to a rope tied to the boat. We sail along and the nets are dragged across the seabed. Soon, the men haul up the nets, one each, and drag them heavy with catch on to the deck. I come over to see their hoard. They shake out the nets and a mish-mash of shell and sealife spills across the boards: seaweed and starfish, cockles and crabs, whelks and urchins, little silvery fish gasping for life and dozens of oysters. The men grab at wooden baskets piled up. Crouching, they sort through the oysters with chubby yet nimble fingers in less than a minute, throwing some into the baskets and others overboard.

Caleb says, 'Culling.'

He takes my hand and spells it.

'Some of the oysters are too young to harvest, see?' he says with his mouth. He takes up a smaller one and spans it with finger and thumb. He shows me the shell covered with pearly discs. 'This is brood stock. Infant oysters.'

He speaks slowly, carefully, to help me understand the unusual words. He flicks the infant overboard. He picks up another. 'This one is nearly mature, see? This is half-ware.' That one is jettisoned too.

'But this one, look. This is mature. Much bigger. It takes them at least five years to reach table age. You can count the layers on the bottom shell. This yellow, these three brown and this rough bit on the edge. That makes five. Now it's legal, ready to eat.'

One man takes a little hammer from his pocket and is breaking loose a large clump of shells. Dead shells, empty of life, are thrown overboard with the detritus and the young oysters.

'We pick out the legals and throw the rest back,' says Caleb. 'When it's all done, we'll take them to the hoys anchored in the bay and they'll ship down to Billingsgate. Cockneys will eat my oysters, then tramp down to your farm and pick your hops.'

We smile at this.

Once the cull is complete, the men repeat the process twice more, throwing the dredgers overboard and hauling up fresh catches. Caleb takes me to the prow, sits with me and watches them.

I take his hand and spell for him, 'Is it a good life, a fisherman?'

'We are not fishermen, as much as gardeners. We grow them and nurture them. Then we harvest them.'

'Like my father's hops.'

'Yes, like that. A farmer's life.'

'Do you like it?'

Caleb looks away and scans the sea for a time. He tilts his head closer to mine and it looks as if he mouths the words silently. I think he does not want the other men to hear him.

'Sometimes I hold brood in my hand and think, in five years that will be ready. And I see my life stretch away in five-year blocks and it feels like a waste.'

'What else would you do?'

'I could go deep-sea trawling. A hunter's life.'

Then he steals a glance at the men, crouched and culling at the other end of the boat. He takes my hand and spells this next slowly and deliberately, pressing my fingers closely to ensure no letter escapes him.

'I might join the navy. I have not told a soul that.'

'I will not tell.'

We stare at each other.

Caleb stands suddenly and marches over to the others. He hauls in a net and culls this last catch. They are done and prepare for return. He does not look at me all this time. We head for shore, the pea-green hills forming a semicircle beside us. I watch Whitstable grow as we near, the railway station fronted by carriages of coal, the docks packed with ships and bobbing boats, the seafront of stalls and tourists and the odd kite fluttering in the sea breezes, the whole town a clutter of fun and hard work and grime and sugar rock. From time to time I glance around to watch Caleb. One man is pointing at something in the water. They all rush to the side and gape and point. Caleb turns and looks at me, fearful.

I stand and he comes to me.

'Don't look in the water,' he says.

I immediately crane beyond him. He takes my hand and says, 'Look away, Liza,' squeezing it so hard I wrench it from him. He stares at me and does not move.

But I have to know. He does not stop me as I step around him and go to the side with the others. In the lapping waves I can see the back of a man, his head fallen down beneath the surface and legs and arms hanging below. It is a drowned man, a fisherman by the looks of the woollen sweater stretched across his back. A wave tips him a little and an arm comes up, the hand bloated and white, the neck twisting and the side of the face visible, black beard bristling across the cheeks and chin, black hair plastered across the white forehead, one ghastly eye like jelly glaring blindly.

I cry out and the men look strangely at me; my alien deaf voice disturbs them. Caleb takes me and holds me. We sway with the cradle-rock of the waves as the boat comes in and we drop anchor. He does not let go and I have buried my face into his chest, the dead man's staring eye haunting my mind. I have seen the dead, but not like this. I have seen the ghosts of the dead, whole, full of ethereal energy, complaints and anger, fear and confusion, their phosphorescence making them seem more alive than the actual life they cannot regain. But I have never seen a dead body. Caleb releases me and helps me climb down into the rowing boat. The other men stay aboard, shouting between boats with other sailors, all gesturing to where the dead man floats. They are busy with sensation as they organise the hauling in of the corpse.

Caleb rows me to shore alone and watches me as he pulls the oars. At the beach, he steps out and pulls the boat on to the pebbles, takes my hand and helps me step on to the stones. I hold his hand and tell him, 'I am all right. It was the shock, that is all.'

'I am sorry you had to see that.'

'Do you know him?'

'Yes.'

'Who is it?'

'A fisherman. We have all known him for years.'

'What was his name?'

'Tom Winstanley.'

Caleb asks me to wait just a moment as he goes across to some fishermen nearby. They are talking about the case, asking questions, pointing along the coastline, shading their eyes as if they expect something to appear out there. I look about me, scan the beach to see if Tom Winstanley has taken up his new existence as a Visitor yet, wandering along in his blue-white light looking for his lost love. There are other Visitors there, a boy, more fishermen, a very old lady shuffling. But no Tom. Not yet.

Caleb walks me home. When we arrive Lottie is there with her parents, flushed from their walk. At first she is smiling, happy to see us, full of questions about our trip. But she stops smiling when she sees Caleb's face and looks straight at me, questioning, fearful that something has happened to me, something shameful. I watch her face as he tells her the news. As Caleb speaks, her countenance changes, in realisation that this is something beyond her, beyond us and this house, but connected by an iron cable to her heart. Her face shows it all, the shock of it, the pity. She bites her bottom lip then covers her mouth with a hand, stares at the floor. There is something else in her eyes, but I am too young to understand it.

Lottie asks, 'Did he go down with his boat?'

'Yes. It was found smashed up on rocks just below Reculver Towers. A tourist at the fort saw it down there, last evening. Tom . . . his body drifted down this way.'

Mr Crowe shakes his head. 'Smashed up? But there's been no tempest in recent days. The wind was up a bit night before last. But nothing too bad. And he's a good sailor, Tom . . . he was. Any other hands lost?'

'No, he was alone on the boat. Had took it out alone, they say. They've towed the boat in and there was nothing on board, no gear, no bait. He wasn't fishing, that's for sure.'

Everyone is quiet. The boys come tumbling in from the yard.

'What?' says Clarence.

But no one answers him.

Lottie goes to her room. I follow and close her door behind me. She is sitting on the edge of her bed, biting her thumbnail. I tap her arm to make her look. Her eyes are looking beyond me, through the walls and down the narrow streets to the sea.

'It was your Tom, wasn't it?'

She nods.

I do not know what to say to comfort her. I do not know what she is thinking.

'Have you seen it yet?' she says. 'His ghost? Has he come to you?'

I shake my head. She looks disappointed.

'Will he come soon?'

'I don't know how it works, exactly. I haven't known anyone who died before. I don't know how long it takes. Between death, I mean, and their first visit.'

'His ship went down at Reculver. Maybe that's where he died. Perhaps his ghost would be there, in the water.'

'Since coming I can say I have seen no Visitors in the sea. Only on the beach. None on boats or in the water itself. Not one. So I am wondering if they cannot go on water, or perhaps they choose not to.'

'Then he would be on the cliffs. You told me last night, the Visitors seem to stay where they died. They don't stray far. They are obsessed with the day of their death, so they stay there.'

'That is true.'

Her face is alight with possibility.

I ask, 'What are you thinking?'

'That we must go to Reculver and look for him.'

A creeping horror climbs up my spine. 'Oh, Lottie. No.'

'Why ever not?'

'I have never sought out the dead.'

'You said yourself, you never knew anyone who died. Now you do.'

'I did not know him.'

'Well, I did,' she says, punching her chest. Resolute and wild-eyed. 'And I want to see him again. I have to know.'

'Know what?'

'What happened, of course. How he died.'

'Do you think it wise?'

'I don't care.'

We make our excuses, say we are going for a walk. Lottie tells me Herne Bay is about five miles. We could walk but the railway would be quicker. It is on the London line, towards Ramsgate. If we hurry, we might find a train this afternoon. She asks to borrow some of Father's spending money for the tickets. I tell her there is no talk of borrowing. It is my gift. We are in luck. A train is due in less than half an hour, stopping at Herne Bay and then a three-mile walk along the coast path to Reculver. We purchase some eel and meat pies with apples to keep us going. The Ramsgate train arrives and the families with buckets and spades pile off, met by beaming relatives. They are holidaymakers, thrilled to be here, glad the journey is over and the sea air fills their nostrils with pleasure. We climb on, a darker mission on our minds.

On the short trip, Lottie quizzes me more on the Visitors. It is a subject new to us. We had spoken about it last night, but mostly about Constance. We had waited up and hoped she would come to us. But she did not and we fell asleep waiting. Lottie still has many questions.

'I know you cannot call the Visitors at will. You said so last night, when we spoke of Constance.'

'Yes. They just appear. But I can make them go. Permanently, I think, if I want to.'

'But why do they come to you? Do you know?'

I have thought long and hard about this. 'Truthfully I do not know. I believe I can *see* them because I had my lenses removed, though that does not explain why I had contact with the Visitors before I had my sight. I am no scientist, but I suspect that there is some part of the air, of the fabric of the world, that my eyes can see. A place where the Visitors live. They are always there, but no one can see them. No one with normal eyes. In a normal eye, the lens stops this, protects the eye from it somehow. When I wear my reading spectacles, I cannot see them.'

'Really?'

'Yes, they vanish, the moment I look through the glass.'

'You have said they shine with a blue or purplish light.' Lottie considers. 'Perhaps there is a part of light in which they live. One strip of the rainbow. The blue part, indigo or violet.'

'Yes, I like that idea. Creatures of the light.'

'But to have spoken to them when you were deaf-blind too, you must have some other gift?'

'Yes, that is more mysterious.'

'Perhaps it is because you were deaf-blind. Maybe everyone has this ability, but our brains are just too busy to accept it. Perhaps the deaf-blind brain is not distracted, is more open to receive other stimuli, like the Visitors. Perhaps the normal brain rejects their messages as mere thoughts, as irrelevant fancies.'

'That makes sense,' I say.

'That would mean anyone could do it, if only they concentrated enough,' she continues.

'Perhaps.'

She falls to biting her thumb again, staring out of the window.

I want to take her hand and comfort her. I have never seen her quite like this. And I think, This is grief. I am not sure that rushing to the cliffs and looking for the ghost of poor Tom Winstanley is the answer. But she is adamant.

When we arrive, we climb up on to the cliff path and walk along the edge of the land. The slate-blue sea faces north to Essex and Suffolk, east to Belgium and the Netherlands. Lottie knows the way as she came often as a child, brought by the vicar who educated her and Caleb. A little weary, I ask to stand a while to get my breath back.

Lottie tells me: 'We'd come here for history lessons. And geography. We'd chalk our homework on our slates and by the time we got home it would all have rubbed off in our bags. Our teacher was always spouting off about the greatness of the empire, our naval victories and brave explorers. He had a big portrait of the Queen in his dining room and in the hall a Union Jack with a caption beneath: "For God, Queen and Country". Caleb lapped it up. I thought it was nonsense. I liked coming out here, away from the stuffy schoolroom, the ink and the paper. I liked to see my geography writ on the cliffs hereabouts, not read about it in books. Caleb would gaze out to sea and say he'd go on long voyages one day to strange and wonderful lands. He said he would sail to Madeira and bring home bananas.'

We move on and before too long, she says, 'Here we are.'

Along the cliffs, russet brown in the afternoon sun, is an imposing ruin, standing sentinel above the boulders.

'Reculver Towers,' Lottie tells me. 'A ruined church, twelfth century. And the remains of a Roman fort and a Saxon monastery. Should be plenty of ghosts.'

I look ahead and luminosity gleams amongst the ruins. I think she is right. If I died here, I would haunt the Towers.

As we near, we peer down across the cliffs to the rocks below, seeking a sign that Tom's boat was there, a scattering of driftwood, a rope, something. But the sea offers nothing, it just broils and spits and splashes against the rocks and ignores us. Lottie keeps looking round at me, watching my face, trying to see what I see.

'I will tell you if I see him,' I say.

'He was dark, very dark.'

I want to say, I know. I saw him in the water. But it seems cruel.

'He was tall. Very tall. Broad-shouldered and bearded. Handsome, yes. He was handsome.'

We reach the base of Reculver Towers. There are Visitors here. The more I look, the more I see. The air is blue with them. There are tourists too, worldly visitors, stepping amongst the ruins and sunning themselves, unaware of their phantom companions.

'Are there ghosts?'

'Dozens,' I say, scanning them. They are dressed in all manner of clothing, from modern garb to ancient robes. I have never seen so many in one place. Some are looking at me. Some approach, but I dismiss them. There is only one I want to talk with today. We walk further. I look and look.

Lottie keeps asking, keeps tapping my arm: 'Is he here? Can you see him?'

We wander around the ruins for an hour or more. Many Visitors come and go. I take to banishing them, to clear the field a little. Women and children first. Then old men. Now there are three men, but one is too short, one too young, one too fair.

'Can you ask them,' says Lottie, 'if they've seen him?'

'They cannot see each other. Remember, they do not know each other exists.'

The three men are roaming to and fro in my orbit, glancing at me from time to time. Trying to begin conversations with me. But I ignore them. None of them is right. I dismiss them all. The hour grows late and the tourists leave too. We are alone.

Lottie's eyes are melancholy. We sit and stare at the view, the sea fading from sapphire to dark emerald to gunmetal grey to black. The sun has gone behind the cliffs and the air is colder. I worry that there will be no trains, that we will have to walk nigh-on ten miles home, with no food and the Crowes worrying themselves to death as to our whereabouts. But I cannot speak to Lottie about this or anything. I am patient for her, as she has been for me these many years.

Finally, when the sun has sunk and the shadows steal about us and the old stones, she says, 'Maybe it takes them a while, after they've died. Before they make their first visit.'

'Maybe.'

'They might go somewhere else, another place, like a waiting room, before they return.'

'Perhaps.'

'Or maybe they never come back from the sea. Maybe they wander the waves out there.'

'Maybe,' I say.

'It must be terrible lonely.'

Tom does not come. There is nothing I can do to help Lottie. I have stared at the sea so long, it seems as if the land has eroded, that we are adrift on the waves. I believe I am borne away from the days of my childhood and the waters below are murky and deep.

11

It is 1899. I am sixteen years old, a young lady. Three years have passed, in which I have perfected my visual signing, my writing and reading, and my ability to lip-read. My education is flourishing. With Lottie, I study English literature, history, geography, art, mathematics and the sciences. Father thinks one day I could attend a university. All this is wonderful and I love my studies. But the atmosphere at home is deteriorating. Father is more and more preoccupied with business, as well as the world beyond the farm. There is daily news from South Africa about the situation between the Dutch republics and the British settlers. It is a complicated state of affairs and at first it has no impact upon my life, here in Kent. I am young and I do not care what happens in a hot country thousands of miles away. I am aware of it from Father's newspapers and his wrinkled brow. It seems he has some money invested over there which troubles him. The news is always bad.

Father explains it to me, that there were Dutch settlers there for many years, and British settlers came later. There was a war back then and the Dutch got their own way on controlling their colonies. Gold was found in one Dutch colony, called the Transvaal. Great Britain provided a lot of the equipment and skilled men to mine it. Everyone profited, but the British settlers have limited rights in the

Dutch republics. Some are treated badly and cannot vote. Our government wants all British males there to have the vote. There is a lot of argument over trying to come to a settlement that will please everyone. Father says the Dutch, who we call Boers, are awful cads who want to make all of South Africa Dutch and boot out the good Englishmen who have helped make them rich. In August we hear that there are no hopes of a peaceful settlement with the Boer republics and that British citizens in the Transvaal are fleeing to the British colonies, particularly to Cape Town, which has become a chaos of refugees. Now there is a new word on everyone's lips, a word that frightens me, even though it is so far away: war.

Father talks about the men on the farm leaving and joining up, that he would have no workers left, and what about the hoppers? He is worried and that worries me. Summer approaches and with it, the hop-picking season. We need hoppers more than ever, as this year it is an excellent yield. Sometimes he voices his concerns to me, but I do not know how to console him. His dour mood and Mother's poor health are becoming a burden to me. I long for the clean, bright sea air. I long for Whitstable. I feel more at home there than anywhere, even my own home. I have never told Father this. I cannot explain it to him or to myself. I feel for the Crowe boys – the little ones – as I would for my own siblings, had I any. The whole family has learned visual signing so they can converse with me. I love them the most for that, that they would invest such time just for me, for my benefit, when they only see me twice a year, for my one visit there and their hopping visit to us.

Even Caleb signs for me. Each year I have visited, he

has taken me on a trip to see the oyster beds. We talk. The men on the boat watch us but cannot read our signs. Caleb is not happy. He tells me things I believe he does not tell anyone, about his life, his frustration, his need for escape. I read his signs, my way of listening. I listen carefully, I watch his eyes as he looks out across the sea to another life he cannot have. I cannot find the words to give solace. I only want to confess the one thing I know for sure, and that is my regard for him. I have not had the courage to tell him at thirteen, or at fourteen, or at fifteen either. Maybe one day I will, when I am of age. But what good would it do? He is a man and I am but a child to him. He pinches my cheek and teases me. Sometimes he hugs me hello or goodbye. He says I am his special girl. He says he speaks to no one the way he speaks to me, that talking to me in signs helps him to think around a problem, to place it in space and time. He thanks me for keeping his confidence. If he knew how I see him, how I think so earnestly of him always, it would shame him and he would not tell me secrets any longer. So I keep my feelings to myself and build my castles in the air privately. Now you know the true reason why I live for visits to the Crowe home.

But it is not only that. I love to see Constance there and share time with her and Lottie. It is not always easy, as sometimes Constance cries as she recalls her fever. I do not tell Lottie about this, only the times when Constance is happy. We have never told the rest of the family about her. Lottie feels it would be too shocking for her mother. She thinks Mrs Crowe would not believe us, as she is a sceptic. And then it would only serve to upset her, as Lottie was upset by me before she believed. I wonder if there is a part of Lottie that still doubts me, and wonders if I tell her Constance's words through lies or some trickery. Especially since, each time we have visited, Lottie and I make our pilgrimage to Reculver and look for Tom Winstanley. But he is never there. We have rambled up and down that craggy coastline looking for him. We have visited the wreck of his boat, his neat cottage, empty now. And there is no sign of him. I have caught Lottie eyeing me in her disappointment and wondered if I spy suspicion there. Why can I not see Tom? I cannot answer. I think only that those lost at sea may not return to land. We have even been on boat trips from the bay near where his boat was wrecked and scanned the waves for hours. But no Tom. There must be another cause. Perhaps some dead choose never to return. For now, it is an enigma.

As much as I value our visits, it is not always the jolly place I remember from my girlhood. Things have turned sour for the Crowes in recent times, too. Their business has suffered of late from falling oyster numbers, as well as changes in who owns their oyster company. They say it has been sold. They do have shares, but now they work for the owners rather than themselves. Then there were the three disasters. First, the Whitstable coast was smothered by an ice sheet that had broken away from the Arctic. They could not leave shore for over a month and when they finally reached the beds, almost all the oysters were dead. Two years later was the flood, where the sea raged through the town and left their neat home up to the skirting boards in filthy, brackish water. Then last year Mr Crowe's cousin, another oyster man, was drowned with his third hand on their yawl when a steamer ran into her port side and capsized her. So much bad fortune in so few years almost sinks the family. Lottie sends most of her wages home every month, but there is never enough. I believe Caleb feels more and more a slave to his work and his family.

This summer, I have an idea. I persuade Father to offer Caleb a promotion, as assistant to the Head Drier in the oast house. Father considers this. He trusts the Crowe family and Caleb has proved himself to be a good, responsible worker every year. It is a sought-after post, a leap up from the hop pickers. He must stay in the oast house all day and night, feed the fires in the kilns, add the right amount of sulphur to colour the hops golden and maintain the correct temperature of the furnace at all times to dry the hops. The trick is not to let them dry out completely, but to distribute the moisture evenly. The old Drier is expert at how to feel and smell that the precise degree of dryness has been achieved, and it is skills such as these, with use of no technical equipment, only years of knowledge, that Caleb would learn. It holds a great deal of responsibility, for himself as well as the Head Drier. They both have beds there in the oast, as the drying needs constant supervision.

In the warm afternoon of his first day, when Lottie is visiting the rest of her family in the hop lanes, I steal across to the oast house and wait for Caleb to go on his break. I have changed my study clothes from this morning and put on a new summer gown, nipped at the waist with a bare neckline. I have brushed out my hair and pinned a blue satin flower behind my ear. Caleb appears at the door to the oast, his cheeks pink and hair damp from the kilns. He sees me standing, waiting in the shade of the cob tree. He stops and looks at me. He smiles. I come to him and sign, 'Good afternoon, Caleb.'

'You look very beautiful today, Liza.'

'Thank you. How is your new post?'

'Fine. It is fine. Hard work. Hot work.'

He looks away and retrieves a rag from his pocket, wipes the sweat from his face and looks back at me, my neck, my hair, the flower.

I sign, 'I am so happy you are here.'

'Me too,' he says and smiles.

I take courage from that smile. 'If only it could last for ever. If only you could work on the farm all year. Then we could meet like this every day. And talk.'

'Yes, we could. We could do many things together.'

'Would that make you happy, Caleb?'

'Well, you know me, Liza. I'm a restless soul. Who knows what could make me happy?'

He smiles still, and I believe he is teasing me somehow. But I am serious. I think, I can make you happy, I can. But I do not say it.

The drying lasts for several weeks and I visit Caleb whenever I am able. He has so little free time and I prefer to see him when Lottie is not around, so there are few opportunities. I try to entertain him with stories from my lessons, particularly geography, as I know he has a keen interest in the wider world. I tell him of far-flung places and their strange customs. One time I show him a picture of a painting, *The Boyhood of Raleigh*, which captivates him.

'That is me,' he says, pointing to the spellbound face of the boy hero, listening to seafaring tales from the experienced sailor. 'I was like that.'

'I know,' I finger spell for him.

He answers in kind, in our old way in the palm, his fingertips rough from work. 'Sometimes I think you know me best of anyone, Liza.'

He holds on to my hand and does not let go. He looks closely at me and as our faces are near, his image blurs. He stands abruptly and signs without looking, that he must get on, that he will see me tomorrow. There are only a few more days until the drying will be done, and I do not see him alone again. Yes, he is busy, and there are excuses. But I fear something has changed between us and I wait, I wait for him to come to me, to explain it all to me, for I am floundering in this new sea of ours.

Around this time, towards the end of the season, Father reveals to me that the Head Drier is considering retirement next year. I see Father's mind working. Perhaps Caleb could be trained up to take over this crucial post. He could stay on the farm all year round and learn all the different stages of the business. The thought that Caleb would work here and live nearby is more than I could have wished from a rub of Aladdin's lamp. But I do not speak with Caleb about it. I cannot find the time alone with him. And most of all I fear that it will not suit him, that he will feel trapped on the farm. But oh, how I want him to want it, to take this chance to stay where I am, to be with me always. I decide it must be Father who puts it to him, that perhaps Father can persuade him what an excellent opportunity it is, what a step up in the world. When the last load of hops is to be dried, Father calls for Caleb to come and see him. I plan to wait alone nearby but Lottie is there. The moment she heard that her brother had been invited up to the big house, she is curious, asking questions of me, and I cannot lie, not to Lottie. I have been economical with the truth this drying season, have kept from her how many times I have sought out Caleb's company alone, when she was out of sight. But I have not yet told untruths to her face. I believe

I could not. So, Lottie and I hide down the corridor from Father's study. When their talk is done, we see Father march off downstairs, his face grim. Caleb appears from the door and we scuttle up to him.

'What happened?' Lottie asks. I watch their mouths closely.

'Mr Golding asked me if I wanted to work on the farm permanent.'

'And what did you say?'

'I said no.'

I knew it, I knew it, but did not want to believe it. I look down at my feet, my head swimming. But Lottie is prodding my arm. They have been talking and I have missed something.

'Caleb has enlisted!' Lottie signs furiously.

I read her signs, but I do not comprehend them. I stare at him. He glances at Lottie, looks to me. His eyes are speaking to me, but I cannot read them adequately. At first I see pity there, but then I wonder, a kind of conflict in his soul? If only we were alone.

'I've enlisted in the army,' he signs to me.

'Not the navy?' I sign, and Lottie looks at me, incredulous.

Caleb signs and speaks simultaneously, for my benefit. 'I go to camp tomorrow. We'll sail out in a few weeks, I think.'

'Sail where?' Lottie says, signing too.

'South Africa, for heaven's sake. Where do you think?'

'And when on earth were you going to share this with us?'

'I just did, didn't I?'

I touch his arm and I sign, 'But there isn't a war there, not yet.'

He looks at me kindly. 'There will be, Liza,' he says. 'And soon.'

Lottie smacks her hands together in sign. 'And what the hell's that got to do with you?'

'It's my country, isn't it? Every Englishman must do his duty for the empire. We can't let the bloody Dutch push us around.'

'Don't give me that rubbish about Queen and country. You're lying! You just want to escape, that's all.'

'Look, I've enlisted and that's that. Leave me be, woman!'

And I can see from his face, his chest and his throat that he is shouting. He stalks away towards the oast house. This night is his last on the farm. Whatever else transpires in these hours, I must seek him out and speak with him alone.

Lottie is too angry to converse with me or anyone. We maunder from the house, each of us waist-deep in our own thoughts. Both of us are sick with it. I cannot explain to her why I am, though I know her reason. There is something between them, a twin consciousness that would be torn if he were to sail away. She fears for his life. I feel ill with it too, but must comfort Lottie, as if my sorrow is but a reflection of her grief. When we reach the hop garden the pole-pullers are taking down the last few bines, wielding their long hooks and using the sharp blade at the top to slice through the bines and bring them to the ground. The hoppers then lay the plants across their knees and pluck the flowers off at great speed with thumb and forefinger, dropping them in the canvas bins. We find the Crowes finishing their last bine, the boys stopping to salute each other, Mrs Crowe laughing, shouting across to other hoppers and nodding. They have heard Caleb's news. I assumed Mrs Crowe would be worried for her son. But no, they are all so proud their eldest is going to fight for his country. The boys shoot at imaginary Boers all down the hop alleys.

The measurer comes and I see him shout, 'Pull no more bines!', as he does every day at this time.

Mrs Crowe nudges me and nods towards him. 'There aren't no more bines to pull, you giddy goat,' and I can see many others laughing.

Our measurer Hodge is a pompous man, proud of his new waistcoat and unpopular. The hoppers are paid by the number of bushels picked and they say Hodge is mean with the weighing out. He comes to the Crowe bin and measures out the last hops into his bushel basket.

'Scoop them up loosely, won't you?' says Mrs Crowe.

He ignores her and sifts through the load. I cannot see his mouth to divine what he says, but he pulls out a bunch of hops with leaves and twigs still attached, holding them aloft as proof that Mrs Crowe has tried to cheat him on the weight.

I tap Hodge on the arm and sign, Lottie translating, 'It was my fault. I picked that one. Sorry.'

Hodge glances at Mrs Crowe who folds her arms over her bosom and smiles smugly. He touches his cap to me and continues to fill his bushels, forcing down the cones as he goes.

'Eh, don't press them down, Mr Hodge. Times are hard, you know.'

'They are indeed, Mrs Crowe. For all of us.'

She turns to us and shakes her head, signs for me and speaks for the family. 'The sooner our Caleb is in Africa, the better for him. Out of this silly business, all of it, on our feet picking the blasted hops ten hours a day, six days a week, and my husband tending those oysters every hour he can and never enough pay for all our hard work. This war will be the making of Caleb.'

This evening, the last night of the hopping, there is the annual hoppers' feast. They throw off their aprons, hats and caps. They eat huffkin cake and drink beer. They dance and sing old hopper songs, about the work and the washing and the lice:

> Now early Tuesday morning,
> The bookie he'll come round
> With a bag of money,
> He'll flop it on the ground.
> Saying, 'Do you want some money?'
> 'Yes sir if you please,
> To buy a hock of bacon
> And a roll of mouldy cheese.'
> I say one, I say two,
> No more hopping we shall do.
> With a tee-I-ay, tee-I-ay, tee-I-tee-I-ay . . .

I watch them laugh and shout around the campfires, the light leaching from the sky and the flames throwing black twisting shadows across the bare hop poles. I wait and wait for Caleb, hoping he will be permitted to take a break from the last night of the drying. He comes late, past eight, and at his arrival the hoppers cheer him and break out in patriotic songs: 'Boys of the Bulldog Breed', 'Tommy Atkins' and 'God Save the Queen'. Caleb plays his violin with other musicians, the same woman who plays her drum every year, another fiddler and a guitarist. Caleb takes a rest from playing and dances with some of the ladies. I watch him move and smile. I know it is my bedtime soon and Father will send a maid to fetch me for my bath, but I want to stay here at the party till dawn. There is a heat and a quickening in the air and I want to breathe it in. I watch Caleb dance and suddenly he turns and walks towards me. He smiles and holds out his hand. I know I must smile and seem the good girl. But when he moves my body around the ground strewn with hop leaves and cigarette stubs, I think grown-up thoughts about him which make me colour hotly. And I believe I feel his body bend towards mine as we dance, his fingers curl into mine as we turn, as if they wish to speak to me in the old way and tell me secrets. I cannot make sense of it. As the dance ends and I must leave him, I catch an ardent glance from him; there is knowledge there and desperate sadness. I am decided what course I will take to make him stay.

I am in bed, and the house is sleeping. My clock reads one. I go to my window and open it. It is a balmy September night with a high, bright moon and the heat from the oast house ovens drifts on the breeze and warms my face. I dress quickly, just a shift and a robe, my hair loose. I open my door and creep downstairs. I pad through the kitchen, the tiles cool under my soles. I take the key from above the scullery door, unlock it and slip out. The grass is damp and soft with dew, the air dusty, spicy, ambrosial. I cross the herb garden and run my fingers across the fragrant plants as I pass. As I approach the oast house, the heat and the smoky, bitter-sweet yeast scent of the drying hops is overpowering. Feeling faint, I stop, touch my forehead and steady myself.

The door to the kilns is open. I peer inside and see the Head Drier asleep on his bed in the corner, blanket thrown aside, head tipped back, red tammy-shanter slipped over his eyes. I tiptoe inside. Caleb's bed is the other side, and I have to come into the room to see him. There is a dim lamp alight in the corner. He is sitting upright on his bed, smoking and staring into space. He wears a white shirt, a few buttons open to the heat, grey trousers held up with braces and grubby boots. His head turns sharply and he sees me. We stare at each other. He does not speak. I stand still. Finally, he drops his cigarette and crushes it underfoot. Stares at it for a moment, then looks up at me. He reaches down, pulls at the laces of his boots and slips them off so that he is barefoot too. He walks to me and takes my hand, but he says nothing and I do not sign to him either. He leads me up the wooden stairs. We pause at a creak on the stair, and he looks round at the Head Drier, who does not stir. We walk up and step into the cooling loft. The heat from the drying rooms is terrific. There is no lamp here, so the only light comes from the moon, casting a white cloak across the hop sacks, the press, the scuppets, the hop fork, the horsehair lifter cloth and the pokes stored on the green stages. There are no Visitors here. They know they are not wanted. We are alone in the world.

There is a pile of sacking in the corner and he bids me sit there. He kneels beside me, and we look at each other. I tilt my head so that his face is clear to me. Everything is his eyes and my eyes. I thank the stars that I can see, that I can look into the eyes of my love this night and he into mine. When he kisses me, I taste tobacco and tea and feel my future, which had stretched before me until this moment, shrink to the size of a pebble and slip into his pocket. I am his now.

Afterwards, we lie together for a long, long time. The

moon still shines and the heat still wafts over us in waves. Our bodies are wet with movement and love and the moisture loosed from drying hops. My hair is long and sticks to his chest, his neck, his face. I know I am a woman now. I wonder if his child will grow in me. I bury my face in his hair and kiss him again. He lays me down and regards me.

'I am a young man again,' he says, smiling.

'I will keep you young,' I finger spell for him.

'I don't doubt it.'

'Where will we go? What will we do?'

He frowns. 'Now? I have to check the furnace in a minute.'

'No, tomorrow.'

'Tomorrow, I must go.'

I sit upright. I look at him very seriously. I brush my hair from my face and sign to him.

'You must not go. Africa is too far away. And war is perilous.'

'I have to go. I've enlisted.'

'But a promise has been made, here, between us.'

He sits up, rubs his eyes, clasps his hands before him and looks up at me. 'I'm sorry. I did not mean to promise you that.'

'But . . . I love you.'

He smiles and reaches out a hand, his fingertips brushing my cheek. 'You are lovely.'

'Do you love me?'

'Yes, my pet. Of course I do. But I am enlisted and must go tomorrow. Today, this morning.'

I am on fire. I sign with ferocity, smacking my hands together at every sign.

'Why did you enlist? Why would you put yourself away from me?'

'Liza,' he signs, 'it is complicated.'

'Explain!'

'You are very young—'

'Not so young,' I interrupt and he holds up his hands, then drops them. He will not sign. He speaks to me now.

'You are a young woman, lately a child. The daughter of my employer. I am not so foolish as to believe there is any future for us, for you with me, who has nothing to offer you.'

'But I do not care for any of that.'

'But your father will, your mother. Even Lottie. You know this is true.'

'I do not, I do not! Father will do as I say, he will want to make me happy.'

'But I cannot make you happy.'

'Yes, yes you can!'

'You know me. You know me deeply. You have seen into my soul. There is a restive man there, a selfish one. It was that man who enlisted. If I stay here, at the farm, at the sea, I will go mad, Liza. I will end myself, I know it. I think you have always known this.'

'But all that has changed. How can you go now? I could never leave you, not by choice. Never. I have always loved you. From your first letter to me. From the first time I touched your face. From the first moment I saw you with my eyes. How can you leave me now?'

'Perhaps in Africa I will make something of myself. Who knows what the future holds? I only know I cannot stay. I will write to you, Liza.'

How can he think this is enough? I am at a loss for

words, and my hands grasp the air for them. Finding none, I thump him in the chest. His eyes harden and he stands up, pulls on his trousers and walks away from me. I am left, alone, my wet shift cold against my skin. I pull on my discarded robe. He stands by the hop press, his hands on his hips, staring down into the opening through the floor, where tomorrow morning he will help fill the hessian pockets with the last of the season's dried hops. He stares and stares into that hole. And I know that his silhouette etched in moonlight will imprint on my memory, the image of him standing there, bare-chested, looking down through the floor of the oast house and making his decision, and it will haunt me.

Then he turns. He signs to me. 'I want to go.'

I run from him and almost trip on the stairs. I see the Drier on his bed, still sleeping the sleep of the just, and I hate him for his peaceful slumber. I run from the oast house and cross the herb garden, the pretty fragrance turning my stomach now. Back in my room, I twist and cry silently in my sheets, desperate that no one in this house or this farm or on earth should know of my great disappointment. My blood does not run, my heart beats very slow and aches very quick. I believe my love has forsaken me and I shall lose him for ever. My hopes are drowned and soiled. My sorrow makes me wretched and I bite the pillow to stop my tears flooding the room. And I tell myself I hate him, I hate Caleb. For leaving me, for not moving heaven and earth to stay with me. And I wish it could be midnight again, before I left my room, before the scent of herbs and the cool grass and the dry heat and first sight of him there on his bed smoking, before he looked up at me with his pale face. Before I lost myself to him. So that

I could relive it, every moment again, every touch and every word his hot hands finger spelled into mine as we moved together, words of desire I will never repeat to a soul, our secret words he left in my hands for me, that convinced me of his love. And I fear I will never lie with him again, that he will leave me and die in Africa; or, if he lives, he will abandon me for another life, for I was just a sweet girl for him who made him young again this one night and who will be crushed like a dry hop in his hand and scattered to the warm wind, forgotten.

12

On 11 October 1899 the Boer republics declare war on our nation. Caleb has been gone for seventeen days. On the eighteenth day my monthly curse comes, and as the blood flows from me into the bath water and colours it crimson, I weep and weep. The thought of his child within me has kept me company in the shorter days and the longer nights and now all trace of him is gone, as if he had never lain with me, as if it had never happened.

We read of the war every day. Lottie and I have made a map of South Africa and put it up on the dining room wall. We follow every battle, skirmish and troop movement with pins, white for us and black for them. We order all the newspapers, which give us disputatious ideas about the war. We thought it was all about the British settlers, who the Boers call Uitlanders, which means outsiders or foreigners. One paper says that the treatment and rights of the Uitlanders by the Boer government is why we are fighting. Other newspapers say this is nonsense, that most Uitlanders, particularly the working men, do not care about the vote. That it is only the stock market Uitlanders who are making all the noise, that they have invented their grievances to create insecurity in the money markets and lower prices. Some say that the aim of the war should be to create a united South Africa, that only British rule would be progressive and Dutch rule is retrograde. One editorial said that the Dutch have no desire or ambition to make the whole of South Africa Dutch, as is commonly believed. And that it is all about money for rich men who want control over the gold.

So, we are confused, Lottie and me. Why is Caleb going to fight? Why are our brave boys risking life and limb, and even dying, in that hot country so many miles from home? Father is very clear: it is the British Empire that must rule South Africa for its own good and the Dutch may go whistle. The Boers are a scrappy nation of ragtags and farmers who will bend under British might and it will all be over soon. He takes us to the Cinematograph at Canterbury to watch a little fiction entitled *A Sneaky Boer*, where a brave British soldier is attacked by the craven Boer wriggling through the long grass. I can see everyone cheer when the beastly Boer is caught and a few handkerchiefs are pulled from pockets and shaken in the air. Then Lottie beside me jumps in her seat and puts her hand to her heart, and I see a puff of smoke issue from the front. It turns out the owners have planted actors in the audience to let off guns to heighten the drama. There is so much smoke by the end that we cannot see the screen. We leave in a flutter of excitement at our entertainment, yet also determined that Caleb and our lads will beat back these cowardly Boers and be home for Christmas.

But Christmas comes and goes and the war does not end. By March 1900, Caleb has completed his training and sails to Africa. We write to him but hear nothing back. For weeks, I am the first to check the post and am disappointed day after day. I have to conceal my distress from everyone. Nobody knows the truth. In the past, it would always be Lottie; she knew all the workings of my heart. But I cannot share this with her. I have not told her anything about Caleb and me, of how I feel for him, of what we did. I believe she would be angry with Caleb, blame him for taking advantage of a girl's callow desire. I fear she would be jealous and a mistrust would grow. That the end of it would be the end of us. It would alter her love for me, snap it and ruin it. I cannot risk losing her, so I decide I cannot tell her. It pains me to keep a secret from her, my soul's companion.

At last, in late September three letters from Caleb come at once. It seems the postal service out there is quite unreliable. But the letters are not for me alone, rather to the two of us, to Lottie and me. Of course, this is how it would be. I could not hide letters from Africa in this house from Lottie or anyone. Caleb knows that. So we go to Lottie's bedroom and she opens them, the elder of us, the sister. I read over her shoulder, searching for clues to his love for me, a message for our future.

Senekal,
Orange Free State
31 May 1900

My dear Lottie and Liza,

Thank you for your letter and photograph. You both look very pretty. I am sorry not to have written at length to you as yet. We have been on the go for months now, what with training and the voyage and setting up things over here. I hope to remedy this now with a description of our first major action, at Biddulphsberg. We have been on the edge of a few skirmishes – and our lads got very frustrated by the lack of action – but this is the first large-scale battle I have fought in. And as you can see from my handwriting, I made it through all right.

I am in the 33rd (East Kent) Company, attached to the 11th Battalion Imperial Yeomanry. This may not mean much to you ladies, but it does work out that I have several Men of Kent about me. We are currently fighting alongside such broad notions of what makes a man British, including the Grenadier Guards, Scots Guards and East Yorks. On Monday, 28 May our British columns under the command of General Rundle numbered around 4,000 and we left Senekal at 1 p.m., moving in an easterly direction for about eight miles. Even on this short march, some men had very bad boots and had to fall out for a while, footsore. We were heading between Sandspruit and Quarriekop to a big kopje on the veldt. (You probably know by now from newspaper reports that this means a hill on the African plain. Kopje is a charming word that means 'little head'. A nice language all round, Dutch.)

We halted for the night about four miles from our destination. Our objective was to give some heat to the Boers around there. I was immediately assigned outpost duty which lasted all night. I spent hours looking out across the misty land, the odd hill breaking the aspect. You could call it dull country, with the same squat farms and hillocks the only interest in hundreds of miles, each one merely serving to make it all seem more lonely. But the skies are enormous and impressive, and the colours on the veldt change every hour of the day with the rising and falling of the light, and it has its own rough loveliness. Some of the moths are splendid, with one landing on my boot six inches across the wings. We see foreign creatures like snakes, scorpions, centipedes and lizards scuttling about, yet also more English familiars such as hares, rabbits and pheasants, to take the edge off the strangeness. 'Arouse' next morning at 4 a.m., then all the tents were struck and packed and we sat on the ground eating breakfast in darkness, but the dawn comes so quickly here it was broad daylight once we'd finished.

We moved on at 6 a.m. on Tuesday, 29 May, advancing towards the kopje. Within 3,000 yards the two Boer big guns opened on artillery to our left. Once you've seen the smoke of the big gun there is a worrisome interval of about ten seconds before something happens. Then you hear the boom of the report, then the whine of the shell which turns quickly into a horrible scream. But hearing the thing coming makes no earthly difference to you, as you have no idea where it will land until the red earth explodes beside you. We went down the slope towards the guns. We couldn't see anyone, but straight away were fired upon very fierce, from all sides it seemed. Bullets buzzed like wasps about our heads. As the Boers have no parapets it is almost impossible to see where they are firing from, as well as the fact that they were using Mausers which emit no telltale puff of white smoke. (We heard later that the Boers' position higher on the hill was well planned. They had some in a dry dam, others in a donga – that's a word for a dried-out lake bed – and more behind long grass.) So they caught us in a duck shoot and we suffered under the crossfire. The order came to 'lie down'. We heard the bugler pipe up, 'Pepper 'em, pepper 'em, pepper 'em, boys' (in a mad moment I thought of your father, Liza, and his bugle calling us hoppers to work!) and recognised the order to keep firing at the big guns.

We rushed on another sixty yards or so, the enemy raining rifle fire on us. I lay on my stomach, firing at the kopje. I emptied my pouches. The fellow next to me – Wallis – got a smack in the leg and called out, 'They have made a rat hole in me!' After that he turned on his back and lay still. I helped him put his coat and equipment at his head for shelter and I did the same. Our coats and mess-tins got shot to pieces by bullets. They saved our lives. We lay there for five hours, pinned to the ground under tremendous fire. Some of the men wore shorts and had awful sunburn on the backs of their knees and were in agony the next day, all blistered up and unable to walk. Wallis called over and over for water. I had given him all mine and had no more. Then he started moaning about the blasted Boers taking all our gold and using it to buy the latest European weapons and how the British are far too lenient on the Free-staters who surrender and take the oath of allegiance then go out and fight for their brothers the very next day and they should all be shot. In the end I told him to put a sock in it. By this point, my nerves were quite jagged.

At 3 p.m. we heard the order to retire. We saw some soldiers fall back and I was about to help Wallis up when we heard a dreadful sound. At first I thought we were being shot at again, as the crackle of rifle fire can sound like dried trees burning. But then a roaring came from behind us and we saw the grass that had been our cover was all alight. We were surrounded by fire! Some of the wounded were dragging themselves through it, appalling burns on their faces. I helped Wallis stand and he leaned on me as we stumbled through. Boers came out of their trenches and helped some of the British wounded through the fire. One Boer lad got Wallis some water and wrapped him up in two coats taken from the dead. They are very fair when it comes to the wounded.

The Boers helped set up a hospital back in Senekal at the Dutch church and Wallis was taken back there with the other wounded. He'll be all right. Do not believe everything you read in the newspapers about Boers. There are brave and honourable Boers and cowardly and dishonourable ones too, like people everywhere, like the Tommies. I must say, though, that despite the foul language and tendency to steal and loot, the character of your average Tommy is good-natured in the face of lack and discomfort, as well as possessing a dogged courage in long advances that test the mettle of the bravest man. The hot dash into battle is exciting to be sure, but the valour it takes to plod on through whizzing bullets seeing men around you fall is a testament to the Tommy's stubborn will to endure and carry on. We can also be very fair with Brother Boer. After the battle, our medics helped them too, particularly their General de Villiers who was shot in the jaw. There was a ceasefire agreed the next day. It is a kind of gentleman's war, as they say, despite pounding each other with explosives.

I stayed behind with some others to bury the dead. We carried them all to a field with a thorn tree nearby. I saw an officer called Campbell write a note and pin it to the tree. I looked at it before we left and it read something like: 'This tree must never be cut down as it is the resting place of those who fell on 29 May 1900.'

It strikes me as a sad thing to be buried in this dry soil, so far from England. A bit like being lost at sea, never to return to your old home ground. There are times in the rage of battle when I am glad to be alive and in this fight, and there are quieter times when I think of how the half-ware are doing and I feel a b----y fool for ever leaving Whitstable.

Please keep the newspapers with reports of our battle at Biddulphsberg for me. If you've already thrown them out, I hear you can get back copies at bookstalls; please do. I will be interested to see what nonsense they make of it. We have seen a few English papers out here and are amazed at the ridiculous lies in them about all manner of things and think most of it is invented in London.

I lost all my equipment to the Boers. I had collected some curious mementos that I was sure would have pleased you. Looting is forbidden, but so far I had found a Boer Bible with a bullet hole right through it, a Free State flag and a shrapnel shell picked up inside one of their gun-pits, but all are lost now. I also had your letter and photograph in my haversack, lost too. I am very sorry for this, as I am in the habit of taking it out and remembering my girls, in this hot, strange and barren place so far from the cool sea breezes of East Kent.

Anything you could send me from home would be very welcome. Our rations are pretty dire. They were cut down recently – on account of the single-track railroad and poor rolling stock – to ½lb bully beef and two biscuits per day. You can smash up the biscuits and boil them in water to make a nourishing gruel that does the job, but they are so hard you risk breaking your teeth to eat them plain. The Kaffirs bring us milk some mornings, 3d a pint and better even than Kent cows' milk. Sometimes we can buy stuff from farmers who come in on their wagons or even the Kaffir police, like sugar or tobacco. But it is dear, jam 1/6 a pound and butter 3s. Most of us can't afford to buy anything but mealy bread. If we get any fresh meat – which is rare, with hams costing 10s – we then must find firewood and cook it, which takes a while on hungry legs. The other night three of our lot were cooking away merrily on a little fire when a Boer shell landed smack in the middle of the cooking pot, sending the meal every which way yet luckily the cooks were unharmed. We heard of a tent attacked by a lion some miles away. Even the ostriches are a bit fierce. Such are the dangers of eating here!

Our kits are pretty patched and ragged by now too, with one Scotchman I saw last week wearing a sack as a kilt. I hear we may be issued new shirts and puttees soon, but think it is a bit thick that we have to pay out of our own wages to mend our boots. I do not wear a beard if I can help it – some fellows keep their whiskers on and look the villain – but my razor is so blunt, shaving can be hard going. It would be helpful if you could send some decent grub and other useful bits and pieces, like a new razor and soap and some thick warm socks as winter will be on its way soon (seasons are all topsy-turvy here).

For now, we are camped out in tents and bivouacs beside the Valsch River not far from Lindley. We have amused ourselves by competing for the best handmade wigwams. I helped build a superior one for the mess, using a mimosa tree as foundation and weeping willow branches for roof and walls. It is a pretty river, yet yesterday was scarred with the sight of hundreds of dead horses floating in a grim procession, evidently killed by artillery bombardment upstream. Just beyond our camp is a small island in the river, where the dead horses catch and gather, the smell in the midday heat revolting. Luckily we can send Kaffirs out five miles west for drinking water, yet we must use river water for cooking, washing and fishing. With any luck, we will be on the move again soon. We are not sure where we are going next, but it is likely we head a little way south, as there is a huge force massing under General Prinsloo around there and we shall make short work of them. We are doing a good job all round, I'd say. We believe in a united South Africa and the only way that will happen is with the British Empire in charge, you can be sure. The Boers may be good fellows but they are hopeless at running a country. We British do need to teach them a thing or two, but I fear we will all learn a lesson before this show is over.

I will write again, when I can snatch the time. As well as all our duties, I write letters home for Wallis and two others too.

Your affectionate brother and friend,
Caleb

Lindley,
Orange Free State
14 July 1900

My dearest pets,

Still no sign of letters from you or home. I know you will have sent all sorts by now, but we get no taste of it. I hope to hear news from you all soon, and at least some socks, as my feet are getting bluer by the day. Who knows when you'll read this request, but some warmer clothes would be most welcome, some of my old fishing sweaters for night time or a woollen cap, as your head gets terrible cold when you have to sleep out on the veldt.

Since I last wrote, I have travelled about the Orange Free State and into the Transvaal with my company engaging in various bouts of fighting: driving in Boer outposts and capturing scattered fighters. I am not yet wounded or dead, so I feel quite lucky. The war proceeds and we are swept along with it. The course of the war is changing. There have been some major battles since it all began. Sometimes our forces do very well, other times we are sent packing. The Boers are highly organised and totally committed to their cause. They have formed commandos which are groups of men who live on the run, engaging in sabotage and skirmishes. Their women and children stay on the farms and supply the men, so that the commandos come and go as they please, blowing up or blocking railway lines, delaying or destroying important supply links to our men (including delivery of your packages). If we carry on angling for big fights, this war of little skirmishes will just go on for ever. So something has had to change. Our latest orders are to cut off supplies to the Boer commandos at the root.

This means burning down their farms. We travel across the veldt. Sometimes it is a farm where a white flag is flown, but then someone fires a shot as we approach. Sometimes the farm is on a list of those that qualify for destruction because their men are away fighting in commando, or because they have supplied local fighting

Boers, or simply because they are within a few miles of a railway line or a sniping incident. The people living there are almost always women and girls, and very small boys, as at a certain age the boys join the men. These families have little say in what the commandos do locally, so have no power over whether they are burned or not. But some do supply the men with food and other goods and are therefore branded rebels. We make an example of these by punishing them, to deter others from aiding the commandos. The hope is that eventually this could lead to starving out the fighting men, forcing them to surrender. But recently orders have come to burn farms that are not on any list, because someone up high says you can't trust any Brother or Sister Boer, they are as bad as each other. It might have begun fairly a few weeks back, when the order first went out to start the burning, but now it proceeds almost at random.

I have attended at several burnings now and this is the way it generally goes. We ride up to the farmhouse. The women are often outside, watching us and pointing. At first, they think we are stopping for refreshments but then our officer tells them we have come to burn their farm. It is a horrible moment and mostly I look away. Some get angry and curse us, or fly into hysterics and collapse. Others are simply downcast and miserable. We give them a short while to get all their things out of the house. Sometimes we help them with the heavy furniture. It is all piled away from the house and they stand amongst their higgledy-piggledy possessions, looking forlorn. We fetch bundles of straw to get the thing going and we set the fire. Sometimes you see Tommies chasing chickens and ducks around to take for food, while others are driving off the horses and cattle or trampling the crops, taking away the wagons or burning them too. We often dig up any newly-made graves; I know this sounds ghoulish but the Boer women often hide weapons and valuables there. I've heard of some Tommies sent to burn stocks of grain and even sheep, leaving them half-dead in agony, rotting under the sun. I want you to know I haven't done this particular act myself. Some of us are sent to the nearest patch of high ground to look out for trouble. More than once I've seen Boer commandos on horseback watching the destruction of their homes from far away – too far for us to bother engaging them – only to turn dejectedly and amble away.

Once we are sure the buildings are burning well, we go, the little group of women left watching their home burn to the ground, holding on to each other. Some of the women cry, while others hold up their chin or even raise their fists to us as we leave. The children always watch the fire with big eyes, like we do on Guy Fawkes' Night. I think the little ones have no idea what the fire means for their future. They are just awestruck by the sight. I'm afraid they will understand it soon enough.

All across the veldt you can see columns of black smoke dotted throughout the landscape, as another farm goes up in flames. Wallis says the Boer men are a mean type of humanity with low cunning stamped on their faces, while Boer children are mostly brutes and the Boer women are stupid and stubborn and they're all spies and deserve what they get. They certainly are stubborn. When they do talk to you, it is astonishing how sure they are of their success. They say they shall fight for ever, that they will never give in, that they are only waiting for us all to pack up and go home. There is a kind of calm acceptance that this may take a long time, that the Tommies will do as they like in the meantime, that their men will be away for months, perhaps years, and that even their homes will be burned and their livelihoods destroyed. But still they believe they will win in the end. I think it comes from their belief in God, that He is protecting them. In every Boer home you visit you see an heirloom Bible in pride of place and find one in many a Boer haversack or pocket.

But it's more than that, it's about patriotism too. They believe completely in their right to that land. They have fought the Kaffirs for it and won that hard fight at great cost. Now they will never give in. It is this attitude – one you find in every home and every heart – that I believe will doom this war to years of fighting. It will take great hardships to break these people. And all that will be left of this land is desert. When you think of those children with frightened eyes watching their homes burn down, this will kindle a deep hatred in them of the British which will last all their lives and surely be passed to their children and their children's children, and so it will go on. The farm burning begins it, and who knows what will end it?

I am sorry to end my letter on such a sad note. But now the fun of the early battles is done, I look into the future of this war and see little but the hit-and-run tactics of Boers on horseback and their endless pot-shots – such excellent shots they are – and us sweeping across the veldt, corralling up who we can, laying waste to the land, and still more Boers will elude us, as we can never catch them all. It is not what I imagined as war, it is not what you will read about in the newspapers. If I had a pound for every time we read that the war will be over soon, I'd be a millionaire. And still the war would drag on.

I am hoping that all is well in Whitstable and Edenbridge, that the oysters are spatting nicely, that the hop flowers ripen in the Kent sun, that life continues there exactly as it has always done and will never change. I have that to hope for, that when I return it will all be as I left it. Here the wind whips up dust into storms and I marvel that the Boers love this dry land with all their hearts. But love it they do and will never give it up. If someone tried to take our oyster beds, churn them to ruin, or trample the Golding hops and set fire to the oast house, would we stand idly by? Would we surrender? Would we forgive?

With best love,
Your Caleb

Frankfort Garrison,
Orange Free State
13 August 1900

My dear ones,

I have a lot to tell you in this letter. I have been present at a great spectacle, perhaps to be one of the most enduring images of this war: the surrender of Prinsloo. I also have a more personal encounter to relate, which has changed my feelings on the nature of this war and its cost. First, the military part. In mid-July, several thousand Boers under General Prinsloo were in the vicinity of

Brandwater. Our forces moved to surround them on all sides. By the 18th of July, the British had broken through at Slabbert's Nek and Retief's Nek. The battle over the next few days cost many British lives and was carried out in the miserable cold and icy rain of the valley and snow in the mountains. The Boers made a hasty retreat, while we edged ever forward on all sides, aiming to block off their escape routes. I came up under General Rundle at Commando Nek and we secured the exit there, luckily with no casualties for our company, as the Boers were nowhere to be seen. They had vanished into the mist.

Once we heard that the trap was set, we marched – well, I'd say sauntered, as there was no hurry now – down to Fouriesberg to see how many lobsters were in the pot. Coming down I saw the marvellous sight of our horses in long snaking columns splashing through the shallows of the river. We heard rumours that Prinsloo had asked for an armistice for six days to take counsel, yet not surprisingly our great leader refused. There was no way out for the Boers by now, only a tiny pass over the hills towards Natal. But that is a British stronghold, so what place for them there? Also, they would have had to leave their wagons behind, something a Boer hates to do, so caught up is his life with this simple item, a life spent before this butchery on the flat veldt with his animals, his rifle and his wagon, on the trek or settling finally at his farm. So on the 29th July Prinsloo and 4,000 Boers under him surrendered unconditionally. We were all astonished at how easily our catch was had. I truly believe those 4,000 souls spoke with one voice, despite any anger from their Boer generals elsewhere. They just wanted to take their wagons and go home.

No home for them though, not yet. We heard Prinsloo asked that all burghers should be allowed to do just that and not be treated as prisoners of war. Our commander General Hunter of course refused – I mean to say, why should the fighting Boers not be POWs? What is to stop them from going back into commandos in the future and killing Tommies once more? Instead, General Hunter was very generous in his offer that they should be allowed to keep their private property and personal effects, including their horses to ride away on, a courtesy never extended to British POWs as far as I know. The actual surrender itself was a picture I will never forget. It took days to complete. The valley was filled with Boer wagons, pouring into Fouriesberg. The Boers themselves came in groups of several hundred, handing over their arms. Each man would have his Mauser taken, the barrels would be opened and ammunition removed, which was thrown on to a huge bonfire that burned all night and day, every now and then a great spluttering of Mauser cartridges exploding in the heat, and black smoke hanging above. The Boers themselves were not proud or haughty, not angry or ashamed. They were only interested in their property and quite cheery about the whole thing. It is hard to dislike them. They were then marched off south to their fate, POW camps or perhaps abroad to British colonies, such as Bermuda, St Helena or Ceylon, a long way from home. You might think that the surrender of this massive number of prisoners would mean the end of the war is in sight, but I doubt it. Rather I think it will serve to encourage the others to fight harder.

The next day, I was called by my commanding officer to complete an unusual task. A woman and her son were part of the surrendering Boer forces. As she was armed, it was decided that she had been fighting with the men. She could not be sent off with them to be a prisoner of war, as there was no provision for women in these circumstances. It was decided instead to interrogate her, as she has been travelling throughout the OFS for months and may have some useful information about Boer movements. I was told that after interrogation she was to be taken to a camp for women and children. She was interrogated for several hours and then I was called to collect her and take her to Harrismith. There is a railway station there from which we were to take the train north to a camp near Johannesburg. She had requested to go to this camp as she believed she had some family there.

The lady I was told to accompany has the wonderful name of Mrs Uitenweerde, but luckily she allowed me to call her by her first name, the much simpler Maria. Her husband, Hermanus (I believe that is correct, though these Boer names are devilish for spelling), was killed at the Battle of Modder River, yet she calls it the Battle of Twee Rivier (which means two rivers), last November. She is a very young widow, perhaps in her early twenties, with a seven-year-old son called Jurie. She must have married very young. After the death of her husband, she left her farm a few miles north of Pretoria with Jurie and followed commando groups in which her cousin Michael fought. Sometimes she returned back to her farm and other times she rejoined the commando. She tired of this life and returned to her farm in June, only to find it had been burned out. I'm only glad it wasn't me who did the deed, as I know I did not set afire any farms up there and certainly not one called

Mimosafontein. Such a lovely name, I would have remembered it.

By July, she was travelling with her cousin's commando as part of Prinsloo's forces and this is how she came to be involved in the surrender at Fouriesberg. She hates the British, to be sure. When she first set eyes on me, she looked me up and down in one swift movement just like Ma used to when we had committed some crime and she was about to reach for the cat-o'-nine-tails. Maria would not speak to me at first, only whispered to her son in Afrikaans. He was a talkative little fellow, but would not speak to me. He looked around her skirts at times to spy on the Englishman, but always hid again if I looked back or winked at him. We arrived at the railway station in Harrismith, Maria directing me as she knew the place, in a civil tone and perfect English, though she spoke no other words to me on this long and bumpy journey over the veldt in the rough Cape cart we had been assigned.

The train was steaming in as we arrived, so I found us a carriage free and we got on. We sat on opposite benches. Each compartment is separate on these trains and the guard has to edge along a nine-inch step that runs outside the coach, as the train speeds along. Rather him than me. I put my hat over my eyes and took a nap for a while, as she would have had to jump off a moving train with her child to escape. There were no dining cars, so we had to wait until the next station before taking some lunch at a restaurant on the platform: cold soup, tough meat and knives so blunt they couldn't cut butter. In all this time, neither the woman nor her son said a word to me. After the meal, she said to the cook in English, 'He pays,' pointing at me and swept out on to the platform, head high. I was like her servant, not her guard!

Once back on the train, I watched her for a while. Her chin still jutted out and her gaze outside was a thousand miles long. Her son slept. I said that we were to be on this train for two days at least, so it would be more pleasant to pass the time of day. She looked me straight in the eye and said, 'What did you do in England, before the war?' I told her and she responded, 'Why does an English farmer like you take up arms against us Boer farmers thousands of miles from home?'

To my shame, I honestly couldn't answer her. I did not know what to say. The conversation ended there. An hour or so later, I tried again. I asked her what had happened in her interrogation and she said that they had gone on and on about how the Boers lived, what they ate, how much longer they would fight, how they managed to blow up the railway lines and so on. Then she added, 'I told them nothing and will tell you nothing either, Khaki.' I said I only wanted to know if they had treated her kindly. She said that Captain Cox was actually very nice to her, that he told her that if she didn't want to speak nobody could force her to, and that he admired her courage. I told her I was glad she was well treated.

'Have you treated Boers well?' she asked.

'I hope so,' I replied.

'Have you burned farms?'

I didn't want to answer her question and looked away. What a coward I was! But my feelings for my fellow countrymen welled up and I felt I was on the defensive.

'Your fellow Boers. Don't they enter the homes of loyalist people and loot them, throw the people out, treat

them very roughly, perhaps even abuse them? Not to mention the way you've treated the blacks all these years. They were in Africa first, after all. When your burghers capture us, they strip off our uniforms and send us starving and thirsty out on to the veldt to fend for ourselves. And don't some of your Boer commandos range around in lawless gangs and mutilate the bodies of dead British soldiers?'

'Lies!' she cried, and the boy, asleep with his head in her lap, stirred. She stroked his hair and he slept on.

We argued for a long while about the rights and wrongs of it all, who did what and when, and it was clear never the twain would meet. But by the end of it, I think we had a new understanding and looked at each other differently.

The passenger trains only run during the day and so by the time we reached Volkrust, the train stopped for the night. The boy woke for some bread and dried meat his mother gave him. I purchased some more food from the station before it closed and gave him some milk, for which his mother thanked me. We talked through the night as Jurie slept on. Maria told me of her life on her father's farm as a child, a simple life of meat, milk and fruit, where they took the water from the earth and the sun grew their vegetables and they sang old songs and read the Bible. I told her of the oysters, the moods of the sea, the scent of hops. We slept for an hour or so before dawn, woken by the train's blast as it let off steam, then jolted onwards towards Johannesburg.

For the rest of the journey, we spoke of the war in better terms. I told her about Wallis and how we escaped the fire. She told me of her numerous escapes from British soldiers, or 'Khakis', as she calls them. She has a different term for just about every category of person you might find in this war: she calls us Khakis, Tommies or Engelsman, she calls her menfolk burghers, she calls the blacks Hottentots. She reserves her sourest face for those of her kind who have collaborated with the British: there are the Khaki-Boers, people who help the British in any way, but worst of all to her are the Joiners, those who have joined and fought for her enemies. When she speaks of us with such disgust, I feel the bile rise in my throat and want to shake her. But I have to remember where she comes from, her life before all this, her youth and her dead husband. Then I forgive her hatred. I only hope that by conversing with me, and seeing the kindness of Captain Cox, she perhaps has a new idea of what an Englishman can be.

Late that afternoon, the train arrived at Johannesburg. We sat and watched the bustling station, the Boers and English, the Khaki-Boers and Joiners and Hottentots going about their business. Suddenly she leaned forward, her arms about her son and a look of great intensity on her face.

'Let us go,' she said. 'Let us get out here. You can say I tricked you. Say I said my son was sick. I got away from you in the crowd at the station. You can say that.'

I told her I could not and would not do that. My orders and my duty were to take her to Camp Irene and that was what I was going to do. She begged me, and her boy pleaded too in perfect English.

'Have you been to the camps?' she asked me desperately. I had not. She told me they were places of horror, where people starved and children died of the cold and diseases raged. 'The angel of death walks through those places.'

I was too shocked to respond. The train lurched on towards the camp, now just fifteen miles away. I assured her that these were only rumours spread around by Boers to stop women from going there for help. I explained that the camps had been set up to welcome and care for refugees, those cut off by the war, those who had lost their men or their livelihoods, to save them from the threat of Kaffirs interfering with them if they were left alone and unprotected out on the veldt. I told her that I had heard that the camps were run efficiently and fairly by the British and no harm would come to her there.

At this point, she grabbed at her hair and almost tore it from its roots.

'How can you be so stupid?' she cried and broke down weeping, her son stroking her face and whispering to her, soothing her, stealing glances of pure hatred at me, her persecutor.

She did not speak to me again. When we arrived at the camp, I walked her to the gates. White tents stretched away in a dozen rows up an incline, the canvas flapping in the cold wind that swept down on them from the veldt. It did look a desolate place, but I could not believe her fears. This was run by the British after all, and if you cannot rely on British civilisation, what else is there? I was not able to say goodbye to Maria and Jurie, as she ushered him away from me without looking back. And I had to entrain and make my way back to Frankfort, a garrison town where the East Kents are to be stationed for the meantime, from where I write this letter to you now.

I trust that she has settled at Camp Irene now and has resigned herself to her temporary fate. After all, once the war is done, she will be able to begin a new life with her son. She is only young. And they say those who have lost their homes will be compensated after the war. She only has to wait and look forward to better times. I will try to visit her there if I can and see she is well.

I am only glad my girls are safe home in England.

I will write again. It does not look as if the war will be over soon, as we hear Kitchener has asked for stores for another six months. I wonder if the British public will get tired of this war too. If the Boers had made a big fight of it and then surrendered I am sure we would be very popular at home and return to street parties and hats thrown skyward. As it is, I fear the country will forget us and we will slink back in a year or two and never speak again of South Africa.

We are to be here in Frankfort for some time. It is a nowhere place of thorn trees battered by dust storms, a sorry place.

Love to you both,
Caleb

To read those words, to hear his voice in them, is joy and pain entwined. Lottie and I weep afterwards and hold on to each other, spreading the letters out on her bed and poring over them. The tears return as I read passages again and my handkerchief becomes a wet rag. Lottie comforts me, she watches me. But she does not question me in my distress. I suppose she knows my regard for him all these years, even without our secret. We talk of his experiences, the danger that surrounds him, the changes in his views that have turned him from the Tommy we read about in the newspapers to this thoughtful man who questions the war. I am proud of him for that, for all of it. But another emotion clouds my thoughts and brings forth bitterness. This woman, this Maria. The way he writes of her makes me hate her. I pity her, who could not? I see why Caleb does. But I am so jealous of her, it freezes my blood. I do not tell Lottie this, of course. She waxes on about what a good man her brother is to care for this woman and child. But in this dark moment I curse her and I will him never to return to that camp, to her, or even to a thought of her.

A Visitor appears beside Lottie's bed. An old man I have seen in the dining room before, dressed in black with a white bow tie; a butler from the old days before I was born. He once revealed that he collapsed while serving at a grand dinner party. He is still mortified that he has caused any inconvenience to his master. He looks at me curiously.

I did not mean to trouble anyone.

I know.

My wife was housekeeper here. She died, when was it? She just went to her bed and said she was weary and did not wake up. No trouble to anyone. An admirable woman, don't you agree?

My tears fall again.

Do you cry for the dead?

No. I cry for myself.

How desperate I was for news of Caleb. Now I feel more wretched than ever.

13

Father has taken to his bed. This morning, as I am coming down the front steps, book in hand, heading for the orchard to sit and read in the spring sunshine, I see him walking up the drive with a hand against his chest. His hair is sticking up at angles, as if he has been swimming. But I learn later this is sweat. His face is red-gold, like the beer brewed from his hops. I run to him and he gasps for breath as he grips my shoulder. I feel his weight release itself on to me and we both go crashing to the ground. Others come running – Mr Davy the head gardener and Maid Edith – and we are helping him up. I see him say, 'It is all right. I'm all right.' He rights himself and brushes down his trousers.

'Are *you* all right?' he signs to me.

I nod and we all walk beside him into the house. He turns and dismisses us, a gentle wave of the hand sending us away with all our unnecessary fuss. But I see him whisper something to Mr Davy. I run to tell Lottie.

She says, 'Don't fret. Your father will make old bones yet.'

But I know Father has not been himself of late. He is worried about the yield this year. There has been powdery mildew on the crop and he has been out with the workers, dosing the crop with sulphur to kill it, checking its progress day and night. I have not seen him so pre-occupied since the beginning of the war. Later, the doctor goes into Father's room and does not appear again for an hour.

Mother asks me to come to her room after her afternoon nap. The curtains are half closed, providing a dimness in which two Visitors loiter. I tell them to go. They are Father's relations and I have no time for them now. Maid Alice is arranging Mother's hair and I sit on her bed, watching as the thick long tresses are trained up over a horsehair pad and pinned into place, Mother's eyes patient yet her mouth pinched in the mirror. When she is done, she sends Alice away and turns to me.

'When can I see Father?'

'Your Father is ill and must not be disturbed.'

'Is it bad?'

'It is his heart. His heart is tired. He needs a lot of rest and then he will get better.'

'Are you sure?'

'Yes.'

'He only needs sleep, and then he will be better?'

'Yes. A nurse is coming from town to tend to him.'

'But I can tend to him. No one will do it better. I must do it.'

'No, you will excite him too much, you know you will. You two will talk and talk and he will never get any rest. Is that what you want, to make him more ill?'

'No, of course not.'

'Then you must leave him alone. You can see him in a few days, when he has rested.' She smiles and bids me go.

I am not comforted by this. Mother does not smile very often and when she does, it is usually a sign that she is trying to cover up something. She has to put smiles on, you see, like a mask.

When afternoon lessons are finished, I ask Lottie if I can walk alone for a while. I creep upstairs and stand in the shadow of the bookshelves outside Father's room. I wish I could hear what is going on inside. After a time, the door opens and a middle-aged woman appears, dressed in the starched white and blue of the district nurse, carrying a basin of water covered with a towel. She closes the door to and looks up.

'Oh!' she cries and starts back. She does not expect to see a girl haunting the landing. 'Get off with you!' she says. 'You'll disturb the patient. Do you understand me? Where's your nanny?'

I can see from the muscles straining on her neck that she is trying to whisper and shout at the same time, from her frown and suspecting eyes that she has remembered I am that deaf girl and thinks perhaps I am an idiot.

I sign at her slowly and full of disdain, 'I am not the fool,' and she glares, perplexed.

I turn, head held high, and march down the stairs very proud. Once outside, I feel desolate. I just want to see Father. Nobody will tell me anything, no one will let me see. I cannot eavesdrop unless I can see their mouths and they know that, they have that power over me. I wander down the path, my head heavy with meditation. As I approach the oast house, I look up to the cooling loft. Where is Caleb now? Is he hot and thirsty? Is he shot at, lying face down in the sandy soil, the backs of his knees burning under the African sun? Is he bleeding? Is he dead? Is he with her? Oh, my love. I shake my head to dispel these pictures. The light is fading. I have just missed the magic hour, when the sun is low and suffuses everything with a golden glow, seeming all the more wonderful since it is about to leave us. It is the gloaming. From the corner of my eye I glimpse a Visitor leaving the side door of the oast house, its blue-white light illuminating the dusky air, so brightly as I have never seen before, walking away from me towards the hop garden. I know that walk so well. I call out to him in my mind, *Father!*

He turns. His face is ivory, his eyes anxious.

The mould is in the hops, he says. *Worse than the cursed fly. I fear we have met our Waterloo. What are we to do, Liza?*

Oh, Father! I cry and fall at the Visitor's feet.

Now, now, my child. Do not concern yourself. God will protect us.

He reaches out and helps me up from the ground, his nebulous touch light as breath at my elbow. I stare at him. His face is unquiet, uncomprehending. He does not know he is dead. They never do. I want to turn and run to the house. Perhaps he is at the door of death, perhaps his spirit is free, but he is not yet gone. Perhaps he can be saved.

Come with me, I beg him. *Come upstairs with me. I have something to show you.*

No, no, my dear. I must check the crops. It's time for treatment. The powdering machine the horses pull keeps jamming. I must get on to Davy, get him to order that new one we saw in the catalogue. I am sure it will be more efficient. Sometimes I wonder if the old ways are not best, when we used to do it manually. But then we would have the sticky stains on our hands and have to rub them with hop leaves, do you remember?

And he drifts away, muttering to himself of hops and crops and mould and sulphur, the everyday stuff of his life. I want to scream at him, that none of this matters any more, but it is the same with them all and they never will learn.

I turn and run to the house, fling open the front door

and bolt upstairs. Mother must hear me, as she opens her door as I pass and I can see her mouth forming words. I burst into his room and see him in the bed. His mouth is open, his eyes are open. He is alone. Where is the blasted nurse? He is alone, he has died alone. I run to the bed and throw myself across his stiff legs. I recoil and look at his dead face, his lifeless eyes livid, like Tom Winstanley's. Mother is at my side, pulling at my arm.

'Come away,' she signs, 'come away.'

But I shake my head, no, no.

I wipe my eyes and reach out to take his hand. No one was there to hold it at the end. I bend down and kiss it. I see Mother reach over and brush over his eyelids. Now his eyes are closed, he looks like he is asleep, head back and snoring with his mouth open as he did in his chair by the fire some nights over a book. But he is not asleep, he is dead and gone. And for the first time in my life, I understand that the body is a painted eggshell, made of flesh and hair so real, so solid that it fools us into thinking it is alive. But the only life comes from within and now his has escaped aimless amongst his beloved hops, and I will never converse with Father again, not the real Father who lived and breathed and understood what it was to be alive and to die. I curse my gift, and despise the Visitors who footslog like cretins in an asylum of their own making, and hate them for accepting Father into their number. And I feel a hot dread of ever seeing his ghost again.

In the weeks that follow, I avoid the hop garden. I do not want to go there and see his Visitor. I stay inside the house, fearful of going outside, yet suffer the affliction of a prisoner within my memories and misery. But as the funeral comes and goes and we stop speaking of Father with every breath,

I miss him more than ever. A threnody sounds day and night in my heart. Nothing serves to lighten my days, not even a letter from Caleb. We write to him, Lottie and I, to tell him of Father's passing, but hear nothing back. I know full well it is most likely beyond his control. If the Boers have hijacked the mail transport, he may well not have received our letter yet and perhaps never will, let alone reply. I know all this and still I blame Caleb for his silence.

Some months after his death, Father's will is read. His fortune is left to Mother, with a very good allowance for myself and a generous annuity to Charlotte for her devotion, to be given for life, whether or not she remains in Golding employ. I am glad this will help the Crowe family, but the money means nothing whatever to me. I am so forlorn and strange of mind. In my sorrow, I have pushed Lottie away. She tries to speak with me, says words such as 'grief' and 'mourning', but I cannot explain it to her. My distress is not only the loss of Father, but the guilt I endure because the man I pine for most earnestly is Caleb. I wear the willow for her brother, ache for him more than my father, more than my own flesh and blood. I hate myself for it, but there it is. I cannot reveal this to her and so she looks at me full of sympathy and I want to fling it back at her, say how little I deserve it. I have no one to talk to, no one who will accept this truth and not judge me. I have never spoken to Mother or the maids about any such thing and have no intention of starting now. I only had Lottie, always Lottie, to share my secrets with. Except for this.

Wreathed in loneliness, I leave the house one evening and go to the hop garden, the same time of day I saw Father last. There he is, sauntering along a hop lane, gazing at the sky. I watch him for a time, thinking of Visitors and their existence, how they are the empty vessel left behind when our life deserts us. I have pitied them, but not understood their plight, not known it in my heart as I do now, looking at Father's ghost. I call to him. He turns and hurries towards me, about to impart information of great import.

Adeliza, the charitable missions are placing great pressure on my back to improve conditions for the pickers. I am incensed. I believe we look after them very well. We house them in brick buildings, we provide potatoes and firewood. The well is not too far from the camp and the beck water is clean and healthy.

The old worries, the old concerns. Pointless now.

Father, I do not wish to speak of that.

What is it, my dear?

I love Caleb Crowe. I have loved him since I was a child. I do not love him like a sister, but as a woman, Father. As a woman loves a man. But I fear he does not love me. He went away to Africa and left me. I know he had enlisted, I know it would have been difficult to escape it. But I believe if it had been me, I would have managed it to stay with the one I loved dearest and best. I have a hope that he loves me, that one day he will come home and renew our love. But on dark days I think he never loved me, is fond of me and took what I offered him as men do, that perhaps he has eyes for someone new. And on those days I curse him and hate him so, it tears a hole in my heart to think of him.

Father considers this for a moment, then answers: *I keep the local pickers away from the Londoners and the gypsies. I never hire tramps. There are never fights on my farm.*

Can you hear me, Father? Are you listening to me?

Of course I am. We are discussing the pickers, are we not? Please, go on.

I can see how hopeless it is, to converse with this husk. But he is the only one I can tell.

I have been thinking. I might go away somewhere, with Lottie if she will come. Travel, as I always wanted to do. I could escape my life here, escape Mother's illness, the rigours of my education, the mooning about the grounds reading novels of romance, the sorrow and comfort of seeing you, Father, changed as you are and yet ever the same. I long to flee it all. I can use the legacy you have left for me to see the world I touched with fleet fingers on the globe you gave me, leave my disappointment behind and begin a new life in a new land. What do you think, Father?

You know I only allow the honest hawkers in to sell them food. And they can use our tokens in the local shops. I always advance their pay if they make a fair case of it. But I refuse to give them subs if I fear they will spend it on jollification in the local taverns. I have the village to consider. Do you not agree?

But I have already walked away. He has not noticed and blathers on. I had hoped that as Father was the first Visitor I knew, and knew so well, I could break through that fog of obsession and reach him, make him hear me. But I believe I never will. And that resolves me. The same day, I tell Lottie my idea. She is in instant agreement and most excited. We consider how to tell Mother of our plans for travel. Mother's weak condition necessitated that in Father's will I was left with some limited power over my own money. Thus Mother will not be able physically or legally to prevent us, but I am keen to attempt her consent. We think of doing a Grand Tour of Europe, to sail to France, by railway to Paris, the Tour Eiffel, Notre Dame, Montmartre. Then on to walk the labyrinth at Chartres, float down the canals of Coulon, out to the coast at La Rochelle to sample the seafood, then over the Pyrenees to Spain. The Plaza Mayor in Madrid, through El Greco's Toledo to the Meseta and Don Quixote country. South to the Alhambra in Granada, the Mezquita at Córdoba, the cathedral at Sevilla. After that, who knows?

We speak to Mother and she is perturbed, yet has little energy to stop us. We begin to make plans and for the first time in months my life has purpose. We purchase clothes and luggage, research western Europe and plan our route. But then a letter comes from Caleb. It is dated months ago, hopelessly out of date, just after Father's death. He would not yet have received our news. I envy him his ignorance. Seeing his neat and looping script again summons every drop of love I ever felt for him in a hopeless flood. I have to press my eyes to stop the tears of gratitude from flowing, as I see my name written by his very hand. And I know, whatever this letter contains, that to escape to Europe may be an adventure, but will never cure me of his love. It is a sickness I will carry with me. I must always defer to Lottie when Caleb's letters come, as she is his sister. But I strain over her shoulder to see, and my heart thumps so in my chest. My first consuming thought is that perhaps there will be a word of love for me in this letter, just a word, a hint on which I may hang a flimsy hope. I read on.

Frankfort Garrison,
Orange Free State
3 November 1900

Dear Charlotte and Adeliza,

I would love to hear your news, yet have received no letters from you for months. How is life in Kent? I am glad to say I did finally receive your packages which all came together, with chocolate and socks, sweaters and sleeping caps. I am afraid it is summer here now and getting hotter by the day, so they won't be so useful as yet. But perhaps I will be here next winter, who knows? And I can use them at night. Thank you for those lovely handkerchiefs embroidered by you, Liza, which I have ruined by blowing my nose on them, but that is their purpose, after all. Thank you all very much for your kindness.

I write from the Frankfort garrison. We are stationed here for the next few weeks at least. It is a cut-off place subject to constant raids by Boer commandos, which affords a bit of excitement. The only other fun is the arrival of supplies. Every month or so a British column of wagons comes to bring us newspapers, clothes and extra kit, ammunition, rations and post. Some men go off with the column that delivers to us, and some of the column's number are left behind here in their place. So there is always feverish anticipation about who will stay and who will go. So far, I have been chosen to stay here all the while. I am quite glad, as it has meant I remain not far from Camp Irene and have awaited my chance to visit there. I have to tell you something now that may shock you, may even sicken you. I am in two minds whether to tell you the real truth about all this, as you are ladies and not used to such things. But I feel that people in England should know exactly what is going on. So I hope you will forgive me. Remember my silly horror stories I would tell by the fire? This is a true one that is all the more horrible for being real.

A few days ago, our patrol picked up a group of wandering Boer women and children. Wallis and I were ordered to take them over to Camp Irene. They were exhausted, very hungry and some of the children were ill. One woman had a scrawny newborn babe, clearly born out on the veldt. The whole group were in a state. Their skin was thick with grime and their clothes were ragged, their dresses tied up with string. They wore gloves and veldschoens (Boer shoes) made from raw sheepskin. Not at all like Maria's clean white apron and her son's shining hair, as I remember it, despite having lived on commando for weeks. But these women had lived alone without protection or supplies. Maybe we would all look a little like this if we had lived wild for many months. These seemed to be a lower class of Boers, with some shoddy ideas about cleanliness and health. One child had a revolting skin rash which looked very angry and its mother had placed upon it a poultice made of cow dung, which she swore was the best remedy. We were allowed only to give them some basic rations and then get them on to the train. We told them they could be seen at the hospital at the camp. But they wept and shouted at us, saying they would never go into the camp hospital, as it was staffed by the English who can never be trusted. They were in a sorry state the whole journey and I did what I could by getting them water. Wallis treated them largely with disdain. I had quiet words with him at one point, when he shouted at a Boer child who never stopped crying. But Wallis is sick at heart of this war and the Boers in particular. He blames them for declaring war in the first place and for it dragging on this long. Sometimes he takes it out on them. He is a good man, Wallis, a good friend. I understand him. But I feel a little differently.

When we arrived at the camp, we saw the women in and they were taken away. The train moved on and we knew the next one coming back was several hours' wait. Wallis was all for getting out of there and waiting at Irene station. But I told him I wanted to find Maria. He didn't approve and told me so, saying some things I won't repeat about her and Boer women in general. I believe he is trying to protect me somehow but I was having none of it and he stalked off alone. I asked a guard about the whereabouts of Mrs Uitenweerde and her son. Records were checked and I was directed to a group of conical tents not far from the hospital. I saw the women we had brought involved in a great argument outside it – a brick building, well-built, with several marquees beyond it for patients; two nurses and a doctor were trying to persuade the women to bring their sick children in to care for them, but they shook their heads and held on to their children ferociously. They would not go in there. 'We would rather die,' cried one woman.

I found the place easily, as the camp was laid out with military straightness in rows of thirty tents, each tent and row given their own number. This may sound orderly, but the tents were pitched very close together on rocky and stony ground, while the pathways between them were littered with rubbish. I stood outside the bell-shaped tent, not knowing how to announce my arrival, as I could not knock on canvas. I called out her full name. Eventually a flap opened and I saw a face. It was a thin, drawn face with dark shadows beneath the eyes, an older woman. I asked her if Mrs Uitenweerde was in that tent. A warm stink of bodies came from within, which made me cover my nose. The woman said, 'It is me.' She stepped out and stood before me. To see this skinny thing, so bedraggled and brought so low, to compare it with the feisty young woman I had met only two months ago, made me sick to my stomach. She looked as if she had aged ten years.

'Maria,' I said and stood there like an idiot. Despite her weak state, she stood straight and pushed out her chin as she always had. She asked me if I had brought her anything. I had to say no, and felt a fool. Why had I not brought her food or something, anything? My only excuse is that I knew nothing of the conditions in that camp, not until that day. She asked me why I had come then, so I explained about the women and said I had to go soon, but I wanted to check up on her and see how she was doing.

'Are you treated well?' I asked, knowing as I spoke what an insult it was to ask this ghost of a woman, who had dwindled to half her size in a matter of weeks.

'Come with me,' she said. She poked her head back in the tent, and spoke in her own language, perhaps telling someone to watch Jurie while she was gone. I asked after his health and she just shrugged. She walked slowly beside me and showed me around the camp, telling me everything she had been through since I saw her last.

I asked about family she had here, the reason she had come to this camp. She told me that before she arrived, there had been a fire in one of the tents which had spread to a number of others and her cousin had been caught in the fire and died of his injuries. She said that people were usually in a bad way when they arrived, as many were taken there by force and allowed to bring no provisions. Khakis burned all the Boers' things before they left, their clothes and bedding, even their own tents which most Boers have, being used to the trekking life. And some British soldiers encouraged the local Kaffirs to loot the house first and take part in its destruction. Some came with only the clothes they stood up in and some were even forced to march barefoot all the way. Some women had been captured after days of trying to escape and came with untreated gunshot wounds.

I knew many women did not choose to enter these camps, but surely it was safer for them to come here than to stay alone out on the veldt, prey to roaming Hottentots while their husbands were away, and with no food or supplies?

Maria said this was untrue, that they had plenty of food on their farms, and knew how to use a gun and protect themselves. She believed the camps were set up to protect the men who had surrendered without a fight – the 'Hands-uppers' as they are called here – from Boer revenge. It was never to protect the women. 'How can you think it is safer to come to this place?' She gestured towards a row of tents and pulled back the flap of the first one for me. Inside, the ground was quite covered with children, lying top-to-toe like sardines. They were groaning, sleeping fitfully, some weeping and calling for their mothers. Maria said, 'They are waiting to die.' I asked what was wrong with them. She explained that there was a measles epidemic, and typhus too. But some were dying from exposure, from the cold nights out on the veldt in the flimsy tents. There is hardly any wood for fuel and the children freeze at night. Some had developed pneumonia and hacking coughs that killed them. Some simply died of diarrhoea.

I told her I'd seen the Boer women we'd brought refuse to go into hospital. Why would they do that, when their children were so sick? Perhaps if they did such illness as this could be prevented. I explained to her how dirty those women were and about their strange remedies.

Maria again looked at me as if I were the greatest fool on earth. 'How can anyone keep clean in these conditions? We are given no soap with our rations, the water supply is limited and polluted and there are no bath-houses. The ground outside the latrines is fouled with s--t. Our tents are pitched on dusty ground and packed with twelve people at least. The rain beats down in the constant storms and floods the tent and we must sleep with no bedding, no beds, in the wet mud. They say some camps have only four in a tent, with ovens for baking and public baths, but we have none of that here. Almost every child who goes into that hospital comes out a corpse. The nurses may seem nice, there may be better food there, but disease is so rife here, and no one trusts the English doctor. There is one doctor here, just one, for thousands of inmates. There are funerals every day and most of the dead are little children. Some die of starvation.'

'You are so thin,' I said. 'I was a fool not to bring food.' I apologised and said I would send her some as soon as I returned to the garrison.

She told me the rations were minimal. Those women whose husbands are away fighting are treated worst of all. They are even given half-rations. 'I'm lucky my husband is dead,' she said grimly. 'On Mondays I get a few pounds of Australian flour, crawling with weevils; a few ounces of coffee, which tastes mostly of acorns and maize. A few ounces of sugar which is black and tastes as if it were the scum skimmed off the sugar boiler. And half an ounce of rough salt. Twice a week I am given a pound of mutton so lean it looks like dog, half-rotten and almost inedible. There are no vegetables or fruit or eggs or decent meat. And no milk for the children or even the babies. Only the sick children receive condensed milk, and that is watered down and often sour. See. The milk shed.'

We had reached a small hut, which let off a foul smell. I did not want to enter it, but put my head through the door and saw empty churns lying on their sides on the filthy floor, crawling with black flies. The bad smell from the shed mingled with a new smell, a worse one, soon a stench as we walked on. The path was stained with black puddles and as I looked up, I saw a trench in the ground on the side of which crouched dozens of children, smiling and holding little bowls in their hands, all gazing down into the trench, which was strewn with lumps of animal intestines, covered in flies. Two men were holding a scrawny sheep stretched across the hole, and one took a big knife and slit its throat, not enough to kill it, but so the blood drained out. The children nearby jumped down and held their bowls beneath the flow, catching the blood and laughing. I thought I would vomit as I watched them stumble back to the tents with their bowls, their cheeks smeared with blood. One was lugging a whole bucketful and another carried the sheep's head, which had been severed once the blood had slowed to a trickle.

I stared at her expression. I was right, it seemed to say, and you were wrong. You should have let me go. You should never have brought me to this place. I turned away, as I could not bear to look at that face any longer.

'Come,' she said simply and took my arm, led me as if I were the one who needed assistance. 'Do you believe me now? These camps were set up to kill us all.'

I had to stop her there. 'This is not true,' I said. No Englishman could even think such a thing. From what I'd seen, I guessed much more likely was bad organisation, no forward thinking, a total lack of understanding of what is required to service a camp of this size.

She told me the man in charge was called Scholtz and everyone hated him, even the staff, that he was a Boer who supported the British. He was rude, rough and petty-minded. Women would rather suffer than go to him and ask for help, to endure his insults and heartless refusals. I said I would report all of this to my superiors back at my garrison. 'If you like,' she murmured, as if the idea of help was beyond possibility. But mostly I think she was just exhausted by our walk. We had now circled back to her tent. She stood before it, tired and wan, looking past me across the tops of the tents.

'There's something else,' she said. 'Someone is bothering me.' She explained that a guard at the camp would come to her tent at all hours of the day and night, calling her to come and walk with him, even to do chores for him. He would watch her while she did them and tell her how pretty she was. 'He brings us little bits of food, or a candle and matches, other small things we need, but never enough. He tries to put his arms about me and I tell him no. But he is getting more rough with me and wants to take me back to his tent. I keep saying no. You do believe me?'

I said of course, and asked for his name, telling her I would sort it out. I said she shouldn't worry any more, that I would speak to this man, report him too. And that I would send her food and supplies for her son, but that if either of them were ill they must go to the hospital, please. She nodded at all of this, but again, that look in her eyes as if it were all a fiction, a story of help that was a dream and would never happen. When I took my leave of her, she lifted the flap of her tent and inside, baking in the heat of that summer day, I could see a dozen bodies lying packed together. Jurie slept in the middle, his bones sticking out, so thin was he. The heat inside was suffocating, the sun beating down through the thin canvas on to that sorry scene, with no furniture, flies crawling up the hot canvas, and slops of matter emptied on the floor and beside the tent.

I begged her not to go back in there. 'Where else can I go?' she said and went inside.

I immediately sought out the office of the camp supervisor, Scholtz. I may be only a private, but I would have a thing or two to say to him. But I was told by a secretary that he was away from the camp on business and I'd have to make an appointment to see him. I asked him if he knew where the guard was, the one Maria told me of. He asked me what it was about and I told him an inmate had complained of his advances.

The secretary merely laughed. 'The Boer women at this camp are of the lowest sort. It doesn't do to take them too seriously. They mistreat their children and are obsessed with death, hanging around the sick muttering, "What a pretty deathbed it is," and such nonsense. They stay in their tents all day and have an unhealthy aversion to fresh air and water.'

I tried to protest but was ordered to be on my way. Nobody would tell me where the guard was. His colleagues certainly closed ranks. But I will go back there, as soon as my next leave is granted. I will find him next time. He will rue the day he ever went near Maria.

I hate to upset you, dear Lottie and Liza. But I hope you can see that you should know of these matters, that England should know. I did not believe it myself until I saw it with my own eyes. Know only that I do not lie, I do not exaggerate and I trust Maria's word. I live now at this garrison, defending it from the visiting Boers who take aim at us. I am haunted by what I have seen and what I know.

The sooner this d----d war is done with, the better. But what will happen to those in the camps after the war? With their homes burned, their livelihoods gone, their men dead or overseas, what chance for the Boers when we have left them alone at last? I am helpless to change these bigger questions, to affect anything but my own small part in it. But I swear to you both that I will do whatever it takes to make that woman's life better, and that of her son. It is the only small thing I can do, in this desert of misery.

I will write again.

Love to you all,
Caleb

14

The Crowes come up to the big house. We received the letter from Caleb only a week ago. It is March 1901, the daffodils lift their heads and the hellebores are nodding. The Queen passed away in January, but we were already wearing black. We see them through the dining room window, Mr and Mrs Crowe, walking slowly and seriously up the drive. We run out to greet them, but Maid Edith has already shown them into the drawing room. We think they are here to pay their final respects to Father, though it has been almost a year. We know they cannot leave home easily or often. I see Lottie's face and she knows something is wrong the moment she sees her ma look up.

'What is it?' she says and Mrs Crowe starts crying.

My gut twists and I think, Caleb. It is Caleb. He is dead.

Mrs Crowe passes over a slip of paper and Mr Crowe says, 'We don't know what to do, love.'

It is a telegram. An image appears in my mind of the telegraph boy knocking on the Crowe door, dressed in red on his red bike, warning, danger. We read it together.

MR AND MRS CROWE WHITSTABLE ENGLAND
= I AM ARRESTED CHARGED WITH MURDER
COURT MARTIAL PROCEEDING SOON = CALEB
CROWE

All I can think is, He's alive, he's alive. The truth of the news does not truly hit me, just the relief that he is not dead. Lottie just stares and stares at the paper, as if it were written in Greek.

'What does it mean?' she asks them. 'Have you heard anything else?'

'No, my dear,' says Mr Crowe. 'That's all we know. We got it yesterday. We tried to speak to someone at the barracks, at the East Kents, but they couldn't tell us anything. They said to talk to the government, but we don't know who.'

I clap to call everyone's attention. 'Mother will know,' I sign. 'She has friends, important ones. She will know what to do. Wait here. I'll send for refreshments.'

It is morning, so Mother will be in her study writing letters or reading. On the stairs, I feel light-headed and grasp the banister to stop myself from falling. Caleb is accused of murder, arrested, charged. In prison, a trial to follow, and what next? If found guilty, death, surely; he will be put to death. Now the truth hits me. And I think, Is it to do with that woman? Is it her doing? Wild possibilities flit through my mind. I knock on Mother's door and push it open. She turns around and frowns.

We talk over sandwiches that no one eats and tea that no one drinks. The others sign and speak at once to assist me. Mother is magnificent. 'I help with a committee to send resources to the Boer ladies in South Africa,' she tells them. 'Through this, I have connections with military wives whose husbands are high up in the army. One is the sister of a general's wife. I will write to her and ask for her help. I will also invite our local Member of Parliament around and enlist his help too. Please do not upset yourself, Mrs

Crowe, Mr Crowe. First we need to find out more. Then we must engage counsel for your son. I will pay all fees relating to his defence – no, no, I won't hear any argument. Lastly, I think someone must go out there, to see how it proceeds, to see Caleb and help him through it, if possible. What do you think?'

Everything seems more hopeful now. Mother will write letters and speak to important people. Matters are in hand. But there is one thing I want to do, one thing I must do, and if I am denied I will defy all orders. But first I must see what the Crowes have to say.

'We want to go to him, Mrs Golding, of course we do,' says Mr Crowe. 'It is a father's duty to rescue his son, or to try. But I cannot leave the oyster beds to rack and ruin and theft. There is no one left to trust it to, now we're not in the co-operative and other men are our masters. We're at war with the whelk trappers and the Essex dredgers, who steal our stock. I can't let my other sons go to ruin while I try to save this one. And if my wife goes . . .'

'What will become of my boys?' Mrs Crowe says. 'A neighbour minds them today, but I'd be gone for months to that God-forsaken place and who would tend to them? Mrs Golding, I believe that parents are meant to guide their children through life, like a ship's pilot. I've always done that for all my little ones, all their lives. But this is beyond me. I just don't know what we can do for Caleb.'

I stand up and everyone looks at me. There is one reason – the best – for why it must be me who goes, a reason I cannot reveal to anyone but Lottie. That I will seek out the Visitor of that murdered man and I will make him confess who killed him. It will prove Caleb's innocence and he will be saved. For now, I must conjure other excuses to persuade the others. 'I think Lottie should go. I would like to accompany her, if she agrees. We are the only ones who can go, as you must stay with your family and Mother is too poorly, you know you are, Mother. Lottie and I are strong and young and healthy and free. We already have everything ready to travel and will do all in our power to help Caleb. Besides, when they see two nice English ladies, one of whom is deaf, they will pity us and give us special treatment. I have the money and the means to finance it, from Father's legacy. What do you say, Lottie?'

My friend claps her hands and we embrace. The parents look on, shocked, shaking their heads. Yet the logic of it will out. On considering the alternatives, there is little argument. If Father were alive, he would have gone; I would have begged to go with him, and would have been refused. Now he is dead, I am the one who assumes responsibility. Perhaps there is this one slender consolation for his loss. It is agreed. Lottie and I are going to Africa.

A week later, we have more news. Mother's contacts have come good and Caleb's commanding officer has sent information. Caleb has been accused of killing a British soldier. He has pleaded guilty; indeed, he gave himself up. He is confined in the Frankfort garrison for now but later he will be moved to a military prison in Pretoria, where the trial will take place in a few weeks' time. Further enquiries reveal that the dead soldier was a guard at Camp Irene. He was found shot dead in a tent and some of his belongings stolen. Caleb has offered no explanation or defence. In fact, he has not spoken a word of it since his arrest. He was not working at the camp and, as far as they know, had little association with the dead man. But we know different. It is as I feared. It is the guard involved with that woman, it must be. I knew she would be trouble. What on earth was Caleb thinking? And then I realise he wasn't thinking, he was blind to thought where Maria was concerned. That bloody woman. We will go to him. We will find out the truth and use it for good or ill to save Caleb. I am convinced in my ability not only to help him, but rescue him. Lottie and I together will get him out of that trap and free him. And damned be that woman if she tries to cross us.

Mother is worried and does not want me to go. She has lost Father, and now I am leaving. I remind her I was to travel in any case. This is a journey to a British stronghold, somewhere we will be protected by the might of the British Army on our travels. And it is for the best cause possible. But she is my mother and does not care for causes where I am concerned. She sees too that she has no sway with me over this; I will go, blow, wind, come, wrack. She sees the fire in my eyes after months of despondency over Father, and perhaps she thinks it would be good for me to do this. Mother books our passage and Lottie and I plan and pack, ordering maps of South Africa and city plans of Pretoria and Cape Town, as well as books on the flora and fauna, the history of the Boers, the British and the Zulus and other African tribes, the peoples and their languages. We want to arrive girded with knowledge, not lumbered with ignorance. We receive a permit to travel in South Africa from Mother's friend's brother-in-law, the general. We are told there is martial law in South Africa and that everyone needs permission to travel. Ours is very specific, a letter to be shown to whom it may concern, that the Misses Crowe and Golding are given permission to travel from Cape Town to Pretoria for the purposes of visiting the said Miss Crowe's brother incarcerated pending trial, and for their return to Cape Town on completion of their business.

Now I must say farewell to Father. He will not understand, of course. He does not comprehend his own situation, let alone mine. I find him, as ever, in the hop garden, staring intently at the new buds just starting to show on the greening bines. I sail tomorrow.

No signs of trouble yet, he says, smiling at me. *New growth looks healthy, very healthy.*

Father, I say. *I am going away.*

To Whitstable?

No, Father. I am going on a ship to Africa. Caleb Crowe is in trouble and I go with Charlotte to help him.

He has drifted already, fingering the buds. *God willing, we'll have no sorrow this year.*

I raise my voice and say, *Listen to me, Father. This is important.*

He looks up from the hop plants and stares at me.

I say again, *I am going to Africa, Father. Caleb has been accused of murder, but I know that he is not guilty. I know it with every fibre of my being, as does his sister and all his family. We go to prove his innocence. We go to free him. I hope I have your blessing, Father.*

He seems to smile his approval. But I know it is the new growth that pleases him, not me.

I love you, Father. Goodbye.

Goodbye, my dear.

For a moment, I felt almost as if it were old times and he were Father as he always was. But he is not Father. I have said farewell for myself, not for him. Goodbye, my Father.

It will be harder to take leave of Mother, for she is flesh and blood and has a hold on me no Visitor will ever have. When she looks into my eyes on the morning of our departure, she seeks there some assurance that I will be well. I hold her hands tight. I kiss her cheek. I sign to her, 'Do not fret for me, Mother. This is something I must do.'

'I understand,' she says. 'You go to save the brother of the woman who saved you.'

'Oh, Mother,' I cry and hold her tight, my eyes filling with tears. She is right, so utterly right, in a way I had never thought to voice it. Yet she cannot know she is short of the mark too, that my love for Caleb is beyond what even his sister knows, it is something no one knows but Caleb and myself. It is a painful love, a love of loss and want, but it is more powerful than anything else I could feel.

We sail for Cape Town on the SS *Majestic*, the afternoon of 7 April. We leave Southampton under leaden skies and a vigorous wind. Our voyage will take almost a month. Before long, we sight the Needles. This is the last landmark of England we will see, as we turn in for the night. We wave farewell to the tall, rocky forms as they recede and the dark sea bites at their ankles. Goodbye, England. In the morning we enter the Bay of Biscay and later spy the Ushant Lighthouse, which belongs to Brittany. A taste of France. Then comes our first storm and the ship rocks so violently we retire to our cabin and moan in a haze of nausea all the following night. The next day we wake to calm seas and discover we have at last cleared the Bay of Biscay, then we see the lighthouse off Cape Finisterre and know we are leaving France behind, waving farewell to our dreams of

Paris. Another time. We sail steadily on, the sea surprisingly calm now, glassy and broad.

We near the Canary Islands. We have passed Spain and visions of broad-skirted ladies dancing the bolero and farruca, and our Iberian plans vanish as the ship steams on towards Africa. We see several vessels sail by, including a troop-ship returning with the wounded. I wish my Caleb were on that ship, that he had suffered the one fate I wished against, injury or sickness, only so that he would not have got mixed up with that woman and her dangerous life. I look down at the tireless seas and spot flying fish defying their undersea destiny and assuming the life of birds for a few magic moments. I understand they do it to escape predators. So there they are, leaping for their lives as we admire them as picturesque. What can they make of us? Some great grey sea-monster that ploughs stupidly through the ocean. One can never know the truth of another's life by looking.

For the next two weeks I stay in my cabin. I have contracted some kind of infection of the chest. I have a fever and the chills, my ears ache and my eyes stream. I am terrified that it is the scarlet fever again and that I may lose my sight, or worse. I am hysterical with Lottie, who bathes my eyes with precious clean water.

I fear I will die. To become a Visitor, tied to this ship for eternity or lost at sea as Tom was, never to see my Caleb more; in the way of Visitors caught in this moment, blind and deaf again to everything but this day, but not even with such as me to offer consolation, utterly alone. So I pull Lottie close, finger spell that I have to tell her something.

'You must rest,' she says. 'No talking.'

But I must. I sign weakly to her.

'When I was sixteen, Caleb and I were lovers for one night, before he went to war.'

'I know that,' says Lottie. She dabs my brow with a cool cloth.

'How?'

'There was blood on your shift the next day. And you wouldn't say goodbye to him.'

'Were you angry with us, Lottie?'

'No. I was worried.'

'Why?'

'That he would disappoint you. And you would have to carry it alone. Perhaps even a child would come and the shame of that. I hoped you might share it with me. But I understood why you did not. I was the same with Tom. I spoke to no one.'

'Oh, Lottie. I wish I had told you.'

'You are telling me now and I am glad of it. But you are your own person, Liza, and deserve your secrets, as we all do.'

'Thank you, Lottie.'

'Rest now,' she says and I close my eyes.

Despite my fever, my soul is buoyant. To think, I have imagined that scene cast in every shade of drama, yet never so simply. I should have known Lottie would find the heart of it and set it right. How could I have doubted the deep-driven foundations of our friendship? Talking with her is like going home.

The ship's doctor is quite calm and tells us it is not scarlet fever. He says I need rest, fluids and a little food once I am cooler. He is right, and I do recover. I have missed all of our passage past the west coast of Africa, as has Lottie, my devoted nurse, as ever. When I am stronger, I dress and come out to promenade one late April morning. I am told the ship will soon sight Cape Town. We are within hours of docking, of stepping down on to the same land Caleb inhabits, a step closer to him.

We watch as the land mass assumes the shape of Cape Town. A tumble of a city down luxurious slopes, topped by the gravity of Table Mountain, an unyielding presence over the city, its white brows of dense cloud flanked by a brooding range of steel-blue mountains. Their immensity dwarfs anything I have seen in little England. The enormity of our coming task assaults me and weighs heavy on my heart. My first thoughts upon landing are of the motley diversity of people in this British corner of Africa. There are the blacks to be sure, skin the colour of which I have never seen, a quick strength in the movements of the black men loading on the docks, a surety I know from the Whitstable dock workers. Working men are the same the world over, it seems, regardless of colour. I see black men dressed in vulgar rainbow costumes, while others wear suits of striped flannel and bowler hats. I had assumed they would all look like the barbaric savages from my books. My ignorance amazes me.

The pungent pot-pourri of Cape Town is spiced with Malays in their eastern clothing and high umbrella hats, all jostling with the others to carry our luggage. If only I could hear, I am sure it would be a cacophony of competing lingos – Lottie puts her fingers in her ears one moment as we laugh at the harlequin madness of it all – skin about us a medley of black, brown and bronze, spattered with the wan faces of other whites. Lottie says she can hear a muddle of languages – from European tongues to something that might be Hindoo – and the welcome English shouts and calls of our compatriots as we approach the roads by the docks. The pavements are thronged with British and colonial soldiers, talking and laughing, trotting and slouching, buying trinkets; sinking their teeth into watermelons and devouring bunches of grapes as they perambulate along, all around beset by the patchwork people of this strange city, shouting and selling to make their living.

I am reminded of watching the flying fish beneath our ship, that it is easy to see the exotic as scenic, but these are real men and women with vital lives of their own, with fears and hopes just like mine, not a mere snippet of local colour for the amusement of English ladies. I must remember that, if I am to navigate my way fairly through this foreign land. Mingling with these fleshy lives are the thousands of Visitors that turn within the boiling crowd and seek out my gaze. Oh, so many, so many of them, so diverse, so many nations and childhoods mingling like ingredients stirred in a thick stew of humanity, and they all look so lost. Some reach for me and stare in desperation, hoping for a friendly face, a voice to guide them in their confusion. I am overwhelmed with them, their blue-white halos glaring as my already dazzled eyes struggle to cope with the colourful chaos of Africa. Before they can speak to me, I banish them. They turn and vanish, and I apologise to them, but I have other business this day.

Our bags are carried by a Malay man who directs us to a line of hansom cabs. He places our Gladstone bag and small tin trunk on the roof, and we get in. Lottie asks for us to be taken to the railway station and no sooner is it said than we are off, careering through the anarchic streets, thick with military trucks. Some British soldiers notice us and wave, one puts two fingers in his mouth and blows hard. We arrive at the station and pay the man in English money, then ask him to telegraph ahead to Pretoria station, that the military prison must be contacted so that we can be met at the station. Before long we are seated in the train headed for Kimberley. We have to change at De Aar, before travelling straight up to Pretoria. We are here in the autumn, and the climate is pleasant enough with a cooling breeze. Yet there is a dense heat layered within the air which is decidedly foreign and unlike any English summer's day.

The land outside the train window trundles by and I am reminded of Caleb's first letter, the flat veldt stretching away from the train broken up by the odd black-stoned kopje or clutch of thorn trees. Kent is a land of red and green: the red-tiled conical roofs of the oast houses and the red ragstone ridge that borders the Weald; the vibrant green of hop cones and the pale green sheaths of ripening cobnuts. This is a land of yellow and brown, sandy and scorched. I see many Visitors wandering that landscape: Zulus striding in their loincloths, eyes on the horizon; the Dutch dead, the white bonnets of the women glowing brightly in their ghostly haze, turning to follow the train with their eyes as they sense my presence. We see animals darting about, identify them from our book learning; leaping springbok and white-faced blesbok stop and stare at the mechanical beast puffing through their territory. Far away, we spy monkeys on the mountains. Above, we are watched by wheeling Cape vultures, and once we see white-necked ravens hopping over carrion beside the track.

One evening at a stopover to buy supplies, we spy something digging ferociously beside a bush behind the station restaurant and think it is an aardvark, that wonderful word meaning 'earth-pig' which should begin any dictionary. It is a shy, nocturnal creature and scampers away as soon as it registers our presence. We are visitors here and it does not know us. How I would like to touch its coarse-haired back and feel the snuffle of its muzzle in my hand. I am exhausted (our journey has taken two days and nights so far), worried about what will happen when we reach Pretoria, bothered by South African ghosts everywhere I turn, and weary of the dust and charged air, so unlike my pleasant England. But I am vibrant with the newness of everything, my first journey into the heart of another world, an experience I have dreamed of since my deaf-blind fingers felt their way across the bumpy geography of my first globe, since my first train journey to London, moving through the English landscape. And now here I am, in that vast triangle Africa, my senses drinking in its beauty and strangeness. I am a true traveller now.

It takes another two days to reach Pretoria. On arrival, we detrain and find our luggage, handed to us by two unsavoury black men in red caps. We stand dishevelled and expectant, hoping our telegraph has been received or even sent.

I sign to Lottie, 'If no one comes, we must make our way to the prison ourselves.'

She replies, 'If we can navigate Cape Town, we can manage anything.'

The two blacks watch us sign, gesturing dumbly with their hands and mocking us. Then a British soldier appears, striding purposefully towards us. He stops and removes his cap.

'Are you the Misses Crowe and Golding? You must be Charlotte, Caleb's sister. And you are Adeliza, have I said it right? My name is Wallis. I'm to take you to Caleb. Here, Kaffir! Carry these bags, quick smart!'

15

Wallis escorts us from the railway station to a small horse and cart, and the luggage is stowed. A native is to drive us, and we settle ourselves behind, Wallis opposite. The driver cracks the whip at the pathetic pony harnessed to the cart and off we trot.

Wallis looks at Lottie and says, 'May I enquire, Miss Crowe?' He tips his head at me. 'Can she understand me?'

Lottie describes my talents.

'The things they can do nowadays,' says Wallis, wide-eyed. He turns to me and moves his mouth in a ridiculous fashion, exaggerating every sound. 'Amazing! Quite amazing!'

I sign and Lottie translates, 'Please speak normally, Mr Wallis. It is easier for me.'

He nods his head and grins. 'Righto then.'

I like Wallis. Lottie does too, I can tell. He talks to us all the way in the cart, shouting above the noise that must emanate from the clopping hooves and the busy streets.

'Now, please don't alarm yourselves, ladies. But I have to tell you that Caleb is in hospital. He's been suffering from dysentery for the last month. It got so bad they've delayed his trial for a couple of weeks. He's all right, never fear. But a bit weak, you know. Not contagious or such any more, but on the mend. I haven't frightened you, have I?'

We assure him not. I am glad Caleb is in a hospital bed instead of a prison, cared for by nurses rather than ignored by guards. And crucially, it gives us more time to investigate.

Wallis goes on: 'How much do you know about his situation?'

Lottie signs and speaks for us. 'We know he has been arrested and charged with murder, that it was a guard at a camp and that he hasn't talked about it since his arrest. Is that right?'

'Yes, that's about the size of it. There's some other stuff though, you probably don't know about. I think I ought to tell you.'

'Is it about that woman?' I sign.

Lottie gives me a quick shake of the head. I sign it again, adding, 'Translate!'

Wallis frowns as he listens. 'If you mean Maria Uitenweerde, then yes. You know about her?'

Lottie explains about Caleb's letters.

'Ah, yes. Well, if you ask me, I think she did it. I think she's the one who killed that guard. I reckon she did it and Caleb is saving her skin.'

Our faces are so shocked, Wallis interjects, 'But that's only me. Caleb won't have none of that.'

'Mr Wallis . . .' says Lottie.

'Call me Walter.'

'Walter, do you have any evidence of this?'

We have pulled up at a low brick building. The pony shakes its head and stamps its feet. Walter glances around, aware our impassive native driver might listen in.

'I don't have any evidence for none of it, ladies. I just know she was a bad one and I never trusted her. And Caleb, well, he was always defending her. From the minute he met her and took her to that camp, he went on and on about her and her boy. Then when he went back and saw how she was living, well, he was full of it. He was going to write to so-and-so and complain to Kitchener himself. But nothing come of it. And he went back there every leave. Then one time, he didn't come back. He was AWOL for a night and there was a big stink. Next I knew he was holed up in a cell at Frankfort. I asked permission to see him and he says nothing, nothing at all. I says to him, was it her, Crowe? Was it that woman did this to you? And he just shook his head and wouldn't say nothing to me, nothing, to his best friend in the army. He saved my life, did you know that?'

We nod.

'I'd walk through fire for him I would, Miss Crowe, Miss Golding. But I can't help him if he won't help himself. That's why I insisted I come to pick you up. I wanted to converse with you both, before you see him. Maybe you can talk some sense into him, get him to give up that woman.'

'Does anyone else think she did it?' asks Lottie.

'She was accused, right off the bat. Everyone in that camp knew that Jackson was after her. That was his name, Private Arnold Jackson. Well, he wouldn't leave her alone. Very pretty thing she is. Rumour was, he . . . had his way, you know. Sorry, ladies. You know what I'm saying?'

Lottie nods. I am not sure. Does he mean Jackson ravished her? I sign it. Lottie thinks a moment, then says,

'Do you mean that the guard had relations with this Boer lady . . . against her will?'

Wallis nods. 'That's a very nice way of putting it. Yes, that's what they say. So when Jackson was found shot dead, they went straight to her tent and hauled her out for questioning. But Caleb, he was there too, visiting the camp while he was on leave. And he insisted they let her go, and says he did it. That they should arrest him. That it was nothing to do with her. And she said nothing this whole time. So in the end they had to take it seriously and they arrested him.'

'Why would he lie?' I sign and Lottie translates. 'Why give up his very life for her? I know he felt sorry for her but . . .'

Wallis shakes his head. 'Oh, it's more than that, miss. Caleb, he was just mad about her. You might say he was obsessed. I don't want to shock you, but I think I can be permitted to inform you that I think him and the lady – no, I won't call her that – the woman. Well, I am pretty sure that this woman and Caleb have had *relations*. More than once. I never see a man so mad for a woman, except when *relations* are concerned, and I'd bet my Kruger pennies that woman had her claws in him, if you know what I'm saying, ladies.'

We alight from the cart and Wallis pays the driver. He takes us into the hospital and shows us down the main corridor. I feel ill as I walk, dizzy from the heat and sick from the knowledge. It had not crossed my mind, it had not. I had thought of Caleb racked with pity, his soft heart moulded by her conniving ways. But *relations*? To think of Caleb with another woman, I stumble and hold my head. Lottie and Wallis take hold of me. There are questions and concerned faces. I am taken to a room to sit down and brought a drink of water.

'It's boiled, miss. Never fear,' says Wallis.

I sip the warm water. Lottie looks closely at me, her eyes tell me she understands, she knows why I suffer. She was right, she said he would disappoint me.

'I want to see Caleb,' I sign.

We are taken to a ward with many beds. In each one a man lies asleep, or tossing and writhing, or awake and staring blankly at us as we pass. One man winks at me and I look ahead, searching for Caleb. All the men look the same, sallow faces bordered with tatty beards, tucked in by white sheets. The room is so full of men the air breathes scanty. By every bed Visitors loiter, soldiers in various states of confusion, exhaustion or anger. They appeal to me, *Where is my package from home? Is Mother coming?* And one Visitor is a solitary nurse, her uniform shining white-blue as she searches for patients she cannot find. We stop before a bed, a soldier asleep in it with a thick beard, sunken eyes closed, hair matted and cheek-bones sharp as mountain crags. It is Caleb.

'I'll leave you to it, ladies,' says Wallis kindly and brings up two chairs for us. 'I'll be waiting outside.'

We sit down and gaze at Caleb. Then we look at each other and grasp hands. We have to be strong now, so I force my eyes to dry and my chest to stop heaving. Lottie reaches out gingerly and places a trembling hand on her brother's. His eyelids flutter and open. He sees her first, then me. His eyes glisten and a fat tear seeps, lost in his whiskers.

I watch his mouth barely move. 'My girls,' I read. 'My girls.'

'Are you recovering?' asks Lottie. 'Wallis says you had dysentery. Are you getting better?'

'You've met Wallis,' he murmurs and his eyes crinkle. He looks at me and his eyes are serious again. We have not looked upon each other since that night. When he left the next morning, I stayed in my room, said I was poorly. How I have regretted this since.

We are interrupted. A doctor is at the bed. He asks to speak with Lottie and they retire. I stay. Caleb closes his eyes. I brush my fingertips against his face. Another tear emerges, others follow. I wipe them away with my handkerchief. I hold his hand.

He will not open his eyes for me. I finger spell, 'Do you love her?'

I wait.

He replies in kind, 'Yes.' He opens his eyes, bleary and damp. 'I am sorry, Liza.'

'Don't give up your life for her.'

His dry, rough fingers move slowly in my palm, painstaking. 'We give our lives to the one we love.'

'If she loved you, she would not sacrifice you.'

His eyes are sharp now, clear. He speaks, 'I did it. I killed him.'

I sign violently, 'I do not believe it. I will never believe it. Wallis says she did it and you are protecting her. But what about us, Caleb? What about your sister and your mother and father, and your little brothers? If you do not care for me, so be it. But do not throw yourself away for this woman, when there are better who love you more, who will be destroyed by losing you. Do not do this to them.'

He has watched me all through, with eyes of fire. He

draws himself up in bed; his face may be thin and gaunt, but his body still has power. He sits up straight and signs to me, 'I did it. I killed that bastard for raping her. And I would do it again. I would do it for Lottie, I would do it for you.'

'I don't believe you!' I sign with ferocity. 'I don't believe you did it. You're lying to protect her. Wallis says she's trouble. A witch, she's bewitched you!'

'If you knew her as I did . . .'

'I do not wish to know her, I wish *you* had never known her. I wish she had never been born, I wish she were dead!'

Caleb shakes his head, then holds it, screws up his eyes and falls back against the wall. Lottie comes back to the bed.

'What is happening here?' she says and shoots me a look.

I turn to the wall, compose myself.

Lottie is speaking reasonably to him. I catch the end of it. She is telling him that she will speak to his counsel and find out what she can in terms of his defence. The doctor has told her there is a chance he may be pronounced temporarily insane. This could help him in the trial. She explains we have brought him English food in tins to help his recovery: meat in gravy, boiled vegetables and fruit in syrup.

'Make sure you eat some of it,' she says and kisses his cheek. 'We will come back tomorrow. Get some rest.'

Caleb nods, exhausted, and falls asleep again before his head has stopped moving. As we leave the ward, I ask Lottie what the doctor has said about his current state of health.

'As Wallis told us, he is recovering. It is a matter of time. He'll grow stronger every day, if he begins to eat well and drink well.' She looks pointedly at me. 'And if he has complete rest.'

I know she is aware of my pain. But she must also protect her twin. She loves us both. A horrible idea enters my mind. If Caleb were to die, that woman would lose him. And he would return as a Visitor, and I would have him for ever. Just like Father. Yet since he came back, all Father causes me is sadness, to see him confused and idiotic like that. The truth is I ran away from England partly to escape him. And Caleb's ghost would still be obsessed with that woman, he would not be the old Caleb I knew, before the war, before the cooling loft, before I was a woman. What I would pay to have my old confidant back, who would sit on the oyster yawl and whisper secrets to me with his fingers. If he could have died then, drowned at sea, he would have loved me, loved me simply and pure. But if the sea had taken him, he might not have come back. Think of Tom Winstanley. To lose Caleb, and then find his Visitor never comes? That would be doubly cruel. What would be the best way for him to die? Then my rational mind steps forward and grasps me by the shoulders, shakes me awake. The wicked thoughts chill me and I shake my head to banish them. But I cannot forget them.

Wallis takes us to our accommodation, a small hotel – whitewashed, trim and flower-bordered – not far from the hospital. It is run by an old German couple who are polite to us, but not friendly. When we try to speak with them, they answer in clipped English then leave our presence as soon as manners allow. Wallis checks our room is satisfactory and is about to leave.

Lottie asks him, 'We want to go to Camp Irene tomorrow. Can you help us?'

'Why would you want to go there then?' Wallis asks, his eyebrows arching. He is an odd-looking chap, with camel-coloured hair and trimmed moustache, pouches under his eyes and big ears. He is so genial though, that his appearance is soon forgotten.

Lottie says, 'We want to talk to Mrs Uitenweerde.'

Wallis wipes his moustache then tugs on it, looking down and frowning.

'I'm sorry, ladies, but I think it may be a fool's errand. She has not spoken since it happened, they say. And if she won't speak up for Caleb, then I don't see as she'd lift a finger for you. And what if she did? If she was the one who did it, she's not going to tell you, is she? She'd incriminate herself and that'd be the end of her.'

I sign to Wallis. He likes to watch me do it and smiles and stares at my hands as I do. Lottie translates: 'We would like to try. We think she may talk to us. As we are females. And I am deaf. Perhaps she will take pity on us.'

'Well, if you insist. But you'll need a permit to travel.'

'We have one of those,' says Lottie. We do not explain that it is limited only to travel between Pretoria and Cape Town, but we are hoping to plead ignorance if challenged.

'And I'd like to come with you. It's only a half-hour from here on the train, but the camp is a dirty place and we don't want you catching anything. I'll bring her out to you and you can talk to her at the gate, where it's safer.'

But we need to go inside the camp, for reasons we cannot explain to Wallis. And we cannot do this while he is hanging about. He means well, but his attentions become infuriating. What can we say to dissuade him?

'Walter,' says Lottie and gives him a lovely smile. 'We feel that our best chance of talking with Mrs Uitenweerde and getting anything useful out of her would be to do it alone, woman to woman. If it is true that she has indeed been . . . interfered with by a British soldier, then the last person she will want to talk to is another British soldier, even one as charming as yourself.'

We are on the train from Pretoria. We are in luck, as no one has stopped us and checked our travel pass. Our first notion of the camp is the sight of long-winged black birds wheeling on the hot currents way up in the blue. Beneath them appear rows of white tents. As we leave the station, a cold wind blasts us and we hold on to our hats. The camp is situated on a hill down which the wind races and whips the canvas into slapping sails. The people must be inside their tents, as we can see hardly any walk to and fro as we approach. But jamming every lane and path and gap between the tents are hundreds of Visitors, almost all of them children. They are so thin, so lost, such dark eyes and bony arms, wretched and stumbling, so many they almost pass through each other as they unknowingly jostle their fellow wraiths. Lottie is talking to the guard and he is frowning and shaking his head. I cannot tear my eyes away from the children. As I step towards the tents, one notices me, then more, and soon dozens of them are circling me, their arms out, their cries and the Afrikaans language ringing in my inner ears:

Mamma, Mamma, Mamma. One carries a baby that screams and screams. I feel a panic rise in my throat as they clutch at me, their wispy grip at my arm, my skirt, even my feet for those too weak to stand. That woman was right: the angel of death rules this place. I turn from them to find Lottie nodding her head and pointing into the sea of tents. We begin to walk.

Lottie stops and makes sure I am watching her. 'Bad news. Maria has gone. She's escaped, with her son. A few days ago.'

I cover my mouth. This is disastrous.

'What can we do?'

'The guard has directed me to a nurse in the hospital. She tended the woman's son when he was ill and was the last one to see them. He says she may be able to help.'

'Did you ask him where the soldier was killed?'

'No, I didn't. I couldn't think of a reason why we would need to see it. I wanted to get into the camp first. Perhaps we can find someone inside who knows.'

We go to the hospital, which is just as Caleb described it. The whole camp had lived in my mind since his letter and he exaggerated nothing. The only detail I could not glean from his words is the experience of smelling the fetor of dirt, excrement, illness and death that pervades the camp like sea fret. Still the ghostly children surround me and stumble after me. I look around for adult Visitors and see only a few women, here and there, their faces covered by their customary white bonnets, wandering between tents, heads bowed as if looking for food on the ground. Each one I ask, *Do you know where the soldier was shot? The British guard, shot in a tent. Do you know which tent?* I ask in desperation, knowing they cannot help me. But my questions are answered with questions; even in a foreign language I can tell when someone is begging me. We stand at the door to the hospital and Lottie calls inside. A nurse appears and looks us up and down. Lottie explains and she disappears, replaced by another, a sturdy young woman in crisp uniform, with a slight smile and curious green eyes.

'Do you speak English?' asks Lottie.

'Of course,' she says. 'My name is Mrs Dedman. How can I help you?'

'This is Miss Golding. She is deaf but can lip-read and use sign language. I am Miss Crowe. My brother has been accused of murdering a British guard here.'

'Oh!' says Mrs Dedman. 'You are his sister? And you have come all the way from England?' She looks at us with sympathy, perhaps pity. 'Please, come and sit with me. I will bring you tea. And call me Henrietta, please.'

She takes us to a tent where two nurses sit with needlework on their laps, cups and saucers between them on a picnic table, talking and sewing speedily.

Henrietta asks something of them, to afford us some privacy I think, as they gather their things in a grumbling fashion and leave, blinking malcontent glances. We are given hot tea and sit with Henrietta, who leans forward with great interest. She asks us questions about the ship, our travels and how we find Africa, about my deafness and how I communicate, about my eyes and ears. She is an intelligent woman, that is sure, and seems starved of interesting conversation. We need her, so we engage politely with all she requires of us. Finally, Lottie grows impatient and changes the subject.

'We came to find a Mrs Maria Uitenweerde and speak to her about the death of Private Jackson. But we understand she has left the camp.'

'Yes, she escaped last week with her son. She took him from the hospital in the morning and went that very night. They slipped under the fence.'

'The guard told me you were the last one to see them.'

'Well, I saw her son that morning. He was recovering from a nasty chest infection. He did survive it but was quite weakened by it. I told her she should leave him in the hospital for a few days more, but she insisted. She took him back to her tent and that is the last time someone on the staff saw them together.'

'So someone else would have seen them, those they shared the tent with. Perhaps we might speak with them? We want to find Mrs Uitenweerde if we can. They may know in which direction she was heading.'

'I can show you her tent, but no one will speak to you there. Her kind were very anti-British you see. They would speak to me because I am Boer, like them, but not like them. I come from Cape Colony to help here. I have lost no one to the war and my family do not fight in it. I am neither loyalist nor nationalistic, I merely hate the war. So they will talk to me, but they do not trust me. If they will not talk to me, they certainly will not talk to you.'

It is hopeless, I see that. The woman is long gone, scot-free. All this way, and she has done a flit. At least we can see the tent where Jackson was killed. But how to ask Henrietta about that? What reason can we give? I sign to Lottie and she shrugs her shoulders.

Henrietta says, 'Excuse me for interrupting. But I may

be able to help you myself. When he was ill in the hospital, the boy Jurie talked about it while he was feverish. The other nurses are English and did not understand him. But I knew what he was saying. He was speaking about his home. One time, he called out the name of his farm.'

'Mimosafontein,' says Lottie.

'That is right! How did you know?'

'My brother told us.'

'He told me, "When we get out of here, we're going home. We're going back to Mimosafontein." He said it had been burned down, but they were going back there anyway and were going to build it up again from scratch. He told me all about it, half asleep. He said they were going to hide in the cellar during the day and at night were going to work on the farm. I assumed he meant after the war. But then they escaped and . . . maybe that is where they have gone.'

I want to know something, and Lottie translates for me. 'Did you tell the British about this?'

'About what the boy said? No, I kept it to myself. They had suffered, suffered very much. I thought, Good luck to them. She had lost her husband, the boy's father. And Jackson – the dead man – he was a bad man. Bad all through. A coward and a bully. And he raped her, oh yes. More than once. Everybody knows that. They say he had it coming to him. We did not even hear the shot, as there was a bad dust storm that day. Everyone was hiding away and the wind was very loud, whistling and howling. We only heard about the murder when we saw Maria taken to the commandant's office. And then people were saying your brother had confessed. Maria went back to her tent, but she did not speak again to any of us staff. Not even when her son was ill. And apart from his ramblings that one time the boy himself didn't say another word after the murder, not even to his mother. That time he told me about the farm he was in a fever, he was delirious, and after that it was as if he were mute. But it may be true, what he said. They may have gone home. Where else can they go?'

'Thank you,' I sign, and Lottie tells her. I reach out and touch Henrietta's hand. 'Why are you helping us?' I ask. I want to understand.

Henrietta looks squarely at us. 'You are good women, I can see that. God has sent you to help your brother. I met him once. He was a good man, I could see that. He tried to help Maria and her son. Maybe he shot Jackson, maybe she did. No one but Jackson knows what really happened in that tent. A horrible business.'

'Can we see the tent, where it happened?' I sign.

Henrietta looks concerned, curious, a little suspicious. 'If you wish. Do you think it will help?' We have our own reason for seeking out that tent, something this woman would not believe or understand.

'We are trying to get a clear picture of events,' adds Lottie. 'We can do very little for my brother, but the least we can do is investigate this as thoroughly as possible.'

Henrietta nods and her green eyes sparkle. 'Like lady detectives, mmm?' She has been helpful and generous with her time, but also she seems to be enjoying this, a little drama to entertain her in which she has no stake.

We take our leave, thanking her again and shaking hands like men. The tent is in row fourteen, number four. Henrietta has told us it is meant for storing cooking and medical equipment, but is used by the soldiers for privacy with their female companions. Not all relations that go on here are rape, it seems. As we count our way down the tents, I begin to banish the Visitors that crowd around, dismissing children, women, Boer men. Soon there are no Visitors left. When we reach the small tent, we peer inside. There are some empty crates stacked on one side, almost blocking the entrance.

Lottie taps my arm. 'Anyone?' she asks.

'Not yet.'

I step around the boxes. There is no Visitor here. It is ferociously hot and I look down to see a dark stain that scrawls across the dirt floor, alive with black flies. It must be blood, Jackson's blood. No one has thought to clear it. Or perhaps it has been preserved as evidence for the trial. But there is no guard, no one to stop us entering and poking about. All very slapdash, if you ask me. But their carelessness is our good fortune. I step outside again and beckon Lottie inside to show her the blood. Back outside, I walk around the full circumference of the tent. I check other tents close by, looking for the telltale violet glow in the air of a Visitor about to appear. But there is no one. I would know Jackson directly by his uniform, as I have seen no other British soldiers as Visitors here, only Boers. I suppose the soldiers get more to eat than their charges. We stay by the tent for an hour, sometimes peering inside, though the heat and the flies drive us out; then we patrol the paths nearby, looking for Jackson. I want to converse with him, I am relying on him to talk of his last obsession as Visitors do, to reveal to us who raised that gun and shot him dead. He is the key to our plan. We must find Jackson. But there is no sign of him.

'It is just like Tom,' Lottie says, wiping her damp brow with a handkerchief.

'But it has been weeks since this one died,' I say. 'And he wasn't at sea. They always wander the place they die, always. Where could he be?'

We decide to search further afield. By the time our train is due, we have circled the entire camp, walked past every tent in every row and looked in every building. We have had enquiring looks from inmates and nurses and guards, but no sign of Jackson. The train is imminent and we must leave. We thank the guard at the entrance for his help and walk down to the station, even looking in and out of every corner there too. Jackson has eluded us. We sit still and exhausted on the train back to Pretoria and observe the South African terrain. I take out my handkerchief and blow my nose, over and over. I cannot rid myself of the stench of that place. The train rushes past the slow lumber of innocent oxen drawing wagons and I am reminded of Kent in September, our own cattle which pull the loads of freshly picked hop cones stored in green bags to the oast for drying. I want to cry at the remoteness of home and I look at Lottie. She is weeping. I have let her down again.

'I am sorry,' I finger spell into her palm.

'It is not your fault.'

'We can go to that farm, Wallis will help us. Maybe we'll be lucky. Maybe we'll find her.'

'Maybe,' says Lottie. 'But what good will it do? Wallis was right. Even if we find her, she will never help us. Perhaps it is best to leave her be.'

'But it is her fault, that woman. It is all her fault.'

'No,' says Lottie. 'No, it is not.'

She speaks no more. It is as if her heart is slow, worn down and made old by her worry and grief. Again, I watch my friend suffer and I cannot help her. I sit and think of that camp, a modern Hades through which sweep the rivers of sorrow, hate and lamentation, the living waiting to die, the dead searching for rest. And I curse the ghost of Private Arnold Jackson for his absence, the British Army for bringing him here, the Boers for declaring war, the money men who want the African gold, the generals for setting up the camp, the soldiers who burned down Maria's farm, Caleb for leaving me and coming to this wounded land. I must blame someone.

16

We return late to our guest-house and are met with raised eyebrows from our German hosts. Our grimy faces, dirty skirts and unkempt hair must be a sight to see. We wash and eat the salted venison left out for us. We both sleep badly that night and are up with the lark, hoping to see Wallis early and discover the way to the farm. We find him after breakfast, looking large and ungainly in the little garden behind our hotel, his face glum, tugging on his moustache.

'Is all well?' asks Lottie.

'I shan't lie to you. Caleb is in trouble. Yesterday while you was at the camp, his counsel came by the hospital and spoke to the doctor. They say he'll be discharged in a couple of days and then he'll stand trial straight away.'

'But he's not strong enough yet,' cries Lottie. 'He needs to recuperate.'

'I know. But they had an army surgeon in to check him over and he says he's all right and fit to stand trial. I think they want to get it over with. It's an embarrassment for them. It's all over the newspapers here and back home. Counsel says they want to make an example of him. And that they might not believe his defence, that he was mad when he did it. There's no history of madness, see? He's as steady as they come, Caleb Crowe. You know that. So counsel says there's not much hope.'

Lottie shakes her head violently and I fear she will cry.

'Then there's no time to lose,' I sign to her, and make her pull herself together and translate. 'Listen, Wallis. We have news. Maria and her son have escaped from the camp.'

'Oh, Lord!'

We tell him the nurse's story.

'We want to go to her farm and look for her. Will you help us?'

'Oh, ladies, if only I could. But I've come to tell you my leave is up. I'm back off to Frankfort this morning. I came to say my goodbyes.'

The thought of Wallis accompanying us had been heartening, but now I see this may serve us well. After all, as soon as she sees a British soldier approach her farm, she would fly. Or worse.

'It is all right. We can go there alone. But first we need to find out where it is. Do you have time to help us with that before you go?'

Wallis says he will speak to the German couple. They have lived in Pretoria for twenty years and probably know the names of all the farms round here. But we explain to Wallis that they barely talk to us.

'They'll take your rent but they hate you all right.'

'But whyever do they hate us?' asks Lottie.

'Germans are pro-Boer, didn't you know? They really hate the British. The Boers all fight with German weapons, Mauser and Krupp. There's even a German volunteer corps fighting over here. The Boers get money sent over from German charity. Germans love them. They think us

British are all big bullies, pushing the poor little Boers about. But the Kaiser can be a bully when he wants to. Never fear though. I'll get these two in order. They'll do what I tell them or I'll make a heap of trouble for them.'

He puffs himself up to full military stance and intimidates the German couple into telling him where the farm is, saying that it is army business and they will be arrested if they do not reveal its location. It is all bluster but they look alarmed and give him directions. He races off to visit army HQ nearby and comes back directly with a crumpled map of the environs of Pretoria. We search across it and find the place the Germans have described. We can take the railway so far, and then we must hire a cart to get to the farm. I recall my blind fingers moving over Father's globe, how smartly I could find a country, sea or landmark when Lottie asked it; excellent spatial sense I had. It serves me still as, once I could see, I would visualise distance as well as divine it tactilely. As I study the map, I memorise our route to Mimosafontein and see it unfurl in my mind's eye.

Wallis is awkward in bidding goodbye. For a moment I believe I glimpse his lip trembling. He promises he will come back on his next leave, but he has no idea when that will be.

'I'll go in to see Caleb again before I get off.'

'Do not tell him what we are doing,' I sign.

'Why not? He'd be proud of you both, going to all this trouble for him.'

'I am not so sure,' adds Lottie, understanding my meaning. 'He will not want us to harass Maria, that is certain. And he may rush to trial if he feels his position is threatened. No, I think it best we keep this to ourselves for the moment, Walter. It can be our secret.'

Wallis cannot resist Lottie and takes off his hat to bow for us. Within the hour, we are on our way. We know to detrain at a little village just twenty minutes up the line. Wallis has instructed us to pay the natives very little when hiring a Cape cart. We haggle and then find our charge, a sprightly pony ready to trot us forth. We peruse the map and head north from the railway station, following a dirt road that should lead us past two farms then to Mimosafontein. The land hereabouts is open grassland, undulating low hills and small clumps of trees here and there. The weather is mild and dry; we are comfortable in our shawls and hats, flurries of wind teasing our hair loose. The land is so vast, so quiet, so dwarfed by the skies that I begin to grasp the appeal. I imagine the Dutch settlers in their wagons trekking across this land and seeing their peaceful future spread out beneath the blue heavens.

As we trot on, Lottie manning the reins and making a good fist of it, it is as if we are on an outing to watch birds, not a life-or-death encounter with a woman I hate to my bones. I steel myself as we see our first farm ahead. But it is no farm, not any more. It is a smoke-blackened husk. We go onwards and say nothing, its vacuity an accusation for which we have no answer. A while further on, we pass another derelict farm. This one looks as if it has exploded, as the roof timbers lie dozens of feet from the wrecked main building, some skewered into the ground by force, their splintered ends cutting a harsh black line through the calm sky. As we ride past, I spy a Visitor at this one, a Boer man, low flat hat askew on his head, beady eyes glaring. He stands before the rubble of his farm, a threshold guardian. He marches forward, raises his arm and shouts something in Afrikaans, his face filthy with dirt and anger. He starts to run after us, gaining on the cart alarmingly. Though I know he cannot hurt us, I urge Lottie to trot faster. As we rush on, he stops, his arm still raised as if in farewell, his spirit dissolving into the air as if he has reached the boundary of the place of his death and cannot travel further.

The next farm is Mimosafontein. We watch it come. It is ruined, like the others. The main building is half burned-out, but two walls are still intact and some of the roof clings on. Low stone walls nearby, which might have housed animals, are complete. There were tall trees growing here once, but they are all dead, hacked off below the lowest branch to murder them. What was once a dam is dry and the earth within it cracked into brown fissures. Weeds proliferate in ragged squares marked out beside the house, perhaps a former flower garden. We pull up outside the front door, still intact and standing ajar; through habit, I knock on it and see Lottie call out, 'Mrs Uitenweerde? Hello, is anyone at home?'

We step inside and find the floor half destroyed by fire, littered with charred and splintery remains of furniture. A sad piano has been smashed into two pieces, useless, its bronzy strings splayed out against the blackened walls. As we pass into the next room, once a kitchen with ruined range and trampled crockery spilling from the axed dresser, we see a huge wildcat perched on the windowsill, fearless and eyeing us with belligerence. Lottie calls out, 'Shoo, shoo!' and we stamp our feet and wave our arms. This is my patch, it seems to say, but like all cats it is too lazy to argue. It leaps down and trots away across the yard.

We scout the devastation. A cow barn stands behind and we go in, buckets up-ended and strands of straw afloat on warm currents. No cows here now, no sign of the people or animals who lived and made it their home. Just desolation, neglect and the wind whistling through the broken beams. A movement in the corner of my eye and I wheel round, looking for that wildcat. A white-blue light emanates from behind a cow-stall. A small head pops up – eyes staring – then retreats.

'What is it?' says Lottie, who has seen me turn.

'A Visitor,' I sign back, and step forward. I look down behind the stall and there is a boy crouched on the floor, his body fringed with a vibrant halo, as if he has only just passed.

Hello, I say to him in my mind.

You are English? he replies.

I am. We are friends. We come alone.

No soldiers?

No soldiers. I am very glad you speak English.

Mamma taught me.

He stands up, proud.

'Who is it?' Lottie asks.

I am going to guess your name. Do you think I can?

No.

It is Jurie.

How do you know it?

I know everything.

Do you know about the man?

Which one?

The soldier who hurt Mamma. He is dead now.

Yes, I know about him.

'Who is it, Liza?' insists Lottie.

'It is her boy, Jurie.'

I did not mean it.

You did not mean what?

He walks out around the stall and stands in the doorway to the barn.

I am sorry for it. I did not mean to do it.

Do what, Jurie? What did you do?

Lottie shoves me. I spin around to see a woman holding a shotgun aloft, aimed squarely at us, shifting it from one head to the other, finger poised on the trigger. Lottie and the woman are shouting at each other.

I see the woman say, 'Hands up! Hands up!'

'Maria . . .' says Lottie.

'Shut up! Who are you? You are English. How do you know my name? What do you want?'

'I am Caleb's sister.'

The gun stops. Maria's eyes widen as she stares.

'I can see it. You are his twin. You look like him. Who is she? The deaf and dumb one?'

The gun nods towards me.

'I am not dumb,' I sign in disgust.

'Hands up, I say! What are you doing here?'

I have to watch Lottie speak, but find it difficult to drag my gaze from that gun.

'My name is Charlotte Crowe and this is Adeliza Golding. We come on Caleb's behalf. We have no weapons. We are alone. We cannot hurt you. Can you please lower the gun?'

'Outside,' she orders and we obey. We are led towards our cart and told to stand near it. There is no sign of Jurie's ghost.

Maria stands before her front doorway, slowly lowering her gun. Now I can see her fully, I see how pretty she once was. She is thin and scrawny, her feet bare, her nails blackened, her hair felted with dust, wild seeds sown in her fringe. But her face is still beautiful, her eyes dark blue and compelling. She reminds me of my gypsy Visitor, all those years ago, bold, feral.

'What do you want here?'

'We want to talk to you.'

'To turn me in? You think you can take me back there and turn me in. Well, just try it!' She raises the gun again.

Lottie holds out her hands in supplication. 'No, I promise you. We come in peace. We just want to talk to you about what happened. We have come a long way, all the way from England, and we have found you at last, and we just want to talk to you, please.'

The gun comes down. 'Go on.'

We lower our hands. Lottie begins, 'We want to talk to you about what happened. My brother says he killed Jackson. He's in hospital now.'

Maria asks, 'Is he all right?'

'He's recovering from dysentery. He has been very ill. He needs time to recover. But his trial has been moved forward and he goes to court in a matter of days. They mean to convict him, Maria. They mean to make an example of him. He will be shot.'

'There is nothing I can do about that.'

'He loves you,' I sign. 'How can you forsake him?' But Lottie will not translate for me.

'What is she waving her stupid hands around for?' scoffs Maria and I want to rush over and take hold of her, throw her to the ground and stamp on her insolent face.

Lottie continues, 'Please, Maria. You and I both know that Caleb did not shoot Jackson. He was a bad man, the worst. We know . . . we know what he did to you. We know. I am sorry, Maria.'

'You are sorry? Sorry?' she spits, her face contorted. 'You silly English women on your little trip overseas, to prance about in your petticoats and tend to your precious brother. What about me, my husband, my family, my country? My son?'

'We know your son has died,' I sign and Lottie speaks for me now.

Maria's eyes fall. 'You saw the grave.'

We do not answer.

'He was eight years old. He had a life before him. I am broken, but he had his life to make, after this war and madness have gone. He had a fever. I could not help him, I had no medicines. He went quickly. He was weak from the last time. And from the walk here, the long walk. I should not have left. I should never have come here. It is all my fault. Poor Jurie! My poor son!'

She is weeping now. Her tears are large and heavy, they stream down her face, drop into the dirt and stain it.

Jurie is here. He stares at the doorway behind Maria, then looks back at me and cocks his head, as if listening.

Can you hear something, Jurie?

It sounds like my mother. It sounds like she is crying, very far away. Across the veldt. Is it my mother? Is she crying?

You can hear people?

Only you and Mamma. I cannot hear others. I have heard no others since some days ago. When I was sick. Only Mamma's voice.

I did not know you could hear the living.

What is the living?

Your mother is well, Jurie. Do not worry.

Ag moet nou nie huil nie, Mamma. Do not cry.

'What is she doing?' Maria is staring at me. She grips the rifle and holds it to her breast. 'Is she mad?'

She is crying because of me. If you see her, tell Mamma I am sorry. I did not mean to do it. I am sorry.

'Jurie killed him,' I sign. Lottie stares at me. 'He is saying he's sorry, he didn't mean to do it. Tell her!'

Lottie says, 'Was it your son? Did he shoot the gun at Jackson? It was an accident, wasn't it? He didn't mean to do it.'

Maria lifts up the rifle. I think for one mad moment she will kill us both. She has nothing to lose.

'What witchcraft is this? Who is she looking at? What do you know about it?'

'If it is true,' I sign and Lottie speaks, 'you have nothing to fear.'

'How do you know about Jurie?' She is shouting now. The gun flicks wildly between us. 'I promised him no one would ever find out what he did.'

'But now that does not matter,' says Lottie. 'Your son has died.'

'It does not matter?' Maria's eyes narrow, her mouth is cruel. I fear she will shoot us now, this moment.

'We mean that no one can hurt him now. You did your job, you protected him the best you could. Now, you can come with us and explain to them that it was not you who killed him, it was not my brother, but your son. And your son is gone now, may he rest in peace. But you can help the living, you can save Caleb, you can free him. If you come with us and tell them, tell them the truth.'

'Are you crazy? I am not going back there. They will lock me up again and punish me for escaping. I'm never going back to that hell, never.'

'But what about Caleb? He helped you. He is going to die for you.'

'He loves you,' I sign and want to scream, I want to fall down and weep into the dusty earth. I hate this woman. I pity her, but I hate her more. I want her to do what we want, then turn into a pillar of salt and never exist or breathe again in this world.

Lottie steps forward, her hands out, pleading now. 'They will understand. They will take into consideration what happened to you, what Jackson did to you. He committed a crime under British law. His crime cancels out your escape. You will not be prosecuted for it, I guarantee it. This lady's mother has powerful friends, they will see to it that no harm comes to you, I promise you, Maria. I promise you on my mother's life.'

'Lies. All lies,' says Maria, her eyes glassy.

'Please,' cries Lottie and falls before her feet. I cannot see Lottie's lips now, but I know she is begging, pleading for Caleb's life. She lifts her head and I see her say, 'Save him.'

I am a thief . . .

I look at Jurie. He is chewing on a fingernail. He is useless to me now. He killed Jackson, but without Maria, no one will ever believe us.

Go now, Jurie.

A thief is a bad thing. Mother told me that. If you see her, you will tell her? I should not have taken his belongings. I never meant to be a thief. But I thought I could sell them, the watch anyway. And the penknife. And we might get some money for them and buy some soap and candles and some food.

What things? What are you talking about, Jurie?

The man's things. I stole them. I took them from the tent after. After I found him with the gun and the blood on his shirt and the blood on the ground.

You found him?

Yes, I found him. He was dead. There was so much blood. Like the slaughter pit. But a man, a real dead soldier.

Did you kill him?

No!

Did you shoot him, Jurie?

No, I did not. Who says I did? They are a liar.

Your Mamma thinks you shot him, Jurie. She found you with the gun in your hand.

I was going to steal that too. She found me and I was so ashamed. I had the things in my pocket and I did not tell her about those. I was so ashamed I could not speak. But she said she would not tell anyone. She said she would look after me and we would get away from there and no one would ever know. But I kept the objects. I put them in my treasure box. The watch, the penknife and the book.

What book?

The man's book. With his writing in it. I can speak English, but I cannot read it. I kept it anyway, his book and his sharp pencil. He wrote in it that day, because I saw the date in it.

When I turn back to look at Maria, my mouth open in shock, she is speaking to Lottie who still weeps on the ground between us. I miss the start of her sentence.

'. . . to me,' she says. 'Now you know the truth, they will come looking for me. You have ruined everything, coming here. All I wanted was my home. And you two

English women have come here with your pity and your lies and you have destroyed my last chance of peace.'

I believe she will do it now. I believe we are about to die. I clap my hands to make Lottie look.

'Ask her, did Jurie ever say he killed Jackson? Did he ever actually tell her he did it? Ask her!'

Lottie drags herself upright and speaks for me.

Maria listens coldly. 'No, he never spoke again. I told you that. What difference does it make?'

'Then how do you know he did it?' asks Lottie.

'I found him holding the gun. He had blood on his hands. He never spoke a word afterwards. When I found him, I asked him over and over, what happened? I found him beside the body with the revolver in his hand. He never spoke a word to me after that moment, not one word. I said I would never let anyone get him for what he had done and he nodded and he cried. I knew he had done it.'

'You're wrong!' I sign. 'He didn't do it. He stole some items from Jackson. He put them in his special box.'

'What?' cries Lottie.

'Translate!'

She does so and Maria frowns.

'How does she know about that? How do you know about that? You can read my lips, can't you? You can understand me. What do you know about my son?'

What was the book, Jurie? Was it a diary?

I think, yes. A book you write in, with dates. Pages and pages.

'Maria,' I sign and Lottie repeats. 'Do you still have your son's special box?'

'No one knew about that, not even Caleb. How do you

know, eh? Again I say, what witchcraft is this? Tell me, or I will kill you. I mean it, I'll kill you both. Who have you been looking at, over there? Tell me!'

She is screaming now. Her finger is on the trigger and I feel the blue-white light may come for me soon, very soon.

'Jurie is here. Your son is here. He is a ghost, a spirit. I can see him, I can talk to him. Nobody knows I can do this, not even Caleb. Only Charlotte. Jurie told me he did not kill Jackson, that he stole some of his possessions, and that is what he cried about, that is what he thought you protected him from. He hid them in his special box, with a book, a diary. Do you have it, Maria? Do you know where it is?'

Maria stares at the space beside me. Jurie has walked away, weary of me now. But is he? He turns and points. There is a small mound of earth behind the cowshed, like a molehill. He points to it again.

I want to walk over there, I want to dig up that earth and look in there. But if I move, Maria might shoot me. I turn and look at her.

'Jurie?' she calls weakly. 'Is he here?'

'Yes.'

Maria's face collapses. 'Jurie? Where is he? Take me to him.'

'He cannot see you, he can only see me.'

'Why? Why you?'

'I do not know. I have never known. But I can see them and they can see me, and talk to me.'

'What does he say to you?'

'He said he was sorry. That he did not mean to be a thief. He said to tell you he was sorry.'

Maria is crying and drops the gun. Lottie should grab it, or I. But we do not. We watch her weep.

'Is he here right now? Can you speak to him?'

'Yes. He's over there, by the barn.'

Her eyes scan the space, desperate to see her son, but fill with tears as she knows she cannot.

'You believe me?' I say. 'You believe some can see the dead?'

'Yes,' says Maria, calmer now. 'I have always known about them. My grandmother spoke of them. I wished I could see them too, but I never did.'

Perhaps other people are like Maria. Perhaps I could tell others one day.

'How is Jurie?' she asks. 'What is he doing, right now?'

'He points at the ground. Did he bury his special box there?'

'Yes.'

'We must see it, Maria. There is a diary in it, Jackson's diary. We must have it.'

'Take whatever you wish. Just take me to my son.'

She steps over the gun, walks to me and stands before me, broken, helpless, asking me with her eyes to do this one thing for her, though she has no right to ask it, only the right of a grieving mother.

I take her arm and she leans on me. We walk slowly over to the barn, where Jurie is still pointing at the earth.

I buried my special box there, when we arrived. I buried it there so Mamma would not know.

'Tell him I knew about the box,' says Maria. 'I saw him do it. Boys are always up to something, their little secrets. I did not care. I did not mind anything he did.'

I explain this to Jurie.

You know my Mamma?

Yes.

Where is she?

She is beside me. You cannot see her.

Is she a ghost?

Something like that.

Can you talk to her?

Yes.

Tell her I miss her.

I will.

I sign to her, he misses you. Somehow, the gesture communicates my meaning and Maria nods, understands because she knows what he would be feeling.

'Tell him I love him. I will always love him. One day soon I will die and I will come to him. I do not want him to be lost here, wandering alone, not to see me, to worry. Can he go on, or must he stay here?'

Lottie joins us, translates for me.

'I can tell him to go away. I've done it before. If I tell them to go away for ever, they never come back. Do you want me to do this?'

Maria looks into the air before us, her eyes searching for something they will never see in this life.

'No. I cannot bear to lose him again.'

'It may be kinder. They are not happy when they wander.'

'No, let him stay.'

I nod.

Maria kneels down and thrusts her hands into the dirt. She digs quickly and efficiently, like an aardvark. The box is unearthed and she pulls it out. She twists a tiny screw on its side and it opens. Inside are many treasures: shells, pebbles, buttons, two pennies with the head of Kruger, a feather. Underneath these treasures are the watch, the penknife and a small journal, navy blue leather with a brass clasp. Maria holds it in her hand.

As I reach out to take the diary, I think of Jackson. Why his Visitor was not to be found, why he did not wander the place of his death as they all do. And I recall Tom, our fruitless search for sad Tom Winstanley who never came back. And then I know.

'Jackson did it,' I sign to Lottie. 'That's what I think the diary will tell us. He shot himself. That's why he never came back. Just like Tom. It was nothing to do with the sea. It was suicide. That must be the rule. Suicides never return.'

Lottie's eyes open wide, she glances out to the distance – her mind travelling through time and space back to her past, to the sea, to her youth – then her gaze returns to me. She nods. Maria hands me the book and I open it. Tiny pages, meant for appointments and reminders, filled with cursive script from the first week of the war until his death, written in smudged grey pencil. I turn to the last page with writing, and Lottie reads it out loud.

'*This is the last will and testament of Arnold Ewart Jackson. I hereby leave all my worldly goods to my mother and father. I have no wife and children and no siblings. I leave everything to my parents, who have always been kind and good to me and proud of me even when I do not deserve it. I know I have done wrong things and I am sorry to all the people I have hurt. I hate this bloody war and I am glad to be shot of it. I am sorry for my parents that they will have to live with the shame of me doing away with myself like this. It is a cowardly thing to do, I know it. But I cannot bear this life any more, I cannot. I wish to shuffle off and not bother with it any more. I cannot live with myself, so when I have finished writing this entry, I will put down my pencil and pick up my revolver and shoot myself in the chest. I am thinking of my parents at the end, as I will not shoot myself in the mouth, it being horrible for the open casket I know they would want. So that is that. I must get to it. Goodbye then.*'

17

'Come with us, Maria,' I sign. 'Come back with us.'

I cannot believe I am suggesting it, but it is what my hands decide to say. When Lottie translates Maria shakes her head, distracted.

I cast an urgent look at Lottie, who adds, 'We will find a safe place for you to stay.'

'We can bring Caleb to you.' Now I am amazed at myself. Why on earth would I offer that, to deliver him – the one I love best – into the hands of the one I hate most? But I do offer it, and I know it to be the only right and true course of action. She looks at me as I say this. I can glimpse in her eyes that she understands me, but they glaze over and she looks past me.

Short of tying the woman to our cart, we cannot persuade her. She will not speak to us. She drifts away, beyond the cowshed and the irrigation ditches out into the wilderness, her head bowed, her arms hanging by her side. Looking for her son.

I say to Lottie, 'I fear she will lose her mind.'

As we settle on our cart, I tell Lottie to call out to her once more, but to no avail. As we trot away the way we came, I see her turn and shuffle back towards the farm. If she stays here, I think she will starve here, die here.

On the way back we are quiet, haunted by Maria. Once

on the train, we are moving closer to Caleb and away from Mimosafontein, her hold on us weakening. We discuss how to convey our good news. How will we reveal our source? We will have to tell Caleb we saw Maria, but what of his lawyer? Will the counsel reveal Maria's whereabouts to the authorities? We cannot have that. We will have to say she left that place never to return. And how do we explain Jurie's involvement? We decide we cannot. We must say we found Maria and she was not willing to come back for fear of imprisonment. But she had found the diary in her son's effects and gave it to us to clear Caleb's name. I know this is the only way, but it rankles. It will seem to Caleb and all who hear the story that she chose to save him, that she was simply waiting for someone to find her so that she could proffer this vital piece of evidence and only her justifiable fear of return to the camp prevented her heroic act. Caleb will not know that it was me, that I am the one who has the gift that solved the mystery, to talk with the dead boy and find the crucial evidence. That I saved his life. He will never know that.

From Pretoria railway station, we walk straightway to the hospital. Caleb is seated on his bed, dressed and shaven, his hair newly cut short above his ears with the curls tamed into a side parting on top. His back is upright as a board – he is stronger, and it is good to see. Beside him an older man with white hair and a stack of papers in his hand speaks earnestly. They turn and look at us together. Caleb's eyes light as he sees us, yet dim as he fears the bad news he must tell us. But we have news for him, and for his counsel. We produce the diary, Lottie imparts all the necessary, the counsel is astounded and leaps up.

'I cannot believe it!' cries the lawyer. 'What marvellous

detective work, ladies. Caleb, do you hear this? Do you understand? You will be free! This proves it absolutely. You will be exonerated, old chap.'

Caleb has listened to everything with intense concentration, but not yet spoken. He takes the diary of Private A. E. Jackson and reads the final entry.

'It is true then,' says Caleb. He looks up at us both. 'You have saved my life.'

'They have, they have!' crows the counsel and takes his leave of us, telling Caleb to remain here while he informs the court of this new evidence. He explains that it may take a few days to confirm the authenticity of Jackson's diary, but he cannot see why all charges will not then be dropped and the trial cancelled forthwith. He bustles off between the beds and with alacrity informs each nurse and the doctor of Caleb's news. There is much shaking of hands.

At last, Caleb smiles and seems to understand his turn of fortune. But I know his face, his eyes, very well. There is something missing there, something not quite right. When things have quietened and Lottie is conversing with the doctor about Caleb's health, I talk with him alone.

'How was Maria?' he asks. 'Where did she go?'

'She was not well. She grieved for Jurie so. We tried to bring her back with us, Caleb, we tried and tried. But she would not come. She appeared to wander out on to the veldt, but the last we saw she turned back to her homestead. She may still be there. We lied to your counsel. We did not want him to know she might still be on the farm, in case he might inform the authorities and seek her as a witness. We wanted her to be free of all that. Did we do right, Caleb?'

He takes my hands and holds them fast. He looks at me deeply in the way I have oft hoped he would.

'You did, Liza. You did everything right. You always have. Thank you. Thank you, my dear. My lovely girl.'

And he breaks down, he cries as I have never seen a man cry. He has hold of my hand and his hot cheeks burn against it and his warm tears soak my skin and his fist crushes my fingers. Lottie comes running and many heads are turning, bobbing, then they look away to spare him.

Within a week, Caleb is a free man. The court ruled that Arnold Jackson 'did wilfully injure himself'. Telegrams have been dispatched to the Crowes and Mother. We receive back grateful congratulations and overflowing joy, straightened into the few clipped words permitted to the telegraphic style. Lottie and I have spent our time discussing our plans. What to do next? Caleb will soon go back to his regiment and we must move on. But to go home? Or to travel onwards, to trace our original plans backwards, by ship to Gibraltar and up through Spain and France from there, to explore Europe as we planned that lifetime before? We cannot think of reasons why not. We have achieved what we came here to do, spectacularly, beyond our wildest hopes of success. Lottie is happy, I can see that. She is content and complete – her beloved brother free – excited too about ideas of further travel and adventure. Our Grand Tour is welcome to me, but only as an escape from a difficult truth, not as an escapade to be embraced.

To me, our time in Africa has not been a thrilling quest, but a trial. I have come through it victorious yet I feel my soul has been wrung too harshly, the life of it crushed. I have saved my love, knowing full well as I did it that I have lost him too. I knew it when I first saw him in his hospital bed and he told me he loved her. Yet when he held my hands and wept, I saw his gratitude, his love for me, his acceptance of my love all these years, my dogged refusal to abandon it. He kissed my hands that day and thanked me, over and over. I believe he was truly saying, thank you for loving me, thank you for that, Liza. In that moment, the desperate need I always had for his regard, for his devotion, for his love and to possess him utterly, the rock of it I had shouldered these many years, seemed to lighten its load a very little. There was in his thanks a kind of release.

Caleb is granted leave for two weeks to recuperate. The morning of his release, he comes to us at the Germans' guest-house.

'I must go to Mimosafontein. I intend to spend these two weeks I have in searching for Maria. Will you help me?'

He does not need to ask. The trip to the farm is not so easy this time. The wind blows strong and we wreathe our poor heads in shawls, Caleb pulling down the brim of his cap to little avail. Just past the second farm there is a dust storm and we are obliged to blanket the pony's head and hide under the cart until it will pass. Hiding under another blanket, all three of us crushed together, the granular wind slapping at our limbs and making us spit, we try to rest and hold on to each other. It is the closest I have been to Caleb for years and I surprise myself. I am not weakened by it, yet strengthened. I, the lonely one, the only child whose blindness and deafness enclosed her from the world, met a woman who saved her from the abyss and loved her. And here is her brother. My brother. Somehow in that moment, under the buffeted blanket, we three become a family.

A voice is calling. It is a Visitor of course. They are the only voices I will ever hear. Beneath our covering I cannot see anything but the three of us, blurred. Lottie and Caleb have their heads down, enduring the storm. The voice is there again. I sense a Visitor approach. I lift one corner of the blanket to look for it. Caleb yanks the blanket back down. I see feet appear, gnarled and buckled men's boots standing firm in the wild weather, the purplish light leaking from the edges of his brown weather-beaten trousers. I slip out from beneath the blanket and stand up to him. It is the Boer ghost I saw on our first journey. Caleb's fingers grasp at my leg. I step away. This Visitor is furious, tormented. The worst I have ever seen, much angrier than my gypsy. He glowers at me as if he would take me by the neck. Dust strikes my body and attacks my eyes. I use my shawl to protect my head as best I can, but I am barely able to stand. He is unaffected by the storm. He inhabits a separate vein of the spectrum, free from worldly pressures. He begins to spit words at me, Afrikaans that I cannot comprehend. He is telling me a tale of great woe. Perhaps his wife and children are in a camp, perhaps they are dead. He tears at his hair as he tells me his story, waves his arm beyond us at the land, he jabs his finger violently at my breastbone, though all I feel is the faintest graze.

Listen, I say. He stops.

Listen carefully. You can hear the voices of your loved ones. Can you hear them?

His eyes express confusion, then disdain. He begins to rant again.

Stop shouting and listen. If they still live, you will hear them.

His face falls serious and he cocks an ear, looks up askance. His eyes widen, his mouth lifts and he is smiling.

I cannot hear their voices. They must be alive. He calls to them, he points at me and laughs. He questions me in Afrikaans. I believe he is asking if I can hear them too.

You can hear them and that is all that matters.

He speaks to them but soon realises they cannot hear him. Yet he is content to listen to them for a time. I will never know what he heard, but I can read in his face the elixir effect their voices had on him.

Caleb is climbing out from beneath the cart.

Do you want to go now? Do you wish to rest?

My Visitor nods his head. His eyes are so tired.

Go now. Go for ever and never come back.

He turns into the wrath of the wind, yet not a hair on his head lifts. He looks his last across his beloved country and he is gone.

Caleb is beside me and grasps my shoulders, turning me so I can read his lips.

'What the hell are you doing?' he yells and bundles me back under.

Lottie peers from beneath her shawl. One look from me and she knows instantly what I have been about. Caleb is back under, complaining, but I am not looking at him. Lottie's eyebrows are asking me if I am well. I nod and smile gently.

The storm passes and we go on to Mimosafontein. We find Maria there, slumped in the corner of the cow barn. I know for a second they think she is dead, but I know different. Her Visitor is not here. She is only asleep. When she opens her eyes and sees her Caleb, she smiles at him and her dirty, tear-streaked face transforms, she becomes the Maria he fell in love with. I will not lie to you, there is a thorny kernel in me that envies them their love, the seed of the angry child I once was who pulled out my hair in clumps and would say now, why her? Why not me? But it is a dwarf, not a giant, and if I can quash it for now perhaps one day I will tame it.

Caleb puts his arm around her, helps her towards the cart. As we leave the barn, white-violet light catches my eye and I see Jurie is here, kicking about in the dust, hands in his pockets.

Hello, he says.

Are you lonely?

Yes, I am.

Maria has stopped. I look up and she is staring at me.

'I will speak with this one,' Maria says to Caleb, nodding towards me. 'Alone.'

'Later,' he says. 'Plenty of time.'

'No, now. She knows why.'

Maria glances back at the cowshed. She nods at me. I understand. I walk with her to the barn. We go inside, so the others cannot see us.

Maria says, 'Is Jurie here?'

I gesture outside. Then Jurie appears in the doorway.

Are you here to stay? he asks me.

Maria sees me watching him.

'Release him,' she says.

I look deeply at her, frown, nod.

'Please do it. Tell him I will always love him. Say goodbye for me.'

Go now, Jurie. Your Mamma says she loves you always. She says goodbye. Go now. Go for ever and never come back.

Jurie says nothing. A gust from the veldt takes him, like breath to a taper.

'Is he gone?'

I nod.

'Thank you,' says Maria.

She takes my hands, enfolds them.

When we come back to the cart, I see Lottie has spoken with Caleb. He does not ask any questions, just helps Maria into the cart, wraps a blanket around her and holds her close. Within minutes, she sleeps.

Lottie and I sit at the front. Nobody speaks. As we approach the sad shell of the first ruined farm, I feel a tap on my shoulder. Caleb is smiling at me. Maria lies across his lap, still sleeping. Lottie looks ahead, directing the cart.

He signs to me, 'Why did you never tell me of your gift?'

'Do you believe it now?'

'If you tell me it is true.'

'It is.'

'Then I believe it.'

We smile.

On our return, we bring Maria to our guest-house.

'We have a visitor for you,' says Lottie to the Germans. They have no love for the British, we know that, but they are devoted to the Boer cause. They take her in and will protect her. They will provide food and shelter until she regains her health. Caleb knows he can return to service, visit her on leave, and one day – who knows when – the war will end and, if both survive, he will surely return to her. Whether he will journey to England, see his family, arrange his affairs, this we do not know. That is his business and, as ever, he keeps it close. Perhaps he will merely disappear from his garrison one night and the Germans will wake one morning to find her gone. That is what I would do.

After that day in the Cape cart swaying back from Mimosafontein, where Caleb and I smiled at each other one last time unobserved, we have not had another second alone together. He spends his fortnight's leave at the guest-house daily, tending to Maria every waking minute. It is quite a test of my new-found peace with him to see him attend to her with such devotion. But the times Lottie, Caleb and I spend together as she sleeps – chatting and strolling, like the old days on Whitstable promenade or down the hop lanes after picking work in the warm evenings at home – are like medicine for my malady. We find some of our old ease in those hours; we are companions again. As Maria recovers, Lottie and I grow to know her a little, to see the strength returning to those clouded eyes of the woman Caleb first met. We edge to a kind of closeness in our discussion of the Visitors, who fascinate Maria; she quizzes me about them most engagingly. By the time we plan to go, just before Caleb's leave is up, I have an understanding of how he came to be captivated by her, most of all her intense and searching mind. I cannot say I find her easy, but I respect and admire Maria Uitenweerde. She pats my hand when we say our goodbyes at the guest-house, and mouths very clearly, 'I hope we are like sisters now.'

My leave-taking with Caleb is public; naturally Lottie is there and even dear Wallis accompanies us to Pretoria railway station to wish us well. It is a busy train with much pushing and shoving on the platform, from which Caleb and Wallis shield us as they lead us to our carriage. There is no still moment to sign a thoughtful phrase to Caleb, but in the seconds before the men leave us to our seats and we have all said goodbye and good luck and farewell and we shall write, he takes my hand swiftly and silently spells in our old way one word for me: 'Sorry.' The same word my mother laid out for me that first time we 'spoke'. I shake my head and look hard at him, grasp his hand and try to spell, 'No.' I will not have that be our legacy, I do not want his pity. But he turns and leaves the carriage and I feel I cannot speak to Lottie of it. Instead, I sit and stare from the window at the bright rainbow of foreign lives and the ghostly blue of the lost Visitors, seeking Caleb in the crowd but not finding him, as we lurch forward towards Cape Town, our ship and the ocean beyond.

18

I sit on a wrought-iron bench beside the lake, beneath the shedding blossom of a cherry tree, contemplating the looking-glass water and the Evian shore beyond. The Alps are masked by morning mist. Only a hint between the fleeting clouds suggests there are mountains there at all. But soon the spring sun will rise and burn away the fog, revealing the startling solidity of this view, ancient stone thrusting up from the restless earth. Beside the lake drift dozens of Visitors, solitary and aimless, staring across at the mountains or eyeing me curiously. I have spoken with many of them since we arrived. My spell in Africa taught me treasured lessons about my Visitors. Now each time I converse with a new Visitor, I tell them if they listen very carefully, they may be able to hear the voices of their loved ones. Some can and it gives them great pleasure. It is a balm to their restlessness which cures their distress. Then I always ask, *Do you wish to move on?* I can help them, if they want it. Many agree and I always sense a release of tension, cool air after a thunderstorm, a sigh of the soul as they depart. After a long day's journey, they can rest now.

I pull my shawl closer about my shoulders. Lausanne stirs, the baker's boy scooting past on his bike, his basket full of warm Swiss pastries for delivery, the restaurants still sleeping after their late night, their shutter-eyes closed whitely to the morning. Lottie slumbers too, within our pistachio room in the Château D'Ouchy behind me. We may stay here a while. We have explored Geneva, the little towns along the lake, neat Morges with its flower-dotted parks, quaint Vevey with shadowed lanes of boutiques to stroll through, and the Château de Chillon with its grisly dungeon, frequented by scores of despondent Visitors. I helped many there. And surrounding it all, the Alps; so still, so set in their flinty way, their mighty permanence gazing proudly at their double in the glassy Lac Leman. I am very small.

I sit solitary beside the lake to read a letter I received last evening. The concierge gave it to me when Lottie was upstairs, and as I saw its hand I pocketed it and kept it a secret. I saved it until now, for I have given up much in the last year. Now I want this one gift of my own. A letter from Caleb. The first letter I have ever received from Africa addressed only to me. We have had communications for the two of us over these months. Caleb's regiment, the East Kents, were sent home in May 1901, their service at an end. We hear Wallis went back to his work in Kent as a painter and decorator. Caleb chose to stay in Africa, and Maria recovered her health and joined him in Pretoria. The war drags its stony wake of chaos into the new year of 1902, the Boer bitter-enders fighting on as Caleb predicted they would. Meanwhile, we pass gaily on in our Grand Tour, through Spain and France, Italy and Austria, to Switzerland. Caleb and Maria returned to her farm. They spend their days reconstructing, pulling weeds, digging wells and trenches, sowing seeds and tending sheep. He is a farmer again. He has found his home at last and builds it himself, stone by stone. He wrote last in January to tell us that Maria is with child. Lottie is delighted to be an aunt. It is good to hear such happy news in his letters to Lottie and me. Yet this one is a letter for me alone, the second only to my first letter almost a decade ago, a child with a doll who had just learned to write and she read of oysters and the sea. In my lap lies my spectacles case. I put on my reading glasses and notice, as ever, that the Visitors disappear when I put them on. I am alone now.

Mimosafontein,
Transvaal
23 February 1902

I write to you, Liza, as it is long overdue. I want to say again to you that I am sorry. I know I spelled this in your hand at Pretoria, yet I could see in your eyes you did not accept it from me. But I say it again all the same, because I mean it most earnestly. I am sorry I loved you in your girlhood and made you my confidante. I am sorry if my absence caused you pain. My only excuse was always your loveliness, your long hair flowing behind you as you raced along the hop lanes in your games, your deep eyes looking into me as we swapped signs on my boat, your hand on the body of my violin as I played sad songs for you. Your miracle of sight made you more delightful than ever and once you were a woman, your beauty would take a much better man than me to resist. When we kept our secret close, I could not write to you alone and wished to, most dearly. I did love you, Liza, I loved you tenderly. But I was an unhappy and selfish man. I saw my chance for escape in Africa and I took it. I had yearned after it for years.

I should not have lain with you that night before I went. It was a wrong deed which I regret for the feeling it inflamed in you and in myself. It tortured me for many moons and there were nights on guard duty, as I watched the summer hail storms rumble towards us across the veldt, when I would relive every moment of that night, every touch and word we whispered in our hands. I loved you as a man but I knew that I did not have it in me to stay for you, to look after you as you deserved, to make a life with you. And though your beauty, so new in those days of your young womanhood, bewitched me, when you came to me in the oast house I should have taken you back to your room and bid you good night. But I have told you, I was selfish and I did what I wanted and hang the consequences.

I do not warrant the love and regard you have always had for me. I am not mysterious and profound. I have no hidden depths for you to discover, only a dull inward nature that would never suit you. I am not trying to fob you off and pretend that I am a rotter. I know you will not believe that. But I do say that the man you loved may have been an image of your own creation, rather than the ordinary man I know myself to be. I must explain to you that it was you who were too good for me, never the reverse. It was to be Maria who saw through me, instantly detected every weakness, every crack in my façade, every untruth with which I fooled myself and my family. She would stand no lies, no nonsense, no sentiment. In that way, she was more like Lottie than anyone. And it is that sharp paring away of my pretence that made me love her. Your love will always be sweetest for its purity. But I cannot live the lie that I am the man you thought you knew. You are the extraordinary one, not me. You are the one with the gift, who used it to save me. I can never thank you enough for what you have done for me. I can never repay in kind the riches you have given to me. I fear my gratitude will always divide us to the same degree it unites us.

Now that I know the whole truth of what you did for me, what you risked for me, I want to say it again: thank you for saving my life. I want to thank you also for helping Jurie's spirit, for setting him free. In that pure and decent act you set Maria's grieving soul free at the same moment. Maria thanks you for that kindness profoundly. I will always love you for that, for your love for me and my family, for your care for Maria, for yourself in all your unique and wonderful ways. I know as sure as that I never will, you will make your mark in the world and do marvellous things.

I hope you are happy, Liza, I wish it most sincerely.

Much love to you, now and always.
Caleb

19

It is the first day of September 1903. I am twenty years of age. At home, it is nearly time for hop picking. The plants tended, pests killed and diseases controlled, the year-round care of Golding Hop Farm's men for our crop results in dozens of strong green bines laden with delicate cones. In Whitstable it is Partridge Day, the traditional moment when the Oyster Company ends the close period, when oysters spawn and the men can harvest. The oyster, soft, cold-blooded mollusc with no foot to move itself, began its journey within the confetti cloud of spawn, to float down to the bottom of the sea and anchor itself to some shell or other hard habitat. It can easily be suffocated by sand or destroyed by rough seas, and if it comes to rest on mud or weed it will die at once. If it survives, it grows, grey as the sea about it. The Crowes and their fellow dredgers tend these infants with daily care, from spawn, to brood, half-ware and mature oyster. Thus man tends his land, his flock and the resolve of these plants, these creatures, against all that would destroy them, is aided by the diligence of their farmers, but something in these beings – the hop seed, the oyster spawn – is determined to survive. I respect the hop, the oyster, for their tenacity.

The Dutch went to Africa. They fought with the natives and dug in, held on fast to the land they claimed as an oyster to its cultch. They built their farms and made a new world for themselves and their progeny. The land brought forth gold and the British came. It was only natural that the land would then be fought for. The black Africans, observing these two nations clubbing each other's heads over the red soil, chose sides and fought too, or starved with the others as the land was ruined. The war is over now, as the Treaty of Vereeniging was signed on the 31st day of May last year. The British had won, and now they own the colonies. Tens of thousands of Boers, black Africans and British died from combat, disease and starvation. South Africa is scarred by war, the farms burned, the fields salted, the people scorched by loss and grief. Some left, preferring exile. Some remained, like Maria and her Caleb, to rebuild a life. They have a child, a little girl called Elizabeth, and they work hard to bring forth fruits from the dry soil to tend her. The odds are against them, but they persevere.

Once I was an animal, human in body, feral of mind. Charlotte found me and held out her hand to me, grasped mine and pulled me free, spent countless hours conversing with me, laying aside her own needs, wants, space and time. Together we forged ahead with shapes, signs, letters and words, to sculpt from that beast a person who could name herself. My nature was cultivated, the weeds of my empty mind cleared and in that clean frame seeds of language grew and flowered. I loved this woman, my father, my mother; and I loved a man. He loved me, in his way. Love can be a kind of possession, a desire to occupy another person's body and soul, welcome if requited, an invasion if not. I saved his life and he made a life with another, a woman who had struggled against the pests and diseases of war, through great loss and suffering, yet survive she did and now their sweet child lives on. My learning, my love and my family have grown me into the literate, educated, adult woman who stands today at the prow of this great ship, the salty air cooling as we cross the Atlantic, the wind in my hair like frigid fingers.

Lottie and I are aboard the RMS *Carpathia*, a beautiful, brand-new ship with four towering masts and bright white lifeboats stacked neatly. The service is superb, the crew starched and courteous, the food tasty and economical. We are bound for Boston, the home of the Perkins Institute for the Blind. This was the place the Crowes' kindly vicar-tutor visited all those years past and brought back finger spelling. He gave it to Constance; and, through her sister, to me. I have been in correspondence with the school for some time. Though only the blind are named in its title, revealing its inception, it caters too for the deaf and the deaf-blind. Hearing the history of Lottie's education of me – first deaf-blind with the manual alphabet, later deaf with visual signing – the tutors at Perkins are most interested to meet us and employ us for a time as tutors to their pupils, be they without sight or hearing or both. I hope to improve my writing and read widely. One day I wish to study for a degree. I look forward to meeting others like me – the deaf – and those who once I was – the deaf-blind. I believe I can aid these young people and that somehow, being with others like me will smooth some of the strangeness of my upbringing.

I wonder how I will feel when I meet my first deaf-blind children. I have never spent time with anyone else of impaired senses. All my life I have been with the hearing and the sighted. I remember hotly how abashed I was of my cloudy eyes when blind, how concerned we were with my noises and grimaces when deaf-blind. When I see these deaf-blind children at Perkins, will I be embarrassed at how I used to be, full of pity? I am ashamed at this feeling. I recall worrying at how Caleb must have looked at me when I was like this. I worked hard to control my blindisms. Once sighted, I rejected my past self. It would be honest to say I sometimes pitied, sometimes hated the deaf-blind child I was. When I see these others, I hope I can reach inside myself and remember how it was to be that child, to be myself with no fear – running through the long grass, gulping down cocoa – that my lack of these two senses did not define my humanity. I hope that my understanding will make me want to reach out to these children and help them as Lottie did me. She was not driven away, did not recoil, yet instead embraced and saw me for the true person inside the oddity. This is what I hope I can do.

For many years, my deaf-blindness was like a monster from myth. My aim was to overcome it. Every monster has a weakness exploited by the hero to win the day. In my darkest memories, I see my early self as a blind monster crashing through the wilderness. But it was not my disability that kept me there. It was my ignorance. Once I found language, the spell was broken and I assumed human form. One does not need sight and hearing to be fully human, only communication. My lack of sight and hearing were not the enemies, only my lack of connection was my monster, my isolation. I was a fish out of water. The ordinary world surrounded me, yet it was not my home. I had to search for my medium. I found it through words. My mind was my true medium, as it is for you, for all of us.

In the Time Before, my mind was a bare house. The walls intact, the door open, but nothing within, no furniture or carpets, curtains or knick-knacks, no memories or images to suggest a life. The cold wind blew through it and its eye-windows stared blindly at nothing. It was a ruined Boer farm, the vacant shell of the Visitor. Only my Visitors haunted my empty house with their invisible, silent presence. Then Charlotte came to me and language filled that house with the stuff of life, as surely as Caleb and Maria fabricated their farm from the ground up. Just as they built upon the burned foundations of Mimosafontein as it once was, a family home rich with laughter before the catastrophe, I believe my mind retained the phantasmal voices of nearly two years of language heard and spoken before my own disastrous fever. When language came, my Visitors spoke to me, their words expressed by the ghosts of voices I had heard before my ears were spoiled. They say a man who loses a limb still feels an itch. So it is with my hearing. Something haunts it. It kept my sense of sound alive. When I gained my sight, I left behind the province of the deaf-blind and stepped into a colourful new land filled with treasures beyond imagining, the play of shape and light intoxicating, the new delight of 'eye-music', as Mr Wordsworth named it perfectly.

Yet I remain and will always be deaf. Deafness is my country, my home. Despite my accomplishments, I am aware that others who are unacquainted with my kind can look upon me as inadequate, assuming that my language of visual signs and spatial grammar is inherently inferior to spoken language, rudimentary, a pantomime. If I am given leave, I explain how much more it is than a sum of its parts, that each sign for each word is not frozen in time and meaning, yet the constant movement and holds of sign speech are closer to music than talking. And speech only has one dimension, that of its linear progress through time; yet sign works in four dimensions, three related to the signer's body: hand shape, location and movement, as well as time. Signers know how complex is the use of the whole arm, the wrist, the fingers, as well as all the fine degrees of eye, face and head gestures and how distinctly these contribute to meaning. As for the misnamed art of lip-reading, few guess at the intricate skills deployed to observe and infer from face, eyes, tilt of head and crease of skin which I use when 'listening' to those who speak.

Yes, I continue to learn my languages and develop my skills. But even before I learned these tricks, I was a person. A human who felt and inclined, extant, surviving. I think back to the flying fish I saw on our way to Africa, the natives I observed but never spoke with, never attempted to divine what moved in their minds. My excuse was my inexperience of their type, their society, and my business elsewhere. Yet, those black Africans I ignored have been maligned through history by such as me, have been ignored and trampled and assumed to be idiots, as I once was – the deaf-blind beast, the idiot child, born a savage and always a savage. But they were wrong about me. We are all wrong about those we label others. I am lucky that it was a young woman who found me, not some cold-eyed scientist to keep me in a glass box – as the insect in the child's jam jar – and study my condition, to affect and improve me for the greater good, as the native to the coloniser. Lottie loved me and wanted to reach me. That was all. Through reaching me, she also found her sister again. I saw my Visitors for the first time. Lottie translated messages from the hearing world for me and I brought news from the spirits to the land of the living. We move between worlds, my Lottie and me. Every human has the capacity for thought, for language, for mind. Every waking moment we negotiate the news from our senses with what sense our mind makes of it, moving effortlessly between the mind's territory and outside. My footfall exploring this globe, my journeys across darkness and silence, and my dispatches from the spectrum of the Visitors – all these forms of time-travel have taught me never to presume, always to observe, to examine with compassion, to learn the oft-hidden nature of what makes us who we are.

The ship approaches the New World. I thrill at my first sight of brief islands of American land as they appear and dip, gathering to form a coastline. Lottie comes beside me, carrying my shawl to put about my shoulders. Our entrance to Boston harbour is an assault on the senses, as all ports are: thresholds between water and land, land and other lands, countries and cultures. Thronging the docks, as I have come to expect, are a host of new Visitors. One turns violet-white and curious, another, another. They await me. I do not pity them or find them tedious, I think only of how I can help them go quietly to their peace. Or if they obsess on business unfinished, what good I can do for the living by acting as their translator, their go-between to heal old hurts, solve old mysteries and put doubt and grief to rest. In the ancient stories, the hero moves between two worlds, the ordinary world of his home, to the special world of adventure. Only once he is the master of both has he earned his freedom to live.

Before I left home, I told Mother about the Visitors. She wanted to be kind, to believe. But she had to have it proven, like Lottie. There are not so many like Maria or Caleb, who accept it immediately, have been on the edge of knowing it all their lives. Mother is a cynic. I took her down to the hop garden and looked for Father there while Mother sat patiently, her eyes betraying her concern. Is my girl mad after all? He came, muttering amiably about the weather.

The wind in the west suits everyone best.

I turned to Mother and asked her to speak, to recite a poem, sing a song or tell a story – but it must be something that Father knew, something about him or a memory they shared. Her eyes were fearful. But she did it for me. I watched her mouth move. She was singing a song. It was unfamiliar to me. Its first lines spoke of sweethearts and flowers, girls meeting boys. I imagined Father and Mother, as they were a lifetime ago, before the babies and the blood, before me.

Father, I said. *Listen. Listen.*

He stopped, standing between two slanting rows of hop bines, the green leaves alive with fluttering. His arms hung loosely by his sides, his mobile face slackened. I had not seen him so at rest since the day he died. He could hear her, he was listening to Mother.

Evangeline? he said. *Evangeline, my love?*

She is here, Father. She is singing for you. What is the song she sings? What memories does it conjure for you, Father?

We are visiting the music hall. I took her there on our first meeting unchaperoned. She had never been, coming from far more well-to-do stock than me, the farmer's son. But I had good prospects, you see. They said my grandfather would lose his shirt if he bought these hop lands, but he made it pay and my father was born wealthy, you too.

Tell me about Mother, about Evangeline, that night at the theatre.

She was the loveliest girl in the room. We sat in the grandest box, it cost me half a week's allowance. Some of the songs were risqué. They made her blush.

Did you whisper to her, Father?

Oh, yes. I wanted to be close to her. I leaned across and told her I'd been inspired to read her namesake, the poem 'Evangeline' by Longfellow. I said to her, 'Let us not wander the wilderness in search of love. We have found it here. We have found each other.' That moment, the way her eyes brimmed with tears, how her hand sought mine and we kissed. We knew.

Thank you, Father. Thank you.

I told Mother his story. She cried, as Lottie did. She questioned me all afternoon, worried it over in her mind all night. By the next day, she had come to terms with it. We spoke of Father, of all the Visitors, of how they wander, and how I can help them find peace.

'Adeliza, you are going away soon, who knows for how long. You have told me how your father's presence is a comfort to you, yet a sadness too, that he will never again be the man that he was. I admit, at first, I imagined a future where, when you return, you and I would walk in the hop fields and share his company. But I see clearly now, it would be wrong. To prolong his time further, to keep him from rest, to serve our own ends. And how I would await your return not only for the sight of you, but for news from him. That is wrong also. You should not be tethered to me or to this place, despite the warm remembrance of home which I hope will always glow in your heart. I want you to be free and your father too. We must say goodbye to him, Adeliza.'

We did it that day.

I love you, Father. You must go now, for ever. Goodbye.

Mother said, 'Goodbye, Edwin.'

He turned and was gone, as they do. No more fears about yield and rain and the mould and the flea. The hops grew silently, alone again.

Mother asked me, 'The five babies I carried before you, Liza. They died inside me. Are they . . . here? Do they speak to you?'

'No, Mother. I have never heard them. I have thought about them many times. I can only think that our souls do not live fully until they cross over into this world.'

'That comforts me. Perhaps they are there, though, but silent. In a place before words, where they cannot speak to you.' She looked down to her belly and placed her hand there.

'I think I would sense them, as I did before I could see. But I can place my hand on yours, here, like this, and ask them to go, to be at peace. Would you like me to do that, Mother?'

She nodded and we closed our eyes, said our own prayers for those five bright little souls and bid them farewell.

I left with Lottie days after. Mother wished me happiness in my travels.

She signed, 'I hope you find what you seek.'

This has played over and again in my mind. What do I seek? It is human to travel, to explore, to be a visitor in strange lands. The world is there to be discovered, we are all visitors on this earth, to walk here for a time, make our mark on it – like my fingertips skimming across Father's globe – and then to move on. But adventure can turn hollow, as Caleb escaped his life to seek adventure in Africa, but saw only the inhumanity of war and discovered instead his home. After the adventure is done, we look back for home, or find a home, or make a home. Is that not what we all look for? The oyster clinging to cultch, the couple rebuilding a farmhouse, the Visitors pacing again and again the day of their death. We carry it with us, this notion of home, a necessary comfort. I look forward to my life, to the green fields and red deserts of knowledge and this new twentieth century that sprawls before us.

For now, Lottie is my home. Perhaps she will find a new home here in America, perhaps I will. Or it awaits me where it always has, bounded by herb-filled walls and the yeast scent of drying hops. We all seek home in the end.

AUTHOR'S NOTE

This book is a work of fiction. However, there are elements of the novel which are based on true events, such as the educational experiences of the deaf-blind from the C19th to the present day; late Victorian hop and oyster farming techniques in Kent; and the Second Anglo-Boer War.

Throughout I have endeavoured to remain faithful to dates of real happenings, such as Boer War battles, for example. Yet certain events have been shifted slightly to fit the narrative. The Whitstable ice sheet actually happened in 1895, not later in time as Liza's narration suggests. Also, the film Liza watches at the Cinematograph – 'A Sneaky Boer' – was made in 1901, and so would not have been seen as early as Liza saw it. I hope the reader will forgive these chronological anomalies, in the spirit of forming a coherent flow within my story.

The reader may query the swift progress accorded to Adeliza from the moment she learns her first word. However, this is based faithfully on the educational experiences of Laura Bridgman in particular – the first deaf-blind child to be educated in America – as well as the autobiographies of Helen Keller. Once the child makes the mental connection between the object and its symbol i.e. the word, then language learning can happen very swiftly, just as a hearing infant's does. This is especially true of any individual with a lively and enquiring mind, and the absolute determination to succeed, such as Laura Bridgman, Helen Keller and indeed Adeliza Golding. Also key is the intensive one-to-one tuition all of these three pioneers received, which is highly unusual for any child today – deaf-blind or otherwise – let alone in the Victorian era, yet it did happen. A detailed account of Bridgman's education can be found in the book 'Life and Education of Laura Dewey Bridgman' by her tutor Mary Swift Lamson.

Regarding Caleb's letters, readers may be interested in some background to postal censorship during the Second Boer War. It was important to me that Caleb be free to write openly about his war experiences in South Africa. So I set about researching the issue of postal censorship. The answer to this is not as simple as it might seem, as I have read many conflicting things about censorship during the Boer War. However, I can direct readers to sources which explain that some but not all soldiers' letters home were censored.

Firstly, in the book 'A Lincolnshire Volunteer: The Boer War Letters of Private Walter Barley and Comrades' by Cecillie Swaisland (published by LITERATIM ISBN 0-9539754-0-1), the author states that 'this was the last major war in which there was little or no censorship. Walter's letters bear no disfiguring black lines, even when he openly criticised the system and his officers. He was able to tell his family back home exactly where he was, what he was doing and how he felt.'

I also studied many original letters from the Boer War that are kept in the Imperial War Museum collection and none of the letters I read had been censored. I have read accounts of letters from soldiers being published verbatim in local newspapers, some with accounts of manoeuvres and highly critical of their commanders. Yet I've seen references to censor stamps on envelopes and also soldier-writers claiming their CO would look at the letter before it's sent. It should be noted too that the trains carrying army mail were sometimes bombed, rail lines disrupted, and post stolen and recovered, so the situation could sometimes be unreliable to say the least. Thus, certainly when I was writing, I felt the situation was flexible enough to argue that some uncensored letters would have come through to England; and therefore, Caleb's letters could be some of these.

An invaluable part of the research for this book came from the charity for the deaf-blind, Sense. They provide wonderful support for deaf-blind adults and children throughout the UK. If you would like to make a contribution to the vital work this charity carries out, please choose from the following avenues:

- through the Sense website:
  www.sense.org.uk/content/make-donation
- by phone to their Supporter Services Helpline:
  0845 127 0067
- by post to
  Supporter Services
  Sense
  101 Pentonville Road

London
N1 9LG
Donations made payable to: Sense

When making your donation, please quote reference CBK12.

Thank you.

ACKNOWLEDGEMENTS

Thank you to:

Simon Porter, for being my benefactor, for knowing it would happen, for putting up with my writer's moods and for everything, forever.

Poppy Mariska Porter-Mascull, for letting me read through drafts in peace while she was eating her tea, for knowing that the Visitors were ghosts and for writing her own brilliant stories.

My agent Jane Conway-Gordon, for getting to the heart of things and for loving both Daniel and Adeliza.

My editor at Hodder and Stoughton, Suzie Dooré, for saying yes, being such a good laugh and a sensitive yet meticulous editor. To Nikki Barrow for her tireless publicity work, not slapping me down for sending too many emails and for her cracking sense of humour. And to Francine Toon and Rosie Gailer at Hodder for their friendly and helpful ways. Also to the reviewers, book bloggers, journalists, other readers and those who attended the book launch; to all of you who have championed this book, I am forever grateful.

My lovely mum Liz Beeson and the oracle Russell Beeson, for tireless editing, love and conviction.

My brothers – Jonny, Robert and David Chadwick – and

my Aunties and Cousins, for whooping and being proud. And to Emily, Alex and Sonny for reading and discussing my work.

Marie and Kevin Porter: to Nana for reading first drafts and all the hot dinners, to Grandad for school runs and being Leo the Lion.

Lynn Downing, for reading so quickly and enthusiastically, with a mother's eye on little Liza, and listening to me drone on. (Love to Abbie and Isobel.)

Kathy Kendall, Theresa Roberts and Ella White, for consuming everything I've ever sent them and the long hours on the telephone.

Francine Koubel, for years of support and our discussions of the novel over Italian meals in London.

Dorothy Judd – an exquisite writer herself – for her grace and goodwill.

Ann Schlee and Daphne Glazer, for expert writing tuition and encouragement.

Kerry Drewery, for being my loyal writing friend and fellow pianist.

Alexis Hepworth, for defending Daniel.

Sarah-Jane Potts and Sue White, for believing in me.

The Media Studies team at AQA – particularly Kim Doyle and Richard Morris – for all the fun and my first opportunity in publishing.

Dr Chris Sutcliffe, for giving me his blessing to leave school teaching and write.

Roger Huggett, Carol Dawson and Tracey Smith, for the gift of the violin.

Debbie Cowie, for responding to novelist hairdo emergencies with flair.

Pauline Lancaster and her family, for being brave.

Alison Parry, for showing clemency and not burning me as a witch.

David Landick the parcel man, who delivered my first novel and always asks.

Rose Kimmings, Assessment and Advice Officer; Ginny Matthew, Senior Children and Family Support Worker; and Emma Blanchard-Moore, Multi-Sensory Impairment Consultant, from the charity Sense, for their valuable time and relating their experiences of working with deaf-blind people.

Bernard Chang, FRCOphth, FRCSEd, Honorary Secretary of The Royal College of Ophthalmologists UK, for his expertise regarding all aspects of Liza's eye condition, operation and recovery. Also to his once colleague Jackie Trevena, who looked up eye diseases for me during one very helpful phone call.

Prof. Denis Judd, Professor of British Imperial and Commonwealth History, New York University in London; and Dr Keith Surridge, teacher of British History for American programmes in London; for their kind assistance with diverse aspects of the Boer War.

Paul McKinnell from Spa Valley Railway for his knowledge of Edenbridge Town Station and the late Victorian rail network.

Staff at the Imperial War Museum Research Room, for their help in finding obscure Boer War diaries, letters and documents.

James, the lad on the bus from Filton College, Bristol who taught me how it feels to be deaf.

My Great-Great-Great Grandfather James Golding born 1810, who farmed on hop land and the real Adeliza Golding born 1868, my Great-Great-Aunt, who died so young and haunted me.

This book is dedicated to the memory of Alison Bonnington, who listened to the story of my first novel over a long lunch in Oxford then frog-marched me to the computer room to start writing it. Thank you, Alison.

READING GROUP QUESTIONS

1. How did the book open your eyes to the world of deaf-blind children in Victorian England?
2. What, or whom, did you think the Visitors were at the beginning of the book?
3. How important were the locations in which the book was set – the hop fields, London, Whitstable and South Africa?
4. Did you think that Adeliza and Caleb should have ended up together, or was he destined to be with Maria?
5. Did you know anything about the Boer War before reading this book? What interested you or even surprised you about the elements of this war presented here? For example, did you know about the concentration camps? Are there any parallels between the Boer War and present-day conflicts?
6. Adeliza has the ability to send the Visitors on their way to find peace. Do you think that this was a comfort for them or for those who remained behind? What influence do you feel the Visitors had over Liza?
7. The Visitors help Adeliza to save Caleb from a crime he didn't commit. Do you feel that this was a turning point in the novel, and if so, why?

8. How do you think Adeliza feels about her deaf-blindness at different parts of the novel? How do her feelings change over time?
9. At the end of the novel, Adeliza and Lottie head for America to help other deaf-blind children. What do you think will happen next?

Thanks to Georgina Tranter, Bridget Ash and Louise Walters for helping to provide these questions for discussion.

JOSIE GRAY INTERVIEWS REBECCA MASCULL ABOUT *THE VISITORS*

What was the initial inspiration for the novel?

I worked with deaf teenagers when I was teacher training and was quite ignorant about deafness. I didn't understand the different types of sign language or the pressure on those students to learn to write and read in English which is different from visual communication. I was hooked and fascinated by their world. The catalyst was a conversation on a bus with a deaf student called James. I wrote some questions on a pad and asked him to explain what it was like to be deaf. He was delighted to tell me and we got stuck in a traffic jam and had a great conversation where he explained things to me. He said he went to clubs like other teenagers and stood by the speakers to feel the vibrations and could dance to the beat. That went in the book: Liza goes to a dance and can feel the beat and thrumming on the floor. That was the spark that made me want to write about deafness. The deaf-blind stuff came in from two main influences; one from watching a TV movie about Helen Keller as a kid and being very interested in how you would experience the world when unable to see or hear. I was fascinated by the scene where Helen learns her first word, which is 'water', by putting her hand in water and learning that an object can have a symbol to represent it. When I came to write I thought, oh my word, what if the character is deaf *and* blind? I thought that would be so hard but part of me likes a good fight. I thought it would be a real challenge to get inside the head of someone without language, who is blind and deaf. I even considered having a black page at the beginning of the novel but in the end I didn't need it. I came up with the phrase 'the time before' to describe the language-less state of the character in the chaotic and terrifying time when she had so little to hold on to.

The novel has a range of disparate themes in it from hop farming to the Boer War, disability to ghosts. Did you know how you were going to bring them together from the start?

A few of the themes were not planned initially. I knew deaf-blindness was going to be a main thrust and that first love was important. I knew it was going to be a kind of *bildungsroman* (or coming-of-age story) of Liza coming to language and coming to herself and becoming a person with the novel ending in her early twenties, as she is just on the cusp of adulthood. That was the shape of it. I didn't know the texture of her life. I started to research the period and found wonderful material for the social background of the story. I wanted something that was interesting in and of itself. Hop farming ticked the boxes because it is so odd and has a gorgeous language all of its own. It is a very singular, high risk business and very tough. Liza's father had to have a stressful life and even though they're well off they're not landed gentry so the money is new money and this adds stress. It was an industry that could make or break you. The Crowe family needed different work but which was equally difficult. As it was based in

Kent I looked at other industries in the area and decided on the coast. I wanted a feeling of space for Liza and going to the sea is a real adventure for her. As a child I grew up in Oxfordshire which is land-locked. Going to the sea was a true adventure as it was a few hours away in each direction. For me stuck in the middle of the country the sea represented freedom. By looking at seaside industries the oysters presented themselves. They provide an interesting image. Their lives are risky, it's hard to create a full grown oyster and like hop farming the industry has lovely language. It seemed picturesque, interesting and also hard for the characters having to fight against nature all the time.

I also knew I wanted Liza's lover to go away to war and I had to choose a war that fitted the period. I hadn't read about the Boer War but it did fit right with the period. It was not really a choice. At first I was not especially interested but then I started reading and fell headlong into it. It has a horrible history in terms of the camps. Many people don't know about them and assume they were a product of the Second World War. I also wanted to include different points of view on the war including the African point of view. Caleb mentions it and says the Boers were visitors too – another use of the idea of visitors in the novel. The war also had to fit in with the development of finger spelling. I didn't want to claim that Lottie Crowe had invented it so I needed a character who had learnt it and brought it to the family and that had to fit in with the time frame and that also determined the need for the war to be the Boer War.

Where did the Visitors of the title come from?

The Visitors were not intended to begin with. The story was going to be set in America after the Civil War but it didn't work out that way and it became clear it was an English story. I had an image of Liza walking across a battlefield and seeing the ghosts of the dead rising up. She saw them and nobody else could see them. I knew she was going to get her sight back as I needed to enable her to move around the world without the help of another person and for that she needed one faculty to be restored. It's a visual novel with a strong visual sense to it and I am a very visual writer. The idea of the Visitors just came and then I had to decide how important they were going to be. I wanted them to be an element in Liza's world but for them to be quite inactive, trapped in time. They do help her to solve a mystery but they don't drive the plot, she does. She drives the rescue of Caleb. I wanted them to be sad and confused and to not understand their own condition. They have forgotten who they are and are in some ways the opposite to Liza. She constantly searches and surges forward. She acts against them but learns to understand and come to terms with them. They can represent fears and regrets as well. I wanted them to be quite woolly at the start and for the reader to wonder if they were in fact just an element of Liza's imagination. One reader commented that they could be interpreted as being like random sparks from the optic nerve. I also considered that if someone was deaf-blind, might they be more receptive to things others cannot experience? If you do have your lenses removed, you could be sensitive to ultra-violet light and hence things that you would not normally see. An unusual brain might just give you different abilities.

The term 'visitors' has many different meanings in the novel. They are Liza's ghosts, yet also can be used to represent the hop-pickers, the Boers and the English in

Africa, the guests who come to see Liza when she's deaf-blind, even Liza herself going to Whitstable and further afield. It's part of the theme of home and homeland, which also resonates throughout the story.

Were you tempted at any stage to give Adeliza her heart's desire in the form of Caleb?
In the planning stages of the story my intention was for Caleb and Liza to go to America together at the end of the story. He would be damaged by his experiences and in need of her. But I got half way through and thought, there's no way this can happen. He fell in love with Maria. I had no control over that whatsoever and that was it. Maria understands him and knows him truly. Liza is besotted but she invents a version of him to suit herself. What they had was first love, it was fragile and beautiful and very painful and ultimately not real. Liza romanticises Caleb and makes him into someone he is not. The adoration of a young pretty girl flatters him and is irresistible to him but he doesn't love her how she needs to be loved. I don't blame him for spending the night with her. He did love her in his own way. In Maria he meets his match. She challenges him and is right for him. I felt the plot would have been forced had I put Caleb and Liza together. It was not the right thing to do.

The women in the novel transcend the gender limitations of the day – did you deliberately set out to give them such pioneering qualities?
Starting with Maria then; Maria is a fascinating woman. She is based on a real woman, Sarah Raal who wrote about the Boer War in *The Lady Who Fought*. She fought alongside

her brothers and experienced some of the same things that Maria experienced. Some women did fight but their secret histories are often hidden away. I found this great book by accident. Raal was a bolshie and difficult woman but I liked her. She escaped from her society.

I didn't consciously see Lottie and Liza as fighting against convention other than them going off to Africa. Male or female I hate constriction and limitation and people saying 'no' for no good reason. I am bloody minded and I don't like restrictions with no good reason for them. Stuff convention and society telling you what you can and can't do! I don't see this as exclusive to female characters either and not all the female characters in the novel are strong. The mother is a weak character whereas the father is the strength in the household. I am interested in people trying to escape limitation and restrictions regardless of if they're male or female but I do like to inhabit a female mind, maybe because I understand it better. There were a lot more restrictions on women's lives in that period and that is something that interests me.

The novel crosses genre boundaries. It could be seen as literary fiction, women's fiction or historical fiction. How do you see it?

I see it as a story. All books that I love are great stories. I see the point of genre and that some readers like to latch on to a particular genre but I see it as another restriction to fight against. I am butterfly-minded and flit between many different things at once. This is the perfect mindset for a novelist, to never be restricted and lack of restriction makes a good story, one that is rich and full of texture. This is how my brain works, it is cross-genre, but that is good in that this is what works for me. Different components make for a good story. Genre is often a tool used to sell books and that's ok but I just want my reader to be able to enter a different world and to care about the characters. I don't want the story to be directed before it is told. I want the characters to do what they want and not to be restricted by genre. Genre is a useful tool but I prefer to use it lightly.

Josie Gray is a freelance writer and arts worker from Great Grimsby. She specialises in community arts projects and works with a range of groups and organisations. She is a poet, playwright and is currently writing a novel. Josie edits the website www.thedock.info – an online resource for writers in the Lincolnshire region and beyond.

THE FRONT COVERS OF *The Visitors*

Anyone can see that the front covers of the hardback and paperback versions of *The Visitors* are very attractive and easy on the eye. Many readers have commented on their beauty. Yet I think there is more to it than that.

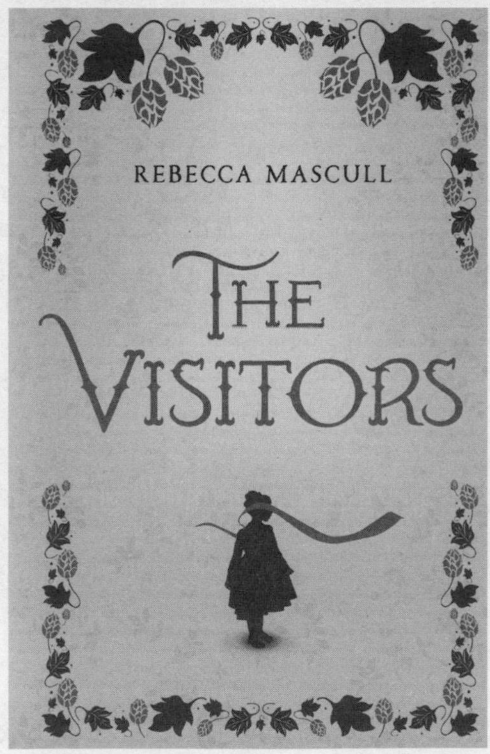

Hardback cover for The Visitors

I was quite surprised when I first saw the draft version of this cover, as I had expected something green. I knew that hops were to feature on the cover, so when I saw the monochromatic scheme shot through with red, it was shocking. Then I realised what a brilliant choice this was. There is something chilling about it, something odd and unsettling. Red is after all a sign of danger. The dark grey leaves and pale background also give it an antique feel; this is magnified by the sepia colouring throughout the cover and the slightly raised texture of the book itself. Also, the fact that the images are printed directly on to the board and not a removable cover serves to suggest that the book itself is from Victorian times. The font used for the title also creates a disquieting mood, with its curious barbs and elongated stance, as well as being in a historical font and again in that alarming red. The figure is charming and being so small gives a feeling of vulnerability. The use of silhouette echoes the historical practice of this art, yet too offers a mystery to the character. The red ribbon across her eyes signifies her blindness and the ribbon her father makes her wear when she has guests. Yet the ribbon flies free (visually repeating the curve of the capital T above) and also signifying Liza's freedom from the confines of her condition. Her little feet are shod in heavy Victorian boots, as they would have been, and furthermore that shadow around her feet gives a feel of solidity about her. The feminine ruffles of the dress are offset by this and give the impression of a girl who stands straight and knows her own mind. The pale leaves in the background offer further decoration and complement the hop leaves, yet their muted tones also offer a ghostly ambience. Perhaps the most subtle and yet still crucial element is the white flash behind the title. Not only does it give the novel's name a focus, it also anticipates the spectral light of the Visitors themselves. The paperback cover retains many elements of the hardback's success. This time, a photographic image of a Victorian child is used and it has been perfectly chosen. Liza is indeed described in the book as having long, thick, fair hair and so this child could well be her. Importantly, her hands are fully visible on the cover, as they play such a key role in her life, as her chief form of communication. Overall, I feel the book covers for *The Visitors* are not only gorgeous to look at, yet also convey in an understated manner a range of themes and moods central to the novel. I for one am thrilled with them. Thank you so much to Alice Laurent at Hodder & Stoughton for her stunning designs.

Find out more about the inspiration behind
The Visitors:

rebeccamascull.tumblr.com

From Anya Seton and Mary Stewart to Thomas Keneally and Robyn Young, Hodder & Stoughton has an illustrious tradition of publishing bestselling and prize-winning authors whose novels span the centuries, from ancient Rome to the Tudor Court, revolutionary Paris to the Second World War.

Want to learn how an author researches battle scenes?

Discover history from a female perspective?

Find out what it's like to walk Hadrian's Wall in full Roman dress?

Visit us today at **HISTORY LIVES** for exclusive author features, first chapter previews, book trailers, author videos, event listings and competitions.